# NOT FOR USE IN NAVIGATION

## THIRTEEN STORIES

## IONA DATT SHARMA

**Not For Use In Navigation** © 2019 Iona Datt Sharma

Cover art © 2019 Katherine Catchpole
Cover design © 2019 Lodestar Author Services

All rights reserved. This book or any portion thereof may not be reproduced or used in any manner whatsoever without the express written permission of the author except for the use of brief quotations in a book review.

This book is a work of fiction. Any similarity to real persons, living or dead, is entirely coincidental and not intended by the author.

# CONTENTS

Introduction ..................................................................... 7
Light, Like A Candle Flame ............................................. 9
Death Comes To Elisha ................................................. 24
Akbar and the crows ..................................................... 31
One-Day Listing ............................................................ 36
Flightcraft ..................................................................... 54
Landfall (your shadow at evening, rising to meet you) .. 81
Birbal and the sadhu ..................................................... 87
Archana and Chandni .................................................... 92
Nine Thousand Hours ................................................. 105
Akbar's holiday ........................................................... 124
Alnwick ....................................................................... 127
Eight Cities ................................................................. 147
Ur ................................................................................ 155
Akbar learns to read and write ................................... 173
Quarter Days .............................................................. 178
Refugee; or, a nine-item representative inventory of a better world ................................................................ 273
A note on Akbar and Birbal ......................................... 281
Acknowledgements ..................................................... 283
About the author ........................................................ 285

# INTRODUCTION

I was asked recently when I was going to start writing "real" fiction. Enough of the spaceships and wizards, Iona! You're not fourteen any more!

There are a lot of possible answers to that. Chief of which is that our genre doesn't need to be defended from those who don't understand its vital relevance. In her speech at the 2014 National Book Awards, Ursula Le Guin put it best: writers of science fiction and fantasy have the unique responsibility to be "realists of a larger reality" – to light the way to a world yet to come.

These stories were written over a four-year period beginning in 2014, and in echo of their times, they are stories about things in flux, points of transformation. I have often been accused of wanton melancholy, and it's true they aren't always cheerful: with extraordinary change comes grief, regret, things irrevocably lost.

But nevertheless, I hope these stories are in Le Guin's spirit: they are about possibility, not constraint. Not for use in navigation, because the world yet to come will be better than anything I could possibly imagine. I hope you enjoy them just the same.

Iona Datt Sharma
March 2019

# LIGHT, LIKE A CANDLE FLAME

On the first day of Sara's appointment as Magistra Descendant to the Assembly of Terravine, Public Works decided they needed grassroots support for the plant.

"I mean, I agree in principle," Sara had tried telling him, as he gestured at his hand-annotated wallcharts. "But for one thing, I'm supposed to be neutral, and for another thing, people might be eating!"

"You see, Magistra Lobo, that's just the sort of avoidant attitude we're trying to eradicate," said Public Works. "Knocking on doors, that'll do it."

The man did actually have a name, Sara thought, while he was talking her into it. It might be Smith or Singh or Park. Light would know.

"It's Nguyen," Light told her.

"I knew it." Sara knocked on the first door they came to and had a moment of dissonance: sometime in the last ten years, she'd stopped recognising everyone in the colony. "Excuse me, citizen. My name is Sara Lobo. Could I have a moment of your time?"

The woman looked at her with narrowed eyes. "Are you here to bang on about cultural ties and the longitudinal view of history? And the importance of holding onto our shipboard and Earthbound past?"

"No," Sara said. "That's the Magistra Ancestral. I'm here to talk about sewage."

※

On day 2, Sara was confirmed in her appointment, the department made a formal proposal to the Assembly and Light fell out of a tree.

"It's really the ideal site," Public Works was saying to the gathered members. "It's a reasonable distance from clean water sources but it also has a decent height of inflow."

"I see," said the Archon, in tones that suggested she didn't.

"All this time we've been getting by with bits and pieces of technology scavenged from the ship! And not even scavenged with thought, or put to use efficiently! Did we really spend generations crossing the gulfs of interstellar space just to dig ourselves giant latrines?"

"No?" said the Magistra Ancestral, after a minute of silence suggested this had not been a rhetorical question.

"And the worst part is this!" he said. "Thirty years ago when we surveyed the place from orbit we just didn't consider the requirements of terrestrial waste treatment."

"I see," the Archon said, again, and Sara imagined Public Works standing there on the bridge as the ship made landfall, pointing at an annotated wallchart.

"If you'll let me show you the plans, honoured Archon," he went on, and suddenly the air above the table contained a revolving three-dimensional blueprint. "See, here's road access. Here are the sandbanks, for the gravel we'll need. Here's the way down to the sea. And, er, this building here—Magistra Lobo, I think that's—"

"It's my house," Sara said, and looked up: someone was trying to get her attention from the doorway. "I'm sorry, Mr Nguyen, I have to go," she said, reading the scribbled message. "My partner has had an accident."

❦

After three decades in part-occupation of a human body, Light had not become resigned to its frailties.

"Let me guess," Sara said, "you went chasing after a missing cat, got five metres off the ground and then forgot you had a body. Right?"

She closed the door and dimmed the floor illumination, so Light's head hurt a little less.

"That is—ah." Light closed its eyes. "Perspicacious."

"The cat's in the kitchen drinking the hypoallergenic nutritional supplement that Nanni Julia won't touch because it tastes like pants. The rest was pretty easy to figure out."

"You—" Light propped itself on its elbows with some difficulty, "—are busy, and you must take care of Julia. . . ."

"Shut up, Light. I've spent my entire day chasing after Nanni Julia and the Department of Public Works. I'd rather look after you. Go to sleep."

Light did, and woke up a short time later still feeling like *it*, as though there were nothing between its body and the chrome and gunmetal sky. A hoarse voice was calling for something to drink. Light pulled one of Sara's cardigans around its shoulders and took some water through to Nanni Julia, but Nanni Julia threw the glass at its face and Light retreated into the open space of the house.

Sara turned at the movement. "Did she—" She made a precise gesture.

"Yes," Light said.

"I'm sorry." Sara waved a hand and the schematics in front of her, reversed from Light's perspective, blinked out of the air. "Light, I don't know why they've got me looking at these things. I don't want to be Magistra Descendant! I don't want to keep a weather eye out for the colony's future. What I want is for them not to be building a sewage works outside my house. And for Nanni Julia to stop throwing things at you. Is that so terribly unreasonable?"

"No." Light was shivering, the sea mist creeping through the gaps in the shutters. "But you could have declined the appointment."

"Eh," Sara said, waving her hand again, "who's ever done that, in the brave new Assembly of Terravine. Come on, back to bed with you, you've had a rough day."

Light woke up in the morning feeling more like herself. She made breakfast for Nanni Julia, who said something rude in Konkani; she fed the cat and returned it to its grateful owner; and then she sat down to consider the blueprints.

※

"I can assist," Light told Nguyen, on day 5. "I'm afraid I have no recent qualifications in the field. But I was intimately acquainted with the process of human waste reclamation for more than two hundred years."

"Et tu, darling Brute," Sara said, but Public Works grinned and gave her a handful of explanatory pamphlets.

※

Day 11 was week's end, and Nanni Julia was well enough to go to mass, but wouldn't sit next to Light. "It's not right," she hissed, "something like you in a place like this," —and Sara rolled her eyes, but Light didn't mind. That morning, Nanni Julia had called Sara by her mother's name, which Light had not heard spoken in decades. She got up quietly and went to sit at the back.

After the service, which centred on themes of growth and renewal, Sara got a determined look on her face and went up to take communion. Light was distracted by a little girl catching at her sleeve.

"Excuse me," she said, "but are you really—it? Her?"

"Both will do," Light said.

"But you're the ship," the little girl persisted.

"Yes," Light said, looking up though the skylight. The ship itself—and Light had taken a long time to reach this place, where she could think in two separate parts of the ship itself and she, herself—was in geostationary orbit above Terravine. Light could feel its passage through space, its weight and tether. "I am the Earth generation ship *Light, like a candle flame*, last of the last."

"Why were you called that?" the little girl asked.

"There was a poem written about me before the journey," Light said. "*Light / like a candle flame / carried out to the stars*. It was thought appropriate, and it advanced no religion, no political position. Who knew what you would be, or become, after seven generations? The poet was a child from Wichita, Kansas."

Who had not been chosen in the ship lottery, Light recalled: who had lived and died in Wichita, Kansas, her body boneless beneath the choking dust.

"What do you do now you're a person?" the little girl asked.

"I was always a person," Light said. But paying rent in two places these days, as Sara had once described it. A piece of a ship's consciousness in a human skin, with that great remainder still out in orbit, rocked by solar wind.

"I mean, now you don't have to go anywhere?"

"I find lost things," Light said. "And I build new things."

"That sounds okay," the girl said, and Light smiled at her before turning away.

Sara was moving across the room, her footsteps ringing on the sunlit floor. "I was right," she said. "A certain person who shall remain nameless—"

"Nguyen. His name is Nguyen."

"—has already delivered unto Father Ignatius his own little homily about growth, renewal and waste processing. Even if I do agree in principle—"

"*Do* you agree in principle?"

Sara groaned. "I look to Terravine's future welfare. I'm supposed to be independent of day-to-day concerns."

Light nodded.

"But what with you and the blueprints, and Public Works and the pamphlets, and now my priest and my grandmother telling me all about how cleanliness is next to godliness, I'm starting to wonder if the Magistra Ancestral's work follows her home. Or to church."

"I'm sorry it's so trying," Light said, and Sara sighed and put an arm around Light's shoulders.

"Are you all right?" she asked. "Before, with the little girl – you seemed upset."

"I'm fine," Light said.

※

Sara committed to the cause on day 19, when a citizen made the mistake of putting their hands on their hips and saying: "How much shitting can one colony of four thousand people do?"

"Frankly, sir, I think you alone contain quite enough—"

"Thank you for your time," Light said. "For statistical information, please don't hesitate to contact the Department of Public Works."

"But in the meantime," Sara said, "if you want your community's water supply contaminated with disease just because you can't get your head out of *your*—"

"Sara."

"—long enough to see that a little construction work and a spoilt view are a small price to pay for—"

The door slammed.

"Sewage disposal is necessary for a long-term sustainable future," Sara said, her hands on her hips. "Do either of you have anything you wish to say?"

Light shook her head, and Public Works just looked delighted. "You read the pamphlets!" he said, and they marched on.

∾

"Light," Sara said, late that night, after Nanni Julia had gone to bed and she and Light were sitting on the curve of the dunes, the tide creeping purplish and bioluminescent below. "Did you have to deal with things like this, before? When you were—what you used to be."

"What I am." Light held a hand up to the sky, occluding the fine dusting of stars. The last observers had been able to see that from Earth, Sara remembered: the same spiral arm, the same galactic neighbourhood.

"No," Light said. "There were no meetings, no petitions. Only survival."

As Sara watched, a bright pinprick described a curve across the darkness, and seemed to pause and revolve against the familiar backdrop. "What's that?"

"That is a salvage detail," Light murmured. "They are searching for aluminium and titanium. To take such things from beneath the ground would take great heat and pressure, and they can be reclaimed from my hull."

Sara shuddered. "I hope they really need them. I hope they're not making toe rings or saucepans out of them."

She meant it as a joke, but Light's eyes were steady on her, blank as smooth metal.

"Do you presume to speak to *me*, Magistra Lobo, of what is necessary? Of what must be kept, or left behind?"

She was shaking with anger, and then it seemed to drain from her, leaving her still and quiet. Sara waited another moment and then gathered Light in her arms, muttering into her hair, *you're here, you're all right*, as though it might assist, or mean anything.

❦

"How can you be on his side?" another citizen yelled on day 27, having come to the door brandishing a petition of his own. Light had been complaining of a headache, which worried Sara after the tree incident, but she'd come along anyway.

"Mr Nguyen is an excellent engineer," Sara said primly. "And if you'd care to listen just for a moment to what he has to say—"

"I've heard the speech," the man said. "All about the need to prepare the colony for growth and expansion! Infrastructure and the bright new future! We came here to get away from that! We came here to live in harmony with the world around us!"

"That's true," Sara said, hesitantly. "But it's also true that we've been taking an amateurish approach to waste processing."

"You're the Magistra Descendant!" the man snapped. "Doesn't that mean you have to look after our *descendants*? You're supposed to stop us repeating all the old mistakes!"

"It's just a sewage works," Sara said, still hesitant. "And we need it. We're outgrowing the initial plumbing arrangements, which were only meant to be temporary in any case—"

"And what will we need next?" the man demanded. "And what will we need to mine, or strip, or destroy, to build it?"

"That's not how it works!" Sara said, falling wholly off-script. "One little sewage works isn't going to lead to—you know, to that! To anthropogenic climate change!"

"And who's going to stop it?" the man snapped. "You?"

He was staring past Sara and Nguyen at Light, who was inspecting her bitten fingernails.

"No," she said. She sounded exhausted and in pain. "Not me."

※

On day 35, the pro-sewage-plant faction had three hundred and sixty-two signatures, to the anti-sewage-plant faction's three hundred and fifty-four.

"Too close," Sara told Nguyen. "It'll come to a vote in the Assembly. Cheer up, man! Pamphlets for everyone!"

He gave her a gloomy look before going up to the public gallery, and Sara took her seat at the table opposite the Magistra Ancestral. She was a quiet woman with a topknot of white hair. Far more befitting the post, Sara thought, appointment by random ballot notwithstanding.

"A full agenda for today," the Archon said. "The first order of business is a submission from the most recent ship detail. Dr. Desai, if you could, please."

She gestured at one of the other Assembly members, who stood up. "It's complicated," she said, sounding nervous, "and there will be a full report to the Assembly in due course, but in brief: this collection detail will be the last."

"Why is that?" asked the Archon.

"The ship is going dark," Dr. Desai said. "Most of the useful constitutive materials have been salvaged by this point, and it's been running with minimal energy consumption for ten years at least. It's a planned obsolescence," she added, hastily. "No one is saying that it hasn't been properly maintained or anything like that. But soon it won't be safe for our people to walk around there any longer. The computer core is intact but it no longer has complete connectivity to the outer shell."

"I see," the Archon said. "We'll await the full report. Thank you very much.

"Now, following a proposal in opposition and a counter-proposal from the Department of Public Works, the Magistra Descendant wishes to make the case for a sewage plant in Terravine, on the western shore."

Sara stood up, glanced above at Nguyen and at the notes in her hand, and then looked straight at the Archon. "One day I'll be superfluous to requirements," she said. "Seven generations from now we won't need a

Magistra Descendant or Magistra Ancestral. We won't need reminding to look to our future or preserve our past. It'll be part of who we are.

"I was six years old when we made landfall. I remember what it was like, to be carried through space, and to know everything was provided for, everything was done. But we're here now. Shouting at each other on doorsteps, producing pamphlets, doing our best to avoid the old mistakes. If we call for help, no one will come. Time to grow up, don't you think? Time to shovel our own shit."

She sat down. Nguyen got up and provided some information on the technical specifics, answering the Assembly members' questions, and after that the representatives of the anti-sewage faction came down from the public gallery and spoke about the need for harmony with one's agrarian environment. Sara barely heard any of it over the litany in her head, repeating itself over and over: *the ship is going dark.*

"Light," a voice said, and Light paused in the doorway. "It's you."

"It's me," Light agreed. She waited, but Nanni Julia did not throw anything at her.

"No," Nanni Julia said. With difficulty, she rose from her rocking chair and walked slowly to the window. Light assessed whether she would require assistance, then stood still. "I mean, it's really you. Light, like a candle flame."

"Yes," Light said. People had sworn by her, once. *Light, like a candle flame*—when one pledged an oath one meant to keep, or dropped a hammer on one's toe. It used to make her uncomfortable.

"I don't like seeing you," Nanni Julia said, fretfully. "You were everything to me. Family, friend, teacher. You were the first thing in the morning and the last thing at night. And now I'm an old woman, and you—you look like *that*."

Light looked down at herself: at the faded tunic, at her bare feet in sandals. At the broken fingernails that Sara had tried to stop her from chewing, at the shape of the bones beneath her skin. "This is where we live now," she said, not knowing if it would be consolation.

"I'll be going soon enough," Nanni Julia said, matter-of-fact. "Off to my life everlasting, and all the flights of angels. Can I tell you a secret?"

"Of course."

"I'm not going anywhere," Nanni Julia said, her voice conspiratorial. "Put me in the hole when they dig it, I can be sewage. I can be the dirt that makes things grow. You brought me here and here I'll stay."

Light nodded, and went to join her at the window. "Shall I take you to mass in the morning?" she asked.

"You shouldn't," Nanni Julia said, again fretful. "You're not a Catholic."

"Perhaps not," Light said. "But I was conceived in sin."

Nanni Julia smiled. "You're a good girl, Light. You were always so good to us. Now I'd like to sleep."

Light helped her back to bed and fluffed the pillows. "Goodnight, ship," Nanni Julia said, as Light was on the threshold.

"Goodnight, Julia," Light murmured, and went out to Sara, who was waiting for her on the path through the dunes.

※

Sara waited until they were by the water's edge, the last of the day's light filtering greenish through the shallows.

"Were you going to tell me, Light?" she asked. "I suppose you weren't. You were just going to let me think you had a dizzy spell and fell out of a tree."

"I did," Light said. She sounded embarrassed. "I did."

"But it's because of *that*." Sara gestured upwards, to where the ship was visible as the first star of twilight.

"It was a planned obsolescence," Light said.

"I thought you wouldn't leave," Sara said. "You'd never leave us."

She was sounding like a child, she knew, and her mind was full of the last memories of childhood: the faint buzz of shipboard air recirculation and the voice who always answered, steady as the stars beyond the glass.

"I will stay as long as I can," Light said, and kissed her.

Sara whispered soft inarticulate things into her mouth, and held her. After a minute she wiped her eyes and said, "Light, they're building a sewage plant next to our house."

"I know," Light said. "You could have voted against."

"Like I could have declined the appointment? You're hilarious."

"I try," Light said. "We could move."

"There's a whole planet, I'm told," Sara agreed, kneeling down to trail her hands in the water. "But, you know what? I kind of like it here."

"So do I," Light said. She got down on her knees to join Sara, tide-phosphorescence gleaming at her fingertips. Sara imagined waking with Light in the early morning, reaching towards her through the wreathing mist.

"Well, then," she said, looking up into the sky. "I suppose we'll be here a little while yet."

# DEATH COMES TO ELISHA

The F train rattles through the joint and it's a passage of glory. The windows shake and the crystals shimmer on their strings and under a sticky sheet and a hundred and fifty pounds of sweat-slicked flesh and beauty Elisha curls his toes and goes still. By the time the Queens-bound local passes in the other direction they've gotten untangled and Félix is standing by the open shutter, watching the train go by. He lets go of the sheet, toasts the oblivious passengers with a lit cigarette.

"Ass-naked for the whole neighbourhood," Elisha says, like his mom would have. Félix laughs. Beautiful to the point of unearthly, but he's the most real thing in this room full of tchotchkes. Healing crystals, incense sticks, long strings of beads: the things clients like. And a half-done tarot spread, abandoned on a side table.

"Hey, corazón," Félix says, gesturing at it and scattering ash. "You never do that for me."

A flutter of eyelashes, an aggrieved tone, like he was complaining that Elisha never made him eggs, or blew him. Elisha rolls his eyes.

"Put some pants on and I will," he says, and Félix laughs again and pulls him in to kiss. Such a fucking hipster, Elisha thinks, tasting menthol, sweet as the affection washing through him. He sits down at the side table and reaches for the cards. Félix leaves his pants where they are but he sits quietly on the window ledge, feet swinging; this is a thing that belongs to Elisha, so he takes it seriously.

Elisha sweeps the cards up, shuffles, cuts, draws. A Celtic cross, some tellers call this. They're imagining Tír nan Òg and shamrocks, maybe, and not Brooklyn under the elevated tracks, here in this sweltering century.

"Ask," Elisha says.

Félix startles visibly, although his attention has been focused on Elisha's hands all this time. It's like he forgot that it's how this goes, that without the question the cards are just paper with pictures.

"Does it all turn out okay in the end?" he asks.

Elisha could curse him for it, that razor-gleam vulnerability. Lately they've all been asking that—the regulars, like the woman from the coffee place with the five kids and one missing, but also the one-time deals: a gawping tourist, looking for a genuine New York experience; a girl who kept using the words *scientific method* as talisman against her own belief; even the twink with "M.A.G.A" patched on the ass of his fuckboy pants. They all check their phones every minute, call their senators every day, and ask Elisha and themselves if this is how everything—the world, the American experiment, everything they've known—ends.

Elisha wanted something easier this time. A dark, handsome stranger, an unexpected gift, a long journey.

But it's what Félix asked and he has to answer, so he lays down the first card: the Ace of Wands. The second: the Seven of Pentacles.

And there it is, the guest from the major arcana: Death.

Elisha does the reading for Félix, not in a hurry, but in a dream. He talks about the Wands, the reaching toward progress; the Pentacles and the gift of distant reward. He picks up the Death card and explains that it can be frightening, for those who aren't familiar with the deck, but remember that it can mean the little deaths, those that fall short of the end of all things. It may be the death of an outgrown self; or the death of an old order that can be remade better. When his own words fail him he reaches for Ecclesiastes: *a time to keep, and a time to cast away.*

Félix is comforted by his sincerity, and his presence. When Elisha asks, diffident but loving, if he would mind sleeping alone tonight, Félix only nods and kisses him. He grabs his phone and his hideous hemp sandals and heads out into the night, whistling cheerfully. Elisha hears him through the open window, the sound fading pleasantly into the susurrus of the city.

Elisha makes sweet tea, adds lemon and mint, sets it to steep. When the door opens, he stands—which is proper, for a guest—but doesn't bow his head. And then he's startled, bemused, as Death stumbles across the threshold, drops to their knees, and rises only with difficulty. Elisha gets them to a chair, murmuring, *Sh'ma Yisrael Adonai Eloheinu Adonai Echad.*

Death slumps on the table, head balanced on their elbows, and lets out an exasperated huff. *I'm not here to collect.*

Elisha is unimpressed. "It's still what I say when you come. You want tea?"

*I don't require your hospitality,* Death says, the same way they do every time. Their coat gets thrown on the bed, their blue-flame blade propped up by the door. *I do not eat or drink.*

"Yeah, hi, I'm Jewish," Elisha says, and pushes the cup over. Death hesitates, then warms their hands on the rim and shivers, huddling into the too-large hoodie, the tattered cloth falling over their face.

Elisha lets them be and moves the tarot cards out of the way. As far as he's figured it out, the rules are this: it must be a random shuffle; a seven-card spread; a sincere reading for another. Money need not change hands, but Death will not come to those who stack the deck.

(Well. Not in advance.)

And perhaps not to everyone, Elisha thinks. But he wouldn't like it to get around that for him, Death follows the cards. They're just a means to ask a question. They're nothing to be afraid of.

"So," Elisha says, as deliberately calm as he can be at this moment. "You're sick?"

Death rises from their chair and goes to perch on the edge of the window ledge, feet swinging. Leather sandals, chipped red polish on their toenails. Cute, like Félix. Death isn't here to frighten.

*Not sick,* Death says. *Something else.*

"Well, you don't look good," Elisha says, hands around his own cup. His mom, who taught him the prayers and how to make tea, used the same blend of spices, in reverence of her own mother's long-ago childhood in Cochin. Elisha's grandmother came to Queens, thousands of miles from her beloved city by the sea, and never left again.

(And were Elisha another woman's son, or grandson, he might be making a fuss right now. He might run out in the street, preaching poetry and prayer: *And death shall have no dominion*, and *death itself shall die*. But Elisha is thinking of every grieving client, every reading done in desperation, of every dawn that brought neither rapture nor resurrection but the real things of real people. Of his grandmother, who died beneath a window that looked over baked asphalt, far from what was hers.)

"All right," Elisha says. "Then what? Why are you here?"

*I am bound by the cards.*

"Like fuck you are," Elisha says. "They're just paper."

He's annoyed. The illumination in the room is limited, tinted by the sodium of the streetlights. Elisha gets up, pushes back the hood. He looks upon the face of Death, and sees:

Exhaustion, mainly. Grief etched in lines as deep as time, eyes like febrile stars. Death sits still with their head propped up on their elbows, and sighs. In that sigh there is the chill of the graveyard, the crackle of the pyre. The shadowy echo chamber of the universe. And death, without the initial capital. Senseless and meaningless and inhuman. Easier to let it happen. Easier to let it all go.

Elisha's hand grips the metal spout of the teapot. He doesn't remember picking it up. It's burning; it's a welcome hurt, a willing surrender. "Shit," he says, snaps back to himself and drops it with a hiss. It clatters hideously loud on the hard floor and the dead-leaf liquid begins to spread around his feet. "*You* made me do that."

*I apologise. It was not intentional.*

"Fuck," Elisha says, annoyed again, but frightened, too, by the apology—by everything passing strange through this place.

And by the look in Death's eyes. Elisha has lived long enough to recognise despair when he sees it.

Do you remember the first time? Death asks.

Elisha nods. He was new, hustling, saw a Rider-Waite tarot deck in a bookstore. And it's not like it's some mystical whatever: you don't have to learn it from your gypsy grandmother. "Gypsy" is offensive anyway, fuck that shit. He bought the deck, read about it, practised, and one night without fuss or ceremony, he did a reading for a client and brought some peace to a troubled mind. The second and the third time were different but the same: small easings of small, human pain. And the fourth time, once the client had gone and taken with her the blistering clarity of the major arcana, Death came to Elisha in stacked heels and glitter.

Elisha freaked the hell out, said his mother's prayers, and cried in the morning when he figured it out. Death came high-femme to Brooklyn because Death was a friend. It was a friend who came to take them home.

*There were so many*, Death says, in Elisha's third-floor walk-up, fifteen years later. *There are so many.*

A gesture, toward Elisha's tarot deck.

*Does it turn out okay in the end?*

Elisha doesn't think about what he does next. He kisses blood-red lips and pushes his hands under the hoodie, and of course there's warmth beneath. Death, who comes in glitter to the queens and for the fearful in jeans; who kisses babies and bows to old men; who comes for an elderly Jewish lady with a cup of tea in hand, to take her where the sun sparkles off the water and the air bears salt.

When Elisha pulls away his ears are ringing and his mouth tastes of ashes. "I don't know," he says, and it's the truth. The Death of the major arcana has fallen from the deck, face down. "I don't know."

Death nods, and pushes a curl out of Elisha's eyes.

"But without you," Elisha says, voice ringing out, "they just die. They just fucking die, okay? Do your job."

Death doesn't answer. But they get up, walk to the door on steadier feet, and reach for the coat and blade.

"It doesn't mean the death of all things," Elisha says, hesitant but earnest. "It can mean the death of an old world, something to be made anew."

The door closes. The F train rattles through.

# AKBAR AND THE CROWS

*(Akbar the Great was the third Mughal Emperor of India; Birbal was his closest adviser and confidante)*

And after the campaigns of conquest were over, Akbar laid down her arms and returned to Fatehpur Sikri, which had been the capital of the empire in her great-grandfather's great-grandfather's day. The great flagships were placed in mooring orbits; the soldiers were made a gift of their vacuum-proof armour, which could be sold for value, and discharged; and the imperial retinue, which had been a spaceborne capital in itself, of generals and soldiers, quartermasters and chuprasi, came down from the heavens and settled around Akbar's durbar, the court of an emperor who must now rule in peace.

It was a dusty, strange place that Akbar found herself in those days. The sun shone, except when it did not. The monsoon rains came, except when they did not. Akbar summoned her court meteorologist. "Sahib," she said. "Tomorrow I wish to hunt. What will the weather be like?"

"It will be fine, huzoor," said the court meteorologist, "except, of course, if it is not."

"Shall it rain?" Akbar asked.

"No, huzoor. Unless it does, in which case it shall."

"Had I asked my military astronomers for the times of the eclipses," said Akbar, "they would have told me the very hour and minute."

"Things are different on the ground, huzoor," said the meteorologist.

Akbar did not send the meteorologist away from the durbar, as his daughters were in school in Fatehpur Sikri, and would be much disturbed by the upheaval. But she was still brooding on the matter when word came from a provincial mantri that famine had struck the world of Kalb-Alrai, some eighty light years off, and starving for lack of grain and digestible proteins.

"How can this be?" Akbar demanded, when the mantri's messenger came with his report.

"Jahanpanah, these things happen," said the messenger, who was not a courageous man. He was thinking of a previous courier with whom Akbar had been displeased, and the jar of ashes that that man's family had received.

"They should not," Akbar said. "Send for the chief agronomist."

The chief agronomist came. He explained that harvests had failed on two of the colonies within the system of Kalb-Alrai; that the closest inhabited systems were still some distance, and in any case their resources were stretched; that food was required for their own people and could not be spared.

"When a supply line was cut," said Akbar, "my quartermasters adapted their plans. They diverted resources from elsewhere in my spaceborne forces. My soldiers did not go hungry."

"No, huzoor," said the chief agronomist. "You are quite correct. Your soldiers lacked for nothing."

He paused over what he would say next. But he was a principled man, unlike the mantri's messenger, who had been sent to the kitchens during the chief agronomist's explanations, and was now drowning his apprehensions in fruit juice and sharbat. Remember that Akbar was brave and skilful, a fine leader who had raised her people to the stars, but at that time she was a young woman at the start of her reign, trying to understand everything new to her. Remember, also, that the chief agronomist had students and daughters and plenty of both.

"Jahanpanah," he said. "Your armies had the best of everything. Where they were in need, the quartermasters requisitioned civilian supplies. Even in those days, some among your people starved."

"I see," Akbar said. The chief agronomist held his breath, wondering if he too would be sent home to his family in a ceramic jar.

But Akbar was not angry. "You must advise me, sahib," she said. "What should be done for the people of Kalb-Alrai?"

The chief agronomist consulted with the court economists, and they brought scholars of xenobotany to the durbar from across the galaxy. Akbar ensured they had access to the best expertise and left them to their work. Her generals had pushed figurines over table maps, taking time and care over their strategising, and Akbar understood that haste would avail them of nothing.

But it was a long wait, and with each day that passed Akbar thought of the hunger of Kalb-Alrai, and the hunger of people she had not known of before she came to this dusty place on the ground.

On the sixth day after the arrival of the provincial mantri's messenger, the advisers produced their report, setting out how the effect of famine might be lessened, if not eradicated, and how such a thing might be avoided in the future. Akbar asked that their course of action be checked by independent scholars, and instructed the imperial treasury to fund its implementation. And when that was done, Akbar rose from her dais and said, "Birbal, walk with me."

Rani Birbal was a poet among Akbar's navaratnas, a witty and intelligent Brahmin, who on happier days needled Akbar like a gadfly. She went quietly with her friend into the great gardens surrounding Fatehpur Sikri, and asked, "How may I assist you, huzoor?"

An emperor, particularly a young and inexperienced emperor, may not show weakness. Rather than speak of what troubled her, Akbar pointed at the flock of black birds gathering around the edge of the ponds, and asked, "What sort of birds are those, Birbal?"

"Those are carrion crows, huzoor," said Birbal. "They pick the flesh of dead things, so the bones are clean, and do not fester or cause disease."

"And how many crows are there in my kingdom?"

"There are five hundred and forty thousand, three hundred and twelve crows in your kingdom," said Birbal.

"How can you be so sure?" Akbar asked. "Very little is certain in this country. Perhaps I shall commission a report and have them counted."

"You may do so, huzoor."

"And what if the number it gives is lower than yours?"

"That is simple," Birbal said. "Some of our crows will have gone on pilgrimage to other kingdoms."

"And if my commission finds that the number is higher?"

"Then other crows have come to visit their relatives in your kingdom, huzoor."

Akbar laughed, and was a little reconciled to the strangeness of life on the ground.

# ONE-DAY LISTING

This is just one ordinary day in Senchai's new life. So far, it's not going well.

People say that the asteroid that destroyed 47 Piscium was set in motion by a passing star. That it was a handful of dust coalesced into rock, with a bare nothing of a molten core, minding its own business out on the far reaches of traversed space, until its nearest star puffed off its outer layers in a radiant twinkling and it tumbled into history contrariwise to the spin of the galaxy. Senchai isn't sure she understands that: how that sequence of relativistic forces led to a crater hundreds of metres across and a cloud of ash blocking out the midday sun. But she's pretty sure, first of all, that she knows what that felt like, that sudden lurch into uncharted territory; and, second of all, that there is a direct causal relationship between that bright burst of stellar energy and the fact that she, Senchai of Signa and Earth and Nazer, respected attorney-at-law, is sitting on her office floor crying into the powdered remains of her morning cup of coffee.

Chrissie does a couple more pull-ups on the door frame, her arm muscles tensing visibly, her feet landing with firm thumps on the honey stone floor, and then realises. "Oh, no, did the vibration push your coffee off the table? Oh, honey, I'm sorry, I'll go get you another one, okay?"

Chrissie's too kind to mention the tears, Senchai notes dispassionately. She leans against the wall, the stone warm against her cheek, and listens to the sound of Chrissie sweeping up the debris and then to the distant whistle of boiling water. By the time she can smell the fresh coffee, she's back at her desk, looking through her case docket for the day, making notes of points of law she wants to check before the hearing. A flash of Chrissie's warm presence and then there's a cup at her elbow; Senchai takes a sip while reading about the original Signan Lands Acts.

Then Chrissie says, "Oh, hey, Senchai, you know we're out of paperclips?" —and Senchai is crying again, really crying, tears dripping down her nose along the same tracks as before, landing with disturbing swiftness in the dust on her desk. For a long moment, there's no sound but her breathing and the rattles of beads in the mild desert wind. The office, like many in Nazer and on 31 Piscium, is built within a natural cave structure. Instead of doors and internal partitions, they have long strings of rough wooden fragments, threaded on twine and cut to fit. The beads rattle. Senchai cries.

"Honey," Chrissie says, after a while, tossing her dreadlocks over her shoulders, "it's nothing to do with the paperclips, is it?"

The ridiculous thing is that it *is* to do with the paperclips, as well as with that same small asteroid rocking through space towards the Magellanic Clouds. They are running out of paperclips because there are none to be had in any of the small retail establishments in town, nor can any be sent for from anywhere else. Everything here on 31 Piscium is bought or given away the moment it's unloaded from the ship holds. What they do have in excess is people, eating food and drinking potable water and using paperclips to hold together the letters they're sending to everyone they know to say they're safe. That the warning system, installed at great effort and expense thirty years before around the colony world of 47 Piscium, worked, and when thousands of tonnes of solid rock and newly molten metal hit the southern continent, most of them, but not all, were already in deep space. Public opinion is divided between those who demand to know why humanity's first foothold on another world should have been on 47 Piscium, a planet known to be the largest of an orbiting field of rocky debris, and have to be reminded of its soft, fertile soils and absence of height or depth; and those who demand why the refugees all have to come *here,* to 31 Piscium, the closest colony world, and why their water is rationed and why are there not enough paperclips.

And those who say nothing, but resolve to eat a little less and wash a little less often, and make do with a lower dose of their medication.

Human melodrama, Senchai thinks: such unnecessary self-sacrifice. Senchai is human on her father's side of the family, but the fact often doesn't figure in her interior monologue.

"If you've got a needle and thread somewhere," Chrissie says, her lips curled up, "I can sew your documents together. I'm sure the court won't mind. I'll do it when I get back, though – just going for a quick run around the block."

Senchai considers telling her about the weight of the paperclips required to hold together the Nazer District Court regulations merely on the subject of the presentation and formatting of court-lodged documents, or about the effect of 31 Piscium's sand-laden air on Chrissie's wholly human physiology, and decides against it on both counts. Because that's it, isn't it: the coffee cup Chrissie brought is warm and comforting, and so is the air in the room, thick with desert heat and solitude. It's what Senchai wants.

Nick comes in an hour or so later, his pupils dilating in the relative dimness. He's sweating from the effect of the desert sun, the crisp creases of his shirt beginning to wilt. He rummages through the piles on his desk, fanning and scattering them, papers making waterfalls into the dust. "Can't be helped," he murmurs, perhaps to himself. Looking up, he asks, "Shall I toddle down and issue then, Senchai?"

Senchai has a flash of something then that could be intuition, or logic, or what the humans still insist on mistranslating as "magic": *signene*, that makes them what they are. "You wish to issue a claim?" she asks. "I will come with you. Chrissie will hold the fort, as you say."

"No probs." Chrissie toasts them with her cup.

Nick and Senchai pause to gather their materials in their arms and set out on the short walk around the corner. On Signa, justice must be done and seen to be done; Signan courts convene by custom under a broad-crowned tree.

The clerk rises at the sight of them walking down the shady street, nodding at them both. "Senchai of Nazer, and" — her eyes rest on Nick — "client? Name?"

"Ah, no," Senchai says. "I am no longer a sole practitioner. I am joined by Nicholas Campbell and Crystal Lorde, both trained on Earth with rights of audience before Signan courts." The clerk's stylus tracks, and Senchai holds up a hand. "Also— we shall be acting only on the Lands Act claims."

The clerk says, "Your family work - small commercial—"

"No longer." Senchai's tone is more severe than she meant it to be; the clerk says nothing more. The first hearing of the day is in session as they move into the clear space of the court. Nick sits down cross-legged, right foot over left, seemingly without thinking about it. Senchai smiles to herself: he has had the training in Signan jurisprudence, after all.

"Allow me to sum up," the judge is saying. "You"— a pause for shuffling papers— "Teller of Nazer, did on the coming of the spring this year sell your neighbour several containers of seed, predicting a standard growth yield for the batch within a ten percent tolerance. It appears that the seeds have yielded…"

"Five times as much," calls a voice from the bench, presumably the defendant.

The judge acknowledges the interruption. "And after that the refugees from 47 Piscium arrived, so we consider this a blessing. You, Teller of Nazer, are now applying for an overage payment in respect of the yield."

Teller stands up and nods his head. "Not for the whole amount," he says. "But for the excess, perhaps the original price could be paid over again…"

"Such a thing is contrary to nature," the judge says, cutting him off gently. "It is" — and he makes the gesture, fingers curled against the grain of the webbing, so the court know the word is coming - "signene. And it is the oldest settled law of our people that where signene lies, no cause of action can. This is how things must be. I elect to dismiss."

The man takes it with no bad grace; he rises, bows, and walks out of the shade of the tree.

"Next," the judge says, taking the brief from the clerk, "the first Lands Act case of the day. Elan, now of Nazer. Advocate? Nicholas Campbell. What did your mothers call you, Nicholas Campbell?"

"Nick," Nick says, standing and bowing, a little clumsily. Senchai places a hand on his elbow to steady him.

"Nick. Speak.

"Ah." Nick hesitates before speaking. "My client, sir. Elon of Nazer."

The judge consults his notes. "Elan of Nazer, it says here."

"Ah," Nick says, uncertainly, "yes" - and Senchai wonders at it. Perhaps it is because he is not accustomed to inquisitorial justice, made nervous by the clear-eyed focus on him. His client sits quietly on the ground, eyes on the judge. "Anyway" —more hesitation — "my client is, in, ah, an unhappy position."

"As are all those making Lands Act claims, Nick. A little more expedition."

"His mother owned land on 47 Piscium. It was left to her sister on her death, of natural causes, last winter. My client would have been in line of succession, eventually. But his mother and his mother's sister, and his siblings and cousins - well, you know. He didn't have any cousins. But the other things. And as his aunt held the land he is a nephew, which is not within the human lines of descent within the Acts. I hope that's clear."

The judge says, "Have you the deeds?"

An apologetic glance at Senchai, a shift from foot to foot, and then Nick is looking at the judge again. "It was rather a mess this morning," he offers, and then pauses. Senchai notices his eyes flickering from side to side, as though he's waiting in fear of something. Her own wrath, perhaps.

The judge sighs, an audible sigh rattling across the space beneath the tree. "It appears to me," he says, "that the equitable resolution to the claim is quite clear. Elan of Nazer, I grant you land under the auspices of my jurisdiction and the Modern 47 Piscium Lands Acts, to compensate and comfort in the loss of your hearth and home; the clerk shall draft the order and you shall take it to the registry in due course. But" - his voice sharpens - "that is despite, rather than because of your advocacy, Nicholas Campbell."

Senchai flinches; the full name is an insult.

"Bring the deeds to the clerk in the afternoon," the judge says.

# One-Day Listing

Nick nods and bows again; the next case is brought up, the next client's name read.

"Advocate, Senchai of Nazer," says the judge. "What did your mothers call you, Senchai of Nazer?"

The issue is purely procedural – a claim under the Acts that was a mere day or so out of time, because of the plaintiff's sudden illness – and Senchai goes through the rituals of the jurisprudence automatically, with her eyes on Nick. She's wondering if she made a mistake.

❧

When the court breaks for the afternoon, all Senchai wants is silence – perhaps just the quiet space of her life as it used to be, before the noise of the impact and the misery and the two Earth-trained lawyers with their endless things to say. But when she arrives back at the office the doors are all open to the sounds of passing people and traffic, and Chrissie, assisted by two volunteers that she appears to have pulled in off the street, is carrying a gigantic purple shrub in a makeshift pot into the office, dropping spiky scraps of foliage and twigs everywhere.

"What," Senchai begins, but Chrissie waves her away.

"Long story, Senchai, don't worry about it. Come on then, I was just about to go get some lunch."

This is what humans do, Senchai thinks with frustration. Somehow without really wanting to, she's following Chrissie to one of the small siesta markets that appear and disappear between lunchtime and sunset. Chrissie stops and expertly haggles over a bowl of vegetable soup with some black market rice. Senchai gives up and buys some of the soup for herself, too. She's not hungry, but then, she rarely is these days. They sit on a low wall to eat it, looking back across the street to Senchai's little frontage with Chrissie's and Nick's names roughly added.

"I wanted to tell you something," Chrissie says, without preamble, once she's devoured most of the soup. Chrissie always eats like that, Senchai has noticed – with the single-minded joy of one taking a sacrament. "When I was a kid my mom died. We lived on 47 Piscium back then."

"I'm sorry for your loss," Senchai says, startled, automatic.

Chrissie shakes her head. "No big deal. I hadn't been back for years when the rock hit. I blew off my high school reunion. But Mom died, and then it was just Dad and me. And I love the Signans, Senchai, I do." A pause. "I don't, I guess. I mean, sometimes I love them, sometimes I don't, like they're my own people. But then it was just Dad and me, humans alone in this little edge-settlement town. 47 Piscium wasn't so big of a place back then and I was young, I acted out." She shrugs. "I want you to know you can do what you want, Senchai. You lost some of your family, didn't you?"

Senchai lets out a sigh because this, *this* is what humans do. "Yes."

"So – you know, I just wanted to tell you, you can stay home when you feel bad, smash some stuff. You want to sit in the corner and cry, that's okay too."

Senchai shakes her head. "What I do is my job."

Chrissie smiles fondly in response at that, and Senchai doesn't understand it. "Senchai, you're doing your job. You're doing it. You got us in to help, and you rearranged your whole practice, and you—"

"And I was here, when it happened; I still have a home." Senchai has raised her voice without quite meaning to, and she knows her eyes are getting wider with emotion from the way Chrissie is moving backwards in alarm. Senchai's father used to say that Senchai had eyes like two silver dollars, which was a human, kind way of saying they were large as a curled index finger and with the implacable surface of quicksilver.

But the moment passes, Chrissie takes another loving slurp of her soup, and Senchai finally feels moved to try her own. It's thin and watery. "Tell me something," Chrissie says, at length. "Your… signene." Though she doesn't make the accompanying gesture, she says the word quietly. Senchai approves. "Didn't you know, that something…"

"That something terrible was going to happen. Yes." Senchai nods. "Some of us did. My mother spent a day crying at nothing; I threw up. I believed it had been my evening meal. Once the data had been collected—"

"It was too late." Chrissie makes a wry expression, not quite a smile. "I guess it's never like fairy tales. I guess we have to go back to work."

"Precisely." Senchai helps Chrissie up, and they walk back across the street.

≈

There are still two hours before the evening session. Chrissie goes out to visit a client at home and Senchai sits down to work, noticing that the purplish shrub from earlier has been moved to a large glass bucket, its roots bathed in water. She shakes her head at it and sits down at her desk, beginning on her afternoon briefs. She works solidly for a short while, making handwritten notes for later reference, when she hears a strange sound, the movement somewhere near her feet. She gets down to her hands and knees to investigate.

"I'm fine," Nick says, irritably. He's sitting, Senchai notes, almost exactly in the same spot she chose in the morning; some of the white dust from the smashed cup is now on his hands. With his head against the stone wall, his eyes are closed. "I'm fine, Senchai. Just... a bad mental health day."

"Ah," Senchai says, understanding a number of things all at once, and goes into the kitchen to heat up some water. Nick doesn't drink coffee, but she pours the boiling water into two cups and adds a precious slice of fresh lemon to each. She puts Nick's cup directly into his hand, so he doesn't have to open his eyes, and sits down next to him to sip from her own.

"Surely," he says after a minute, still aware of her presence, "you have better things to do."

"No." Senchai takes another sip from her cup. "But I will leave if you wish."

He opens his eyes at that, glances at her quickly, but doesn't say she should leave. "Thanks for this," he says, after a moment, gesturing gently with the cup. With some interest, he adds, "I thought... well. I thought

Signans weren't too good with this" – he taps the side of his head – "sort of thing."

"Historically, they were not." Senchai thinks about that, and drinks more of the lemon water. "People with illnesses of the mind were feared. For... what they might do." She makes the gesture with third finger and thumb in conjunction, to avoid saying it: it is not right to use the word around a person already upset. "What you mistranslate as magic."

"Ah," Nick says, and she admires his wry, lawyer's intelligence, evident even here on the floor in the dust. "A little bit of paranoia in the wrong person, then crash bang boom."

"Yes. It is thought," she goes on, slowly, "that this is why such illnesses are not common, with us. The genetic component to the condition has long since been" - she pauses, delicately - "eradicated."

"Ah," Nick says, again. "Well, that's... terrifying."

His voice is still wry, but he seems to shrink for a moment, pressing further against the wall. It takes Senchai another minute to perceive the disjunct in their understanding. "Do not think it was not a terrible thing," she says, quickly. "The worst of things. If someone were to threaten you for your illness, I would pick up that thing there" - she points to the purple shrub with its spiked leaves and twigs - "and make your defence."

Nick laughs, shakily. "I believe you would, Senchai. And then bring an action for the damage inflicted on your property by their face."

"Sometimes that is necessary," she says, primly, because she thinks it will make him laugh again. It does, a little, and she leans back against the wall in unconscious echo of him, enjoying the warmth of the cup.

"Senchai," Nick says after a while, "may I ask you a personal question?"

She considers. "Yes," she says, "like for like."

"That's the Signan way." Nick nods. "You and me, we look similar on the outside, but inside we're completely different, right? I guess I don't mean you and me, I mean, humans and Signans. We're different. Different species. But you... you're half-Signan and half human. Is that because of the" - he made the hand gesture - "signene? I'm sorry to use the word, if it offends you."

"It does not offend me," Senchai says, calm. "Electricity will create an arc across space, to complete a circuit; so it is with us. When the physical things of the world are not enough, the signene will fill that space."

"Equity sees as done what ought to be done," Nick says, and she nods, pleased with the analogy.

"Quite. So it is with us; so it is with me."

"Can't have been a lot of people like you around, when you were growing up," he says. "Guess you spent a lot of time alone."

"Quite," Senchai said, irritated at the softening of his expression.

"It's okay," he says, and she resists the urge to ask him, indignantly, why he is suddenly consoling *her*. "It's okay. Chrissie and me - we can learn to be quiet." He looks up at her, his eyes bright and his hands shaking.

"Like for like," she says, sharply: that's the Signan way. For every secret given and every confidence demanded, an equal and opposite reaction. "Nick. Are you taking your medication?"

His head snaps up, eyes bright with anger for a moment, then swiftly fading. He glances up at her again, and down at his feet; it takes him a moment, but he is a good lawyer and he knows the rules. "I just, I saw it," he mutters, "and I thought, what can I do, I can do pro bono, but I did that before, Senchai, I did that before a planet got obliterated. And they were saying can you do with a little less. Can you manage without the full dose? And I thought I've been medicated half my life. They've got plenty to be anxious about right now."

"You self-sacrificing idiot," Senchai says, and is alarmed at the degree of fondness that has come into her voice. "Nick, the evening listing will begin soon. Are you ready?"

"It's my job to be," he says, and it's hers, too, so she gets up to return to her desk. But she touches his shoulder briefly, and catches the flash of his smile.

❧

"Next. Nizramuddin of 47 Piscium, now Nazer. Advocate, Nicholas Campbell, whose mothers called him Nick." A pause; Senchai wonders if the judge is going to offer a comment on Nick's earlier performance, but the pause lengthens into nothingness and the moment passes.

"I had only one mother," Nick says, ironically, "as is more common among my people, but that is correct. May I proceed, sir?"

"Do." The judge pauses again. "Although my clerk reports you have not, once again, provided the deeds to the land. This is a Lands Act claim, is it not, Nick?"

The judge is matching him for ironic, and Senchai breathes in deeply, but Nick meets the judge's eyes with equanimity. "Yes, sir. The crux of the case revolves around that particular point. My client was born on 47 Piscium to a family who had been working its land for as long as there have been humans and Signans to work its land."

*Had been*, he should have said; there is a minute pause while Senchai and the whole court notice that, and then let it go.

"The land came to my client from his mothers," Nick says. "The land came to them from theirs."

"I understand the nature of the thing," the judge says, not unkindly. "No one demands that the refugees stopped to gather the deeds to their land as the klaxons sounded."

Nick nods, and Senchai shakes her head, for some people did do just that. When the first family stumbled into the office with their arms full of crackling yellowed paper, she remembers that she took a long look around the room, wondering what she would take, should the planet-wide alarms start blaring at that very moment and pull her world from beneath her. She looked, and did not decide.

"However," the judge continues, "there is the central registry of land proprietorship."

"With respect, sir, there is not." Nick puts his hands on his hips and leans back slightly. "Land registration on 47 Piscium, as here, recorded transfers, assignments and mortgages of land. When my client's ancestors arrived on 47 Piscium all those scores of years ago, they made landfall on what would be their own land. Their own land: never for value given; never in other hands."

Senchai can see the anxiety in his wringing hands, but Nick's voice is steady.

"And now, if you'll forgive me for a moment," Nick says, and Senchai follows his gaze away from the judge to Chrissie and the clerk, struggling slightly with their burden of a giant purplish shrub, dropping foliage in a long trail behind them. Others seated on the ground shuffle rapidly out of their way to let them pass, and the judge looks on as they set it down in between of him and Nick. Chrissie puts a hand on Nick's shoulder as she returns to her spot on the ground.

"This is what my client brought," Nick says, a little dangerously. "This is what came with him in his arms from a dying world."

"Nick," the judge began, and is perhaps about to say something familiar to Senchai's ears about human melodrama, but Nick sighs and the sound is strangely loud, even in that outdoor, quotidian space: it sounds like exhaustion, tempered with hope.

"The water in the twigs and leaves has been replaced by ours," he says. "The rest endures."

He bows, and straightens, and it's over. Nick's breathing is coming rapidly when he sits down next to Senchai, and there is a slightly jerky cast to his movements, but somehow Senchai isn't surprised when the judge grants the application for land for the client, despite the lack of deeds. "It is held," he says, "to be within the spirit of the Acts."

Later, Senchai, Nick and Chrissie walk quietly along the shady road, winding beneath the canopies of other trees.

"Signene," Senchai says, after a while, making the gesture with her eyes on Nick. "What could not be done, has been done."

"I'm human, Senchai," Nick says, tiredly. "I don't think that's how it works."

"You have been here some time," she says. "You will become like us." Tentatively, looking around for passers-by, she makes the sign again, fingers curled into thumb, and places it against his skin, at the hollow at the base of his collarbones. Too late she remembers his anxiety and that perhaps he might not wish to be touched, but his eyes on her are calm and kind, not unhappy, as though he understands it's a blessing. He holds her gaze for a moment, and then she takes her hand away.

"We should eat before we head back," Chrissie says with determination. "It's getting late."

Senchai nods in return. The light of explosion from 47 Piscium took time to cross space, so for a few minutes, it existed as it did before, peaceful in the night sky. Perhaps, she's thinking, this is the same thing: shocks and sudden tears taking their time to reverberate through the ground. Perhaps if they eat together, and take their time over the meal, there will be no more time, tonight at least, for solitude, and sorrow.

"My treat," Nick says. "Somewhere quiet."

Senchai smiles at that. They keep walking, beneath the trees, beneath the cooling evening sky.

# FLIGHTCRAFT

She's started to get post through the door now, circulars, letters from the local council, bills, all addressed to Talitha Cawthorne. That was the name she gave the gas board, when she moved in, and the water board, and the name she gave to the lex-engineer who needed it for the new telephone connection, and it was the name on her birth certificate, once.

"Lovely old-fashioned name, Talitha," her landlady said, when she signed the lease. "Arise, little girl, arise? I used to know my divinity, a long time ago. Although I suppose people call you Tali."

"Yes," she said, because that was true, or at least, she remembered being called that, years ago; she wondered if she'd still turn around at the sound of it. "Thank you. Perhaps you can direct me to the nearest grocer's?"

It wasn't far, up on the road towards the airbase. And now this is her third weekly shopping expedition, picking up eggs, bread, Heinz tinned soup, cheese. She leaves the bicycle leaning against a railing – Downham is safe as houses, the estate agent has said – and walks along the road from the little grocer's, past a bookshop with law and lex textbooks in the window, up to a café with a row of tables by the window. There are a couple of other customers: a woman gesturing wildly at the chalkboard menu, and a man moping into a coffee cup the size of a soup bowl. She sips her own drink and looks up at the little biplane rising and circling from the base, diving, looping the loop. She knows the place used to be RAF Downham – it's been in civilian control only a few months – but it seems to have held on to its skilled craftspeople: the plane corners and turns with eerie, tight precision. And perhaps, she's thinking, drinking in a little self-awareness with her tea, it's why she's here, after all. She could have gone anywhere, but she's come to a place where they still fly.

The woman at the counter has stopped gesticulating and is now crossing the floor with another soup-bowl coffee cup and a plate of biscuits balanced precariously on a tray. Talitha frowns, looking at all the chairs that she'll have to avoid tripping over, gets up and says, "Can I help you with" – and then it's too late.

"Shit!" the woman yells, stumbling against the table. The hot liquid makes a boiling arc above, and Talitha's mind works overtime – Scottish, from the voice; probably demobbed, to be yelling profanity in public places; possibly stationed at the base here in the town? – before she notices the coffee has slopped over the table edge, soaking into her shopping bag. "Oh, I'm so sorry," the woman says, reaching down to pick up the things spilling out across the floor. The liquid has got into the soup tins so the paper wrapping is coming away, the ink on the inside of the labels blurring into featureless smudges. The metal is visibly tarnishing and the woman groans. "So sorry, I'm going to make your soup go off. Look - what's your name?"

Talitha takes a breath. "Talitha."

"Look, Talitha, give us your napkin, will you?"

Talitha gives it to her. The Scottish woman pulls a soft pencil from her pocket with hands that are covered in inkstains. Working quickly, she sketches a sequence of symbols on the napkin and hands it back to Talitha. "Quick patch," she says. "When you get home wrap it round the tins with an elastic band, it'll do the trick. I really am sorry. I've lost my assistant at work, everything's at sixes and sevens, it's a wonder I can keep my head screwed on, but that should fix it."

Talitha inspects the napkin, folds it carefully and puts it away in her pocket. "Thank you, ah…"

"Cat. Catriona McDonald." She looks up at the big wall clock and hisses through her teeth. "Shit, shit, I'm late! Nice meeting you. Sorry!"

She flies out of the café, leaping over a cardboard box in the way of the door and disappears in a flash of movement crossing the glass. Surprising herself, Talitha laughs. She finishes her drink, picks up her bags, lets her hand close on the napkin in her pocket, and starts on the walk home.

꙰

Cat thuds into the hangar, slams her coffee down, finger-combs her hair and gets her breath back just in time for the outside door to swing open. She looks up, hoping she's giving the impression of calm competence, and says, "Audrey Knapp?"

"Yes. A pleasure to meet you." Her new client reaches out for a handshake and Cat winces at the amount of ink on her hands. But Mrs Knapp turns over her palms, inspects them with interest and no displeasure, and Cat thinks perhaps she, like Cat herself, considers the stains honourable badges of the trade.

"Catriona McDonald," she says, a little belatedly. "We've corresponded."

"Of course, Miss McDonald." Mrs Knapp smiles at her, but her eyes are on the great structure behind them, the glowing bronzed surfaces of the metal. When she seems to recollect Cat's presence and turns, she's distracted again: this time by the coiled scrolls on Cat's beautiful carved oak desk, the mess of discarded brushes.

"Perhaps you'll call me Catriona," Cat says, smiling. "Or Cat, everyone does."

"Then you must call me Audrey." Mrs Knapp finally drags her gaze back to Cat and smiles back. "Tell me how this is going to work. You said you'd figured out a new method of lexical locomotion – can you explain, please?"

"With pleasure." With sudden decision, Cat walks to the back of the workshop so the whole scene is spread out in front of them. The prototype craft dominates the space in its struts. "You know, of course," Cat says, "that I'm used to working with smaller aircraft. Biplanes, mostly." Almost unconsciously, she looks up to the giant hook in the roof from which they are hung, and the old Moth they're using as a model. "You've seen the wings in the process of the workings. I can have craftspeople in here eight hours a day with their brushes, painting the lettering on the outer surfaces. I suppose if there were no need for that, we could use something other than canvas for the wings."

Audrey nods. "But she's going somewhere where canvas won't cut it, I'm afraid."

Not for the first time, Cat wonders what is taking her on this journey – this middle-aged woman of no particular background, deciding suddenly to cross oceans by air and devoting a large portion of her not-inconsiderable resources towards it. Looking at her, Audrey seems to guess what she's thinking. "Peacetime doesn't agree with me," she says, with a studied lightness. "My former husband departed in search of a quiet life." She gives Cat a small, conspiratorial smile. "Now tell me how we're doing this."

"It occurred to me," Cat says, "that you don't have to see the lettering, even on an aircraft – it's just how we happen to do it. Now, if you take the heavy paper" – she points at the burgeoning scrolls on her desk – "and load it safely into the skin of the vessel, for example in the vacuum spaces between the layers of plating, then…"

Audrey smiles. "I understand."

She starts forwards, going to inspect the work, and Cat hangs back to wait for her verdict. Suddenly, a voice pipes up: "How do the letters make it go, then?"

Cat turns to the stranger coming inside from the rain. "Hello?"

"I'm Toby," he chirps – a boy, not quite a young man. "That's m'mum over there. How does it work?"

Cat is thrown off balance for a moment. She considers, then draws a piece of paper towards her.

Quickly, she sketches a basic form, and the paper crumples in her hand, becomes a folded swan.

She hands it over to Toby, who accepts it joyfully. "Wow! That's brilliant! How did you do that?"

"It's like mathematics," Cat says. "Once it's written, it can't not be true. See?" She takes the swan back and adds a descending stroke to the character on the neck. It takes flight and flutters around Toby's head.

"Brilliant!" Toby says again. "Do you think I could learn how to do that?"

Cat inclines her head. "Possibly. In earlier days I'd have said you were too old – I started learning when I was twelve." She smiles at the memory. "But the war has turned everything topsy-turvy. If you have the talent, you could be teachable."

Toby is delighted. "Can you show me now?"

Cat grins. "That's not quite how it works. But sit down over there and I'll see what I can do."

He sits down obediently at the empty desk and she gives him the first exercise from memory. It's no struggle, to remember being twelve years old with a sharp pen in her hand, sketching *open* and *close* and *open* and *close*, making a child's four-fingered fortune teller with the concentration of a chartered craftswoman working on a de Havilland.

"That's kind of you," Audrey says softly, and Cat startles; she hadn't noticed Audrey stepping back from her aircraft. "Sure he's not in anyone's way?"

"He's not," Cat says. The base at Downham is filled with junior craftspeople, but Cat's own assistant and right-hand man left her service only a week earlier to return to civilian life. Cat explained in vain that they were no longer *RAF* Downham; they were civilian lexical engineers working on civilian aircraft. "Not good enough," he said, and departed for a life presumably connecting telephone lines or mass-producing Fords or some such thing. She knows in her heart it's wrong to blame him; she had been feeling it herself in those latter days, the grief and weight of seeing their craft become a part of the government war machine. "I'll need to recruit someone new at some point, I suppose, but right now it's an empty desk."

Audrey nods, her eyes serious. "Right, Miss McDonald," she says. "I've seen what I need to see. I'm impressed with your work. Let me have a quotation for labour and materials and we'll see about getting this thing done."

Cat blinks, surprised. "I thought – I mean" – she pauses, aware she's about to self-sabotage out of nervousness – "that's a very quick appraisal, Mrs Knapp, I had this meeting booked in for the whole afternoon."

"You were head of the engineering corps here, weren't you?" Audrey snaps.

Cat nods, a little unsure of where this is going. "86th Lexical. I had captain's bars, but it's professional courtesy, really. I never ordered enlisted men about, I did my own job throughout the war."

"You were in charge of this place," Audrey continues, implacable, "and you, and it, are still here. That'll do for me. Toby, come along."

"Wait!" Toby cries, and waves his little square of paper. It's half-squashed and covered in inky smudges, but he holds it quite still in his palm and Cat sees the movement.

"Well done," she says, and looking at his bright, sweet face, and Audrey's serious one, makes an impulse decision. "Toby," she says, "would you like to stay a while?"

※

Talitha is sure it's the right door, with the right voice filtering through it, for five minutes before she brings herself to turn the handle and go in. Inside, the open hangar space is familiar, airy under the rafters and filled with light filtering through dust motes. There is a biplane at the far end – de Havilland Giant Moth, provides the part of her mind that never forgets such things: single-engine and four-hundred mile range – half-occluded by a swarm of craftspeople, sharpening the smudged flying forms and doing something to the structural lexicography. Something experimental, that same part of her mind adds, and Talitha turns away sharply.

"Can I help you?" asks a voice, and Talitha looks at the junior craftswoman with her hands on her hips. "This is a working hangar, I'm afraid, it's not safe for—"

"Don't be overzealous, Lindy," says a familiar Scottish voice, and Talitha wheels around. McDonald is there, her arms full of scrolls of paper. "You're my friend from the café, aren't you? Let me just – hey, Toby, put these somewhere, will you?"

A boy scurries across from the other side of the hangar and does so, seemingly delighted to be asked. "So good to see people happy in their work," McDonald says, sounding quite sincere.

"Your apprentice?" Talitha guesses.

"Not quite." McDonald sits at the edge of a desk – there are a half-dozen of them in a row at this end of the hangar, although only three seem occupied at present. "But the lad has a fancy for the craft, so he's spending a week or two with me to see if it's for him. Lindy, this is – Talitha, isn't it?"

Talitha nods.

"This is Lindy, she's helping out on that monster thing over there." The 'monster thing' is the Giant Moth. Lindy nods stiffly and returns to it without another word, striding determinedly across the hangar. "And," McDonald continues, "she's still not quite on board with the whole civilian aspect of our work, these days. I think she misses the barbed wire." She grins. "Anyway, Talitha, what can I do for you? How did the tins hold up?"

"Oh," Talitha says, suddenly brought back to herself. "They were fine, thank you. Ah, you left this in the café the other day, I asked the owner where I might find you, and..."

She trails off awkwardly, but McDonald takes the sketchpad from her. "Thank you!"

She flips through it and Talitha catches sight of a whole multiplicity of forms, some for flying, some for strength, some for precision, some she's never seen before. "Are you in the trade?" she asks, curiously. "Not many laypeople know how valuable one of these things is."

The paper, Talitha knows, has metal filings in the weave – so even a perfectly-executed form will not take, and a craftswoman can practise without accidentally turning her sketchpad into a paper aeroplane. "No," she says. "But I picked up a little bit in the war."

"Right." McDonald nods. "A lot of people did. Well, listen, if you want to come back at twelve, I'll stand you your lunch, all right? It'd have cost me ten times as much to replace this, after all."

Without waiting for agreement, she turns away to her not-quite apprentice and starts giving him a list of forms to memorise; she breaks off in the middle of the last to call some instructions to the team working on the Giant Moth; she breaks off from that to try some new form of her own on her newly-returned sketchpad; then asks the boy to repeat back the first five items on the list. A little bewildered, Talitha goes back into the cool, heavy spring air, and thinks it chilly after the warmth of the space inside.

They have lunch at the same café, though not at the same table. Cat orders toasted sandwiches and tea for them both and goes to fetch them when Mrs Daly behind the counter calls her name. "That the girl who's taken Amelia Pennyroyal's spare room?" she asks Cat. "Odd fish, that. No one knows her here. See if you can find out what brings her to Downham."

"You're a terrible old gossip, Mrs Daly," Cat tells her, and picks up the tray with utmost concentration. She makes it to the table without incident and Talitha looks up and smiles.

"Thank you," she says. "You know, this wasn't necessary."

"Not a bit of it," Cat says, biting into cheese, ham and pickle. "Eat up, it'll get cold. Maybe I should have ordered chips as well. I can, if you want?"

Talitha laughs, surprising herself once again. "I forgot that," she says. "Lex engineers are always hungry. I worked with one chap who had scrambled eggs on the hour. It was quite endearing."

"I've read theories that say it's some of our energy that makes things fly," Cat says, composedly. "Even if it's not, it's thirsty work. Where were you stationed?"

The sudden shift in conversation startles Talitha. "A long way from here," she says, after a moment. "Up north. You know," she adds, "there's money in wires and cables, these days. Telegraphic lex engineers, household appliances, that sort of thing."

Cat nods. "And there always will be. When I'm old and not on the top of my game any more, that's what I'll do." She has a craftswoman's dispassionate assessment of her own skills, Talitha notices. "But right now – Toby, wee Toby, you met him. Well, his mother has an idea for a new kind of plane. Further, faster, with proper long-range cargo. It's all to do with a stronger physical skin, maybe made out of metal. When I can't fly any more, that's when I'll do household appliances."

Talitha nods in return. "Metal, though? Won't that stop the forms from executing?"

"Somewhat," Cat says, "but it's not an absolute effect, it depends on other factors and I'm hoping we can work around it. I'll show you the diagrams if you like."

"Miss McDonald..."

"Cat."

"Cat," Talitha says. "Should you be telling me this? If it's a private commission, and—"

Cat sighs. "You sound just like Lindy," she says. "Listen, Talitha. I was born into the trade. I got my charter mark when I was twenty."

Talitha whistles involuntarily – she knew, of course, that Cat's talent was something out of the ordinary – but perhaps, hadn't quite grasped the extent of it. She says nothing.

"And during the war," Cat continues, "I had to do some things I wasn't proud of. I built new, improved lightweight planes that dropped new improved heavy artillery, and I put planes back together faster than the medics could put together the pilots. And I did it all behind the barbed wire up there." She motions to the window and the road up to the base. "No apprentices and not accountable to anyone, though my charter swears I'll teach my craft to anyone who asks. They can do proprietorial washing machines, frankly, I don't give a damn. But anyone who wants to fly gets to learn how."

Cat knows when she's finished speaking that she must be flushed with emotion – it's a practised spiel that nevertheless works its way through her body every time, like a form through canvas. But she looks up and Talitha is smiling at her, tentative, luminous. "I understand that," she says.

"We could do this again," Cat says, suddenly. "I mean, it's nice to have company at lunchtimes. It's been lonely since everyone up at the base started to leave."

"I'd like that," Talitha says, and she's smiling again.

"What happens," Toby asks, "If I do this?"

He picks up his pen – privately, Cat notes his grip has got much better: firm between forefingers and thumb – and rests the nib on his own wrist. He glances up at Cat, then stubbornly begins to sketch a form, a simple one for flight that's on the list that she drills him on every day. He reaches the end, smudges the ink and then looks disappointed. "Oh."

Cat breathes in and shoves down her immediate reaction, which is to grab the pen from his hand. "What were you hoping for?" she asks, keeping her voice gentle. "That you could sketch out *avis-alpha-b* and up, up and away!"

"Alpha-b?" he asks, distracted, and she shakes her head.

"A little beyond your pay grade, I think. You need to get *avis-unmarked* absolutely spot-on before we do the variations. And soon I'll have to think about getting the first-year syllabus for you. I'll make a note."

"Cat," he says, a hint of a whine coming into his voice. "Tell me."

She relents after a moment, putting a hand on his shoulder. "Toby, you mustn't try and do forms on yourself like that. Not on yourself or anyone else. Do you understand?"

"Why not?" He looks up at her in confusion, and Cat reminds herself that he isn't like she was; he wasn't born into this life.

"There are long textbooks about it," she says, after a moment, "which you'll have to read before you get your charter mark." His eyes shine at that and Cat realises that it's because she's talking about his charter mark, as though it's a given that he will get it, some day. "But for now: think about it like robbing Peter to pay Paul. You can't burn up the energy in your own body that way. What's the First Axiom of the craft of flight?"

In his frustrated expression, Cat sees herself at his age, and smiles beatifically. Finally, he says: "Remember Icarus."

Cat nods. "That's right. Don't do that, Toby. It doesn't work, and it's not" - she hesitates - "it's not right. Promise me you won't do that again."

Toby glances up at her. "I promise."

"There's a good boy." She ruffles his hair and he ducks away, heading across the hangar presumably in an attempt to escape both form drills and gestures of affection.

"That's not quite it, you know," Talitha says, emerging from the shadows behind the prototype. The aircraft is about half-done and is beginning to take on a personality of her own. Cat can't quite see the shape of her yet, except in shadows and absence, like a dry patch under a tree in the rain. It'll come.

"What's that?" she asks, as Talitha walks out from under a wing.

"What you said to Toby." Talitha looks at her, her eyes dreamy. "It's not quite right. There are some forms which will work on skin. If someone else draws them."

"Oh," Cat says. Before she can think of anything to say, Talitha is gone, edging back into the dimness behind the aircraft, heading for the door out to the sky.

～

Cat formally declares Toby her apprentice after he's been hanging around the hangar for a month. "Getting in the way," Lindy says, but Cat knows that's not right. The lad has fetched and carried messages, stirred great pots of ink, trimmed brushes, got up early and stayed late. Cat herself was born into pre-war privilege, the daughter and granddaughter of flight craftswomen; she respects the boy scrabbling for his start.

Audrey is grim but accepting, when she visits next. "God knows it's in his blood," she says. "His father was a craftsman. A mediocre one, mind you, never stretched to anything but rivets and joins. But it's a trade for the boy."

Cat smiles, then feels herself grow abruptly serious. "I'll do my best by him," she promises, "but my best isn't what it might have been. Before the war I'd have sent him to Woolwich for his theory, and he could have come here for his practical, but since the war—"

Audrey holds up a hand. "I'm grateful for whatever you can give him, Miss McDonald."

"Call me Cat," Cat says, for at least the fiftieth time, and smiles again. "Would you like to see how the work is progressing?"

"I would, thank you," Audrey says, and this time, as Cat shows her around the bare skeleton of the aircraft, she's less nervous: she knows the work is good. She and her people have been scratching forms and grammar on scraps of paper, making tiny models to dart around the hangar; they've been testing materials out on the hill, in the full blast of the wind; they've been consulting the sort of textbooks the craftspeople often leave for the academics. The aircraft doesn't yet look very different from any other of its size - the forms have been done on the usual heavy paper and then laid on the surface of the metal plating; Cat means to have them put within the skin only when everything is complete - but she's aware on a subconscious level that this one is different. A different presence, she thinks to herself, then smiles at her own fancy.

"It looks like you're making good progress," Audrey says, with reserve; Cat thinks that she probably doesn't say anything she doesn't mean, and keeps on smiling. "Have you considered a name, yet?"

"For the type?" Cat shakes her head. "Not yet. We might have to move away from the" - she gestures at the Giant Moth they were using as a model, now on the other side of the hangar from the prototype - "insect theme."

"For the particular craft." Audrey is hesitant. Nervous, Cat realises. "I don't know what the custom is, with these things - for the builders of the craft to name her, or for..."

"Oh," Cat says, and then, gently, "I think you should name her. If she's your" - Cat pauses - "unquiet life."

Audrey gives her a half-smile. "In that case," she says, "I suppose I'll have to think of something."

And after that, Cat thinks she's forgotten - after another week, some of the metal plating is appearing, and craftswomen in the hangar are calling it the Beast and the Thing and other such hefty monosyllables, so Cat thinks she's not the only one to have felt the presence of it, sitting squat in the hangar - but then Audrey asks, in a routine letter that otherwise deals with quotations for further materials, how they're getting on with *Margaretha Zelle.*

"Mata Hari!" Talitha says, startled, when Cat tells her.

"I had to look it up," Cat says, ruefully, over a cheese bloomer. "I don't know much about - well, anything that's not flightcraft."

"That's understandable," Talitha says. She seems amused, taking a bite into her own sandwich with piccalilli. It's a bright, breezy day, so they're sitting on the hill on the grass and holding on tightly to the sandwich wrappers. "I don't suppose you've ever had much time for anything else."

"And you should forgive me if I'm wrong," Cat says, tentatively, "but wasn't she a spy for the other side?"

"Brave as anything, though," Talitha says, and Cat is content to take her word for it.

~

Not long after that, Cat needs a favour.

"You're afraid of flying!" Talitha says, and chuckles. A shared and excellent steak pie has just rather robbed them of any great urgency to return to work.

"Not at all," Cat says, primly. "It was part of my training. But" – she pauses – "Miller, my old assistant, you know. He used to do it. When they wanted a craftsperson along on a test flight."

"Seems to me they ought to have one along on every test flight," Talitha says. "I'll do it, Cat. But you should try it sometime."

"Oh, no," Cat says, "no" - and then almost gets knocked flying onto the grass. "Lindy!" she says, stepping backwards. "Don't rush about so! What is it?"

"You've got to come," Lindy says, breathless and incoherent, "I called the fire brigade but they won't come in time, you've got to, Cat—"

She turns and runs back up the hill, her wildly scrabbling feet pushing up tufts. Cat follows her up and into the hangar, pushing open the little door with her eyes on her feet, so it takes her another second to look up and swear extravagantly. *Margaretha Zelle* had been hung from the roof: now she's half on the floor, great strips of paper hanging from the now-bent hook, and one of her wings is almost broken off, turned into a shapeless mess from the impact. "Is there someone under there? When did it happen?"

"Toby," Lindy says, tearful but steady, "he was looking at the forms, he was trying to figure out the pattern. Just a minute ago, Cat, he wasn't under the fuselage, he was under the wing, he might be—"

"Shut up, all of you," Cat snaps out, with military sharpness. "Not a word! Now."

In that textured silence, the paper flaps in the draught, a drop of water falls from the roof, and from the left wing of the stricken aircraft, two metres down and along, something - someone - taps. "Toby?" Cat says, loud and clear. "Tap twice if that's you."

Tap, tap.

"Tap if it's just you under there."

Tap.

"And once more if you're hurt."

Tap.

"All right," Cat says, clapping her hands. "The fire brigade have to come all the way from King's Lynn, we can't wait for them."

"Cat," Talitha says, urgently, "the plane's on the edge." She gestures at the hook, at where part of the structure remains suspended. "If we pull or tug at it, we might bring the whole thing down. It might crush…"

"Understood." Cat breathes. "We need to lift it. Not manually, you know how. None of you distract me for the next two minutes." She's getting down on her knees as she speaks, drawing forms quickly on the sheets laid out on the hangar floor. It's only the skill of long, long practice that keeps them neat and true. She draws strokes in abbreviated forms, crossing out rather than erasing her mistakes, waiting for them to execute; she thinks for a second about the hook she hadn't even considered, designed to hold up aircraft made out of canvas and not metal, then pushes away the thought. It's not useful.

"Cat," Talitha says, gently, "I can help" - and Cat wants to cry over the junior craftsmen who departed for telephone engineering, rather than do this work that matters.

"Do the groundwork," she tells Talitha, screwing pieces of paper into tiny balls and throwing them north, northwest, north-northwest. Talitha follows them and lays down the right forms for rigidity and tension, not with textbook perfection, but with the fluid essentials.

"You'll put yourself into a coma if you try this with no help," she says, without looking up. "There's not enough push in the forms for you to lift this alone."

Cat gestures wildly and put in a cross-stroke. "No other option."

Talitha holds up her pen and pulls up her sleeves, exposing the unmarked skin of her forearms.

"You're mad," Cat breathes.

"It's energy," Talitha says, with head back down. "It will fuel" – she draws a form in the air, and Cat breathes in sharply – "under the wing, if you – look, Cat, we don't have time to argue over this. Say yes or wait for the fire brigade."

Cat stares at her for another moment, then pulls up her own sleeves. "I didn't mean *you*," Talitha snaps, a little panicky, then begins to draw. Cat's fingertips are on the edge of the sheet and as the forms take shape something crackles at the paper's edge. Cat stares at it in bemusement, not thinking about the pain, as the fire catches and carries along the sheet and in its wake Talitha sketches out form after form, ones Cat only knows from textbooks, with no time to perfect her work before it's sacrificed to the flames.

"Done," Talitha says, and the two of them look at each other, then both reach downwards. Cat has time for fear, feeling her eyebrows singe and the roaring heat inches from her bare hands – and then they press the new sheet of paper down onto the aircraft wreckage, the flames leaping across. They only have a minute or two, Cat thinks, before the metal starts to heat up.

"Now!" Talitha yells, and Cat adds one more form with a hand that barely grips, simple enough for an apprentice to have done it – *avis-unmarked*, a stylised bird, for flight – and the broken pieces explode upwards.

Before Cat can move, Talitha dives in, grabs Toby, covered in dust, with blood showing at his mouth, then goes back to check there's no one else there. "Go!"

"Get back!" Cat presses both hands down, bloody and ruinous, destroying all the forms. The mess of the wing rattles down like unholy rain, Cat's knees hit the ground and the last thing she remembers is the sound of steam hissing, and Talitha's voice, soft and determined, as she calls to the others, as she pours water on the flames.

❧

"Mrs Knapp," Cat's saying, not for the first time, "I'm so, so sorry" - and Audrey stamps her foot.

"Cat, with all due respect, shut up," she says. "It's a fat lip and a broken leg. Toby's had worse playing cricket. And even if he hadn't, it wouldn't have been your fault."

"He's my apprentice," Cat says, stubborn and frustrated, "he's my apprentice, and I should have protected him, and I should have..."

"Cat," Audrey interrupts, "if you must make a martyr of yourself, go back to fixing my aeroplane. I will take Toby home for a while and run him back to you when he's ready. A very good day to you both."

She bows, turns on her heel and stalks out of the hangar. In the ensuing dusty silence, Talitha sighs. "She's right," she says, tentatively; Cat has not been easy to talk to, these last few days. "It's not your fault."

She waves vaguely as she says it: *Margaretha Zelle* is still spread in pieces across the hangar floor, though the remaining craftspeople have been working hard to remove the destroyed pieces, as not to warp the whole. Before Cat can say anything else, Talitha adds, "How's Lindy?"

"She says she's feeling a little better," Cat says, sounding defeated. Other than Talitha herself, Lindy had the worst of the smoke inhalation and falling debris. "She's going to stay with her sister-in-law for a few days."

"Glad to hear it," Talitha says, and then stops short. "The first part, I mean. And - Cat. What about you?"

"What about me?"

"How are you?" Talitha asks, insistent. "Cat, you lifted that wing more or less entirely by yourself. I know I helped make the thing susceptible, but you made it fly." She pauses. "I've seen what happens when people do mad things like that."

"Mad things like that," Cat repeats, with something in her expression that Talitha can't read. After a moment Cat gets to her feet, slowly and stiffly – Talitha wasn't wrong that what she did has taken the energy out of her - and beckons imperiously. "Come with me, please."

Curious, Talitha follows. Outside the hangar, on the grassy hillside, Cat sits down on a soft tussock and leans backwards, looking right up at the sky. She doesn't speak for a couple of minutes, and Talitha reaches over and touches her shoulder. "Cat?"

Still silence. Cat takes a number of deep, steady breaths. Talitha is starting to wonder if she's ever going to speak when Cat finally sighs and says, "So. These forms." She pulls back her sleeves as she says it, showing the damage: the lexical cuts are healing faster than the burns around them.

Talitha looks across at her face. "Yes. What about them?"

"I'm not sure," Cat says, mild. "I've been wondering, you see, if you might have used them in the war. If that's how you know what you know."

"You've worked it out, then," Talitha says, dispassionately.

"Have I?" Cat says, still looking straight up. "I don't know what I've worked out. I do know the old stories, about people who work with skin, and blood, and all those things that are neither ink nor paper."

"Mostly," Talitha says, sighing, "I worked with ink and paper. Mostly, but not always."

"Can you tell me?"

"I probably shouldn't." Talitha shrugs. "It was a place up north, somewhere near Loch Laggan, if you know it. If an aircraft came down with something interesting in the visible lexicography, that's where the pieces were brought. And..." - she pauses, then goes on - "with them, they brought the pilots."

"I was approached, myself," Cat says, matter-of-fact. "Just a few weeks after the declaration, actually. Someone came up to me in a café in Soho and said they'd known my father. They probably did, at that. Told me about the importance of the war effort. And how everything could be a weapon in the wrong hands. Asked me to consider a role in *special operations*, italicised, and awaited my answer."

Talitha shakes her head in return, impatient. "You said no."

"I want to say I thought about it," Cat says. "I want to say I had that kind of... courage? But I sent him away and he didn't come back. Tell me, what forms did you use on the pilots?"

"Lapidary forms, with proprietary modification." Talitha shrugs again and gestures. "If you work them on rock, it crumbles."

"Jesus Christ." Cat puts both her hands over her eyes, and Talitha flinches.

"We didn't all have the luxury of the long way around," she says, more sharply than she'd meant; she does not care about Cat's opinion of her, not about this. "We didn't all have the kind word, the fair start. We weren't all like Toby, or..."

"Me." Cat hasn't moved. "All of us raised in the grand old tradition. Remember Icarus. Help all who ask for it. Thou shalt not kill. Did you—"

"Yes. When it could not possibly be avoided."

"For information?"

"Among other reasons." She pauses. "You saw the value of generating energy in a hurry."

Cat looks up at her, something awful in her eyes. "Christ."

"Cat." Talitha stands up and takes a step downhill. "I did what I did. And I saved Toby's life. Yours, too, in the war. A dozen times, perhaps, without your knowing it. If you call it dirty work, well, I'm not here to answer to you."

She's trembling a little as she walks down the hill, but not too much. She's thinking about the pretty little room she's renting from an old lady who's kind to her, and how she came here where they still fly.

"Talitha." Cat scrambles to her feet, swaying slightly. "Stop, please."

Talitha says, over her shoulder, "Perhaps you should have waited till the fire brigade came from Lynn. Perhaps you should have let the undercarriage tip and crush Toby's bones."

Cat makes a frustrated noise and holds up her palms, still partly bandaged, all the exposed flesh shiny and raw. "Talitha…"

"Your own skin was in the form you made," Talitha says, and she'd meant to walk away, but she's turned on the spot, facing up. "Burnt away. Don't talk to me about clean hands."

"I'm not, for God's sake," Cat says, staggers and lands on the grass, makes a muted noise of pain, and moves no further. Talitha takes one more step, and has a sudden memory of meeting Cat in the village cafe, the rising arc of boiling coffee, the tins of tomato soup that are still sitting on her shelf at home, now sealed for all time, or at least until she stops having lunch with Cat every day. With a groan, she starts back upwards.

"You did your own war work, Cat," she says, half with anger and half something else, as she gives Cat a hand to steady herself with, and sits back down beside her. "You told me yourself."

Cat just looks at her. "I know."

"And," Talitha says, cuttingly, "you implemented what I learned. What I got from them, and the improvements you made…"

"I know."

"You might not have done the work, but you—"

"I know!" Cat puts her head in her hands, then looks up. "For goodness' sake, Talitha. I know what I did."

"Well, then," Talitha says, hands shaking.

For a moment, there's only silence. Then Cat leans back and breathes out, and her expression slowly loses some of that bleakness. "Believe it or not, Talitha, before the accident I was planning to offer you a job."

Talitha stares. "What?"

Cat nods. "Lindy and the juniors are good and sweet and Toby has promise, but I need a real second."

Talitha's still staring. "You want me to be your assistant?" She pauses. "I mean – you still do?"

"My right hand. " Cat gestures with her actual right hand, the bandages making the point. "Will you consider it?"

"I don't have your qualifications."

"We'll put you in for your exams when Toby does his. Will you do it?"

Talitha says, "Even if I do, I won't apologise for who I am, Cat. Nor what I did. I don't need your forgiveness."

"I used to build efficient aircraft," Cat says, softly and sadly, "delivering efficient artillery, on top of people. I don't know what happens, about that." She spreads her palms. "I told you before, I don't know much that isn't flightcraft. I don't know about what's written, what's true. Thou shalt not kill and all that. But I've got to rebuild that damn aircraft, Audrey's bought her goggles. I've got to get the new syllabus for Toby, and I need to send a get-well card to Lindy and I need to put in an order for a few hundredweight of wing canvas and I need to not be sat on my arse on a damp hillside, and I need your help."

Talitha grins, suddenly. "All right," she says. "On one condition." She holds out a hand to Cat, who takes it, and between them they get Cat to her feet. "When she's built, you'll fly in her."

"Oh, no, no," Cat says. "Don't even think about it."

Talitha shakes her head. Despite the chaos in the hangar, out here in the wind and the sun, she can imagine *Margaretha Zelle* clearly, how strange and beautiful she'll look, with forms hidden within her skin and so much more than she seems. "Don't worry," she says, giving Cat a shoulder to lean on, "I'll teach you how."

"All right," Cat says, sounding entirely defeated, "if that's what it takes" – and Talitha laughs as they go on up the hillside, into the curve of the sky.

# LANDFALL (YOUR SHADOW AT EVENING, RISING TO MEET YOU)

At one point, it was a source of consternation to Earth's constitutional bodies that the original Mars mission made landfall on Christmas Eve. It was a diverse, multinational and strictly *secular* leap of faith into the unknown; with three hundred and sixty-four other days to choose from, the particular date was felt impolitic.

Magnus never worried about it too much. "They'll speak of one longer than the other," she used to say, and all these years later Evan sees her point.

She still wishes Magnus wouldn't roll into a room full of children and official visitors, on Landfall Night, and say: "And it came to pass in those days that there went out a decree from Caesar Augustus, that all the world should be taxed."

"Magnus." Evan taps her foot and resists rolling her eyes upwards. Heavenwards, perhaps. The sky above the Tharsis Montes is blue with the translucency of eggshell, shifting through a blink-of-an-eye twilight to a depth of black never seen on Earth. The Milky Way dusts across it. Even through ugly fibre-optic tinsel and the silicate dome glass, it's beautiful to the point of pain. "That's not the line."

The kids are getting restive. One of Evan's students pulls at her sleeve, which is undoubtedly a precursor to *Evan I have to pee* or similar. Evan taps her foot again. "Magnus, please."

"Sorry." Magnus doesn't sound at all sorry. She leans back in her chair and rolls back a few centimetres. "O brave new world that has such people in't! I will show you fear in a handful of dust. That's not it either, is it?"

"Magnus, will you just say the fucking line."

The official visitors – from Terran Central Administration, by way of several months' journey time – look alarmed. The kids all perk up at once. Evan groans.

"Once upon a time," Magnus says, leaning out of her wheelchair so she's almost at eye-level with the nearest child. Magnus despises children with less of the open hostility with which she despises the rest of the human race, which is one of Evan's favourite things about her. "This was called Dome 2B. There were five domes and fifty people and a lot of duct tape and a broad range of talents. Don't do that."

A child pauses in the act of hitting his neighbour with a Happy Landfall Night card.

"Good," Magnus says. "We contained multitudes. We were combination botanist-linguist-polka-dancers. The best and the brightest the planet had to offer, at a hundred thousand dollars – you don't know what those are, kids, thank the Lord for that – per kilogram. Very efficient. Very pioneering."

None of this is the line either. The line is: "Teachers, technicians, surveyors, and more! Mars needs you!"

There's going to be a voiceover after that, and maybe some inspiring music, but they want the strapline spoken by a voice that speaks from history: the first commander of the first Martian colonisation expedition. Though with a calculated background of domesticity, Evan thinks: by the twinkling fibre-optic lights of a Landfall Night celebration and the faces of humanity's only extra-Terran children.

"Very pioneering," Magnus says again. "The Martian Colonisation and Exploratory Mission can go to hell."

She sweeps out, wheels soft on the carpeted floor. Evan checks the ratio of adults to children in the room, and goes after her.

❦

Dome 2B was initially constructed of meteorite-resistant polymer and the will to survive. These days it's made of glass, with the peculiar orange-purple shimmer that comes from the local mineral impurities. It encloses pods and modules and the internal components of a rudimentary spaceport structure. But along with what came with them, they have enclosed what was already here: precious square metres of the Martian landscape, under glass so they can breathe, but real sand and grit and dust underfoot. Evan knows to find Magnus at the very edge of the dome, her fingers outstretched to the inner surface, not quite brushing it. The surface will be unbearably cold to the touch, with planetary night well-advanced on the other side.

Evan waits a while before asking, "Well, what's wrong with you?"

"Nothing," Magnus says shortly, and lays her hands on the glass. Evan hisses and grabs her wrists, pulling her away.

"You're going to give yourself frostbite, you silly cow," she says. She would usually have much more to say on the subject of Magnus's self-destructive tendencies, but this time she trails off. Beyond the curve of the dome, the landscape stretches out before them, windswept and lonesome and every inch enticing. Evan stares at it, then down at her oldest friend's fingers bluish with cold, and feels frightened and miserable.

"Before we came here," Magnus says, gently. "Before we came, and we saw, and we conquered our own little space, and went forth, and multiplied. Before all that. They said to me, it will take all the years of your life. It will take all you have. Best to make peace with whatever gods you believe in."

"Magnus…"

"Because it won't be by their holy rites that you are laid to rest. And I said, yes. Yes. Take me there, and you can take all I have."

Evan looks up. At this time of year, it's easy to pick out the light that wanders among the fixed stars. Earth is bright tonight. Close-to it would be brighter still, the dark side strung across by the necklace of the equatorial stations, and the space elevator cables descending into the atmosphere. What was an extraordinary journey will remain extraordinary, but those technicians, surveyors, scientists, teachers, and – such luxury, and after thirty years, such necessity – artists, and primary school teachers, and lawyers, and town planners, will come at a payload cost of a hundred dollars per kilogram.

Magnus follows her gaze. "But here we are. Here we are, still. Holding welcoming parties. Making recruitment posters."

She's crying. Evan looks down again at Magnus's hands, half-frozen, reaching for further worlds to conquer. "We'll outgrow the domes," she says, carefully. "There will always be more to do."

"Yeah," Magnus says, and finally pulls back from the edge, blowing on her fingers to warm them, and wiping her eyes. "Like, for example, trundling back in to make a bloody speech all about technicians for a brighter tomorrow."

"We do need technicians for a brighter tomorrow," Evan says. She turns to look behind her, at their footsteps and wheel tracks in the reddish soil. On impulse, she kneels down to bury her hands in that crumbly dirt. Magnus watches her with something sad and sweet in her expression, and they go back inside together.

※

And it's a beautiful Landfall Night, in the end. The children make little presentations to the visitors from Terran Central, and one of them shows off a working scale model of a space elevator. The original mission crew sing their old embarkation songs. Evan nibbles on hydroponic fruit on sticks. When the evening is wearing long and the festivities are almost over, Magnus consents to being recorded for the colony recruitment message. "We can't offer you riches," she says, brusque and uncompromising as ever. "We can't offer you palatial accommodations or reliable plumbing. Only the sincerity of our need for you, and the sight of another world's sky. I promise you, it's worth the trip."

"I believe you," Evan says, into the silence that follows, and Magnus ducks her head in embarrassment. Evan smiles at her: her friend, Dr Prathiba Sengupta Magnus, who showed them fear in a handful of Martian dust, and promise, and beauty, and ambition, and will be laid to rest beneath these red-ochre sands; who has been holding a block of grilled tofu between two fingers for at least half an hour and probably ought to go to bed.

"Come on, mission commander," she says, and Magnus smiles, rolling after her. "You know, next year, it'll be a much bigger party."

"I hate everything," Magnus says, still clutching the tofu, her face alight with righteous misanthropy, and with the gleam of a thousand stars.

# BIRBAL AND THE SADHU

There was a little girl in Akbar's kingdom who had suffered greatly during the wars of conquest. Her parents had been soldiers - volunteers, for even in the darkest times Akbar rarely conscripted - and had gone from Earth to join the fleet near a star called Rā's al-Hamal. But before they reached there the ship had been overtaken by dacoits, who had been roaming between the fixed stars for unarmed craft (for the armament for the ship would have been provided by the armies' quartermasters). The little girl's parents were killed, and she too would have been killed had her mother not taught her the combination key for an escape pod, and how the device was to be operated, and how to be strong and go on though she was deathly afraid.

The escape pod was picked up by the outermost fringe of the fleet formation, and the little girl brought to a military medical station. Her injuries were treated and a message was sent to Earth to whatever relatives could be found. After some time the little girl's chacha came to the medical station to take her home to Agra, and although it was a time of great sadness for the family it was also a time of gratitude. Back in the city of her people the little girl took prasad at the puja for her returning and tasted sweetness amid her grief.

But the seasons changed: the summer came, and the monsoon, and she did not speak again.

Her chacha was not lacking in means, and he loved her very much, the daughter of his oldest brother, and he took her to the finest doctors. And those doctors said, a young, healthy body takes a little time to heal, but a mind grown old before its due time will take longer. Her chacha understood that he must be patient, but he was uneasy, and wished there were something else he could do. Which was why when a sadhu came to the district, and spoke of his great power of healing the afflicted, the little girl and her chacha were among those who attended him. The sadhu called her forwards for his blessing, his hands outstretched. The little girl went to him, and for the first time in a year she spoke.

"I know you," she said. "You are the dacoit who killed my parents."

"No, bacchha, no," her chacha said, torn between his joy at her speaking and his horror at what she said.

"I am a holy man," the sadhu said. "The child is mistaken."

"No," said the little girl, in front of all those gathered there. "I am not mistaken. This man is a pirate and a badmash."

The sadhu had disciples who followed him in his journeys from town to town, and they came to the house where the little girl and her chacha lived. They told him that he must look to his niece, and see that she caused no further trouble.

## Birbal and the sadhu

Her chacha did not know what to do. But his wife, the little girl's chachi, knew that such a thing must be settled in a higher court than gossip and rumour, and so it happened that the family came to Akbar's durbar, to explain their quandary, and ask for counsel.

"Children lie," said Abdul, a courtier among the navaratnas, whose son had troubled him of late. "They lie often, huzoor. They speak of their fine results in their examinations, and then their teacher comes in the evening with a frown on his long face and a plan for remedial instruction."

"You are a good father, Abdul," Akbar said. "And this little child who comes to me for help has no such father, no mother, no sister. I must be all of those to her."

Akbar dismissed the navaratnas and the attendants, and took the little girl into the gardens where the sun was too bright for secrets. "Child," Akbar said. "It is said that you have told your chacha that this holy man is not holy, but killed your mother and father, and took their ship, and left you drifting. Is that so?"

The little girl said, "Yes, that is so."

Akbar was satisfied, and returned to the durbar.

But matters could not rest there, for the sadhu had also come to Fatehpur Sikri to complain that his name was being slandered, and to demand hearing and remedy, as was his right. So Akbar came to Birbal and said, "Birbal, a little girl does not come to her emperor in deception, and a holy man should be honest in all things. But they cannot both be speaking the truth. What shall I do?"

And Birbal said, "Leave it with me, huzoor."

Now in these times of peace the vast phalanxes of Akbar's armies had been disbanded, and the attention of the empire brought to agriculture and art. But women and men with lifetimes of service do not come down to earth so easily. Old soldiers, who had come to Fatehpur Sikri in honourable retirement, nevertheless rose before the sun in the winter and took their exercise on the training grounds. Without constant exercise and drill, their muscles and bones would have atrophied in space. Here on the ground they had not cast off that habit. When Rani Birbal came to them and spoke of a little girl whose parents might have been their brother and sister in arms, they were pleased to assist.

On the fifth day after the arrival of the sadhu at Fatehpur Sikri, he came to request audience with Akbar, to once again plead that he was but a holy man who had spent all his days on the soil of his native land. In the durbar the morning's dispatches were being read and the clerks from the imperial treasury were delivering their accounting. Akbar's attention would be occupied for some time.

When the sadhu turned away, to reprise his request for audience at a later hour, an alarm was heard throughout the durbar. It was a piercing alarm with a sharpness of rise and fall, distinctive so that it could not be mistaken for anything but what it was.

Akbar, who had spent her life in space, put a hand to her left shoulder. The navaratna Abdul, who had been on the flagship as a young man, put his hand to his. The little girl put her hand to her left shoulder and her chacha put his to his. In the exercise yard the old soldiers made the same gesture together as one. They were each reaching for an emergency air supply, although none had it to reach for. If you have been in space, you have heard the sound of a depressurisation alarm. Though it may be the dust of Agra beneath your feet and this world's sky above your head, your body remembers what it must do.

Rani Birbal, who had never been to space, did not make this gesture. Neither did the remaining navaratnas. And neither did the little girl's chachi, nor the dispatch riders from the south, nor the accountants from the treasury.

But the sadhu did. And although he tried to remove his hand from the position which had betrayed him, it was too late.

"I see you *have* left the soil of your native land," Akbar said, after the sound of the alarm died away. "And I see that you have lied about more than this. Thank you, Birbal."

The sadhu, who was not a sadhu, was taken away from the court. Once he had been revealed in this way his disciples ceased to follow him, and people came from the villages around the city to report that they had been swindled by him rather than healed. The little girl returned home with her chacha and chachi. Although she was never as bright and happy as a child as she had been before her parents went into space, she was grateful ever after to Akbar, who had been mother and sister to her when she had neither of her own. And for some time afterwards Rani Birbal was obliged to take her exercise in the yard with the old soldiers, who thought she must learn discipline as well as wit.

# ARCHANA AND CHANDNI

"Your sister is such a sweetie-pie girl," Manju Auntie was saying, sticking a pin in Archana's middle and then hissing between her teeth. "Oof, beta, hilo mat, this all is coming down." She undraped the sari entirely and Archana resigned herself to standing in petticoat and blouse in the middle of a public bathroom. "She will be getting married next, hai na?"

"Not for a long time," Archana said. "Owww, Auntie, the pin—don't, not there—ow. Okay. She's out on deep-space exploration. But she always says. . . ." She trailed off before she could finish the sentence about Tara-didi's breathless missives all about *Sasha this* and *Sasha that*. Sasha was from Russia and had beautiful cheekbones and was also Tara's ship's chief engineer, not that that fact had come up all that often in Tara's letters. "Right now it's just me."

"Ah, you," Auntie said. "No, no, beta, it is Chandni I am meaning. She is a sweet girl. Not at all modern! She will drape your sari at her marriage even, ha."

"Chandni?" Archana said, confused, and then the floor lurched under her feet, so Auntie squeaked and

Archana hung on to the faucets for dear life; when the world righted again she pulled off the petticoat and blouse with no further ceremony and fished a shift dress out of her bag. "Come on, Auntie," she said, "they all saw me in my finery, now all they care about is the food"—and then ran for it before there could be any argument.

Out in the space of the corridor it was quiet, except for the soft echoes of the welcome-to-the-wedding party drifting along the ventilation shafts. Definitely the sound of a lot of munching going on. "You," Archana said, "are such a cow."

"Aww, didi!" Chandni appeared at her left shoulder, as she always did. "You're so mean."

"And tipping Manju Auntie into the urinal wasn't mean?"

"There wasn't a urinal," Chandni said, sulkily. "I had them all ripped out, they make me smell. And I wouldn't have let you fall."

"Huh," Archana said, not quite convinced. "And why'd you do it, anyway? Can you even get married? Like"—she warmed to the topic—"with a giant baraat and everything?"

"It'd have to be light-years across." Chandni frowned and bounced her hair over her shoulders. Such beautiful hair, Archana thought. Chandni looked young for her age and always would. "It's not the same for us. Though I'm sure I'd look nice in red."

"You mean, you"—Archana pointed to Chandni's pretty pink anarkali and the roses in her hair—"or *you*?"

That time she pointed to the wall, to indicate the exploratory mining vessel *Chandragrahan*. Both

Archana's baby sister, though. She suspected Auntie had just forgotten.

"Both, I think," Chandni said thoughtfully. "Later on can I try on your lehenga? The one for the reception day?"

"Do you really want to do that?" Archana asked, surprised. "I thought you were—you know. You're a ship, kiddo."

Chandni glared at her. On her baby face, it looked more adorable than anything. "Yes," she muttered, "but I'm *not at all modern*."

"Well, then, of course you can," Archana said, amused, and they went back down to the party.

꩜

Lupita was not on board. First, it was Archana's father who had been doubtful—"Beta, it does not seem right"—and then Supriya Auntie had made noises like *chee, chee*, and after that Chandni had refused to open the docking bay doors.

"Not till afterwards," she'd said when Archana complained, and later, in the privacy of the room they were sharing for the wedding festivities, she added: "Dad doesn't like it! And I can't. You know."

Archana took a deep breath. "Chandni, we've been living together three years."

"I know," Chandni said, conciliatory, but the docking bay doors stayed firmly shut and Archana gave in.

"Just a week," she said brightly to the screen, "and it's been two days already, it'll be fine! Christ, you look so hot and I miss you so much, let's run away to Oort Station and elope."

Lupita twirled in her dress for Archana's benefit. "That bad, huh?" she asked, laughing. Her voice was crystal-clear, as though she were right there in the room, or as though someone somewhere were paying special attention to the quality of the connection. "And tomorrow's the blessing ceremony, right? We'll see each other then."

"For, like, five minutes," Archana said, "and there'll be some guy chanting Sanskrit at us."

"If that's what's on offer I'll take it," Lupita said. "Hey, is that your room? What's with the"—she squinted and came closer so for a second the screen was entirely her nose—"florals?"

Archana looked at the pastel extravaganza walls with a sigh. "Chandni," she said. "Every room I've ever shared with her has ended up looking like this after a while. Before you ask"—she held up a hand—"yes, it's a ship, yes, there's a tonne of space for all of us. But Mum thought it was important we shared a room growing up, for socialisation."

"Chandni's or yours?" Lupita stepped back. "I'm kidding, I'm kidding. How are you holding up?"

"Urgh," Archana said, morose. "All the aunties spent hours draping me. And undraping me. And pretending not to understand me when I spoke English. And complaining about my complexion."

"You have a lovely complexion."

"Shut up, what the hell even is a complexion."

"I don't know, but I'm sure you have a lovely one." Lupita grinned at her. "See you tomorrow, honey."

"Yeah," Archana said, and the screen went black. After a minute Chandni sidled in, still immaculate in the same pink anarkali.

"I'd have given you longer," she said, "but Naya is a bugger, na." Naya was the orbital station where Lupita was staying. "Don't you know there's important traffic on the channel, blah blah. This *was* important."

Chandni really did believe that these goodnight chats with Lupita were important, Archana thought, trying to take comfort in it, but that night the bed seemed empty and cold. Chandni was curled up at the bottom of it and taking up three extra pillows, and that was nice enough, but she gave off no heat.

※

There was a package from Tara-didi in the morning, delivered via orbital station pickup with a note stuck to the outside. *Should be opaque to little sister's sensors*, she'd written. *Us bad girls need to stick together.* Archana only had time for a quick peek at something pointy-pink with four speed settings before Dabbu Auntie barged in to call her to the beautician. "She has come from Naya Bharat!" Dabbu Auntie announced. "To thread your eyebrows! You want to get married with those so-shaggy caterpillars? Come!"

"Auntie," Archana said, "Lupita already knows what my eyebrows look like. And Chandni can probably do them better, and less painfully, with a narrow-beam laser"—but Dabbu Auntie clapped her hands and strode forth, and once in the beautician's chair Archana was poked and prodded and seared (with portable, not ship-mounted, lasers) while her mother wrung her hands and tried to be diplomatic and encouraging.

"Archana always had such different interests, na?" she said to Dabbu Auntie, who only sniffed, and the beautician made a noise like *aaaaaie!* at Archana's bitten-down fingernails.

"That means butch," Archana said helpfully, but no one was listening to her, and later, she kept her voice soft when she asked: "Mum, would you have liked it better if I'd been into this"—a gesture at the rows of nail polishes on offer, prismatic, sugar shimmer, and classic red—"stuff? When I was growing up, I mean."

"Married woman now! Should take more care," Dabbu Auntie said, and Mum just looked apologetic, so that seemed to be that.

Chandni had gone all out for the mehndi party, decorating her observation deck with streamers that trailed sparkles and changed colour with reference to the elliptic plane. The girls from grad school had brought bottles of bubbly and put on music, and no one had told any of them that they wouldn't be able to touch anything while they waited for their mehndi to dry, but the girls who were still waiting held glasses to the lips of the ones who'd had it done, and Archana had to admit it was pretty fun.

"Thanks for inviting us all," said Lily excitedly; she'd been in Archana's first-year class on Structural Engineering for Interstellar Mining Operations, and they'd made friends originally because she reminded

Archana of Chandni. "I mean, this is just super, isn't it? And I've read up loads on Indian weddings, I don't want to put my foot in it by mistake. Is it true that the night before the wedding the bride's girlfriends steal the groom's shoes? I guess"—she grinned—"the other bride's shoes."

Before Archana could reply, an arm was put around her shoulders. "Arré, bacchha," said Supriya Auntie, "time for talk-shalk later! Mehndi time. You want to look beautiful for your wedding, no?"

Where Mum had got the mehndi-walla and his three minions out here beyond Ceres, Archana had no idea, but she went along with it quietly enough as she was put in a chair and told to extend all extremities. The mehndi-minions chattered in Hindi while they produced cones of the stuff, doing beautiful intricate patterns across her fingertips, her palms, her ankles and wrists. It was customary to hide the beloved one's name somewhere in the design: Archana wondered if they'd left enough room for 'Lupita.'

"Mum," she said in English, "I don't think they know I understand them. They keep talking about how giant my feet are. Also I have to pee."

"Don't you dare." Her mother looked up and laughed. "Just be patient and bear it, okay, beta? I'll send them for Lupita too if she wants it. Will she want it?"

"Maybe," Archana said, honestly unsure. "Let's keep them on hand and get Chandni to ask her."

"Sure," her mother said, said as much to the minions, and went off to speak to Chandni's local terminal; Archana shifted slightly in her chair and tried to convey, through gesture and movements of her eyebrows, that she could do with a break. The mehndi-minions looked at each other blankly and Archana sighed and let it go.

"Lily?" she called. "Come offer the bride a libation, why don't you."

Lily grinned, bowing with the glass before holding it up to Archana's mouth, which made her snort with laughter into the bubbles. One of the mehndi-wallas turned to his friend and said in Hindi, *she's simple, like a little girl*, and Archana was patient and bore it.

※

Chandni gave a dance performance the night before the marriage ceremony. "For our friends in the audience who may be unfamiliar," she explained, standing on the little stage at the front of the ship's main function room, "we call this bharatnatyam. It's a classical Indian dance form that is thought to be thousands of years old."

When she began, the room became quieter, if not silent. "Oh, wow," Lily said, her eyes wide, "that's beautiful. How come you never did anything like that?"

Archana tensed up, then forced herself to relax. The room was full of people clearly entranced; a minute ago they'd been intent on the buffet table or showing off their mehndi. Archana didn't know if Lupita had had it done, but her sisters and cousins certainly had: they were here tonight in beautiful borrowed saris and shouting in joyful Spanish at monolingual aunties. They were all getting along fine.

"I don't know," she said, at last. "I guess—I wasn't interested. I knew what I was like pretty early on, you know? Staying home from family parties and driving Mum mad with the state of my clothes. And Chandni—well, she knows every human language now, pretty much, but she went to Saturday Hindi class to please Dad. Took dance lessons from when she was twelve. She was"—Archana smiled, suddenly, looking up at Chandni in mid-execution of a smooth and graceful form—"perfect. She is perfect, isn't she?"

"You're pretty great too, Archana," Lily said, and Archana grinned.

"Thanks," she said, and would have said something more, asked about Lily's kids or her thesis, but was drawn away by an arm around her shoulders.

"Arré, beta, five minutes only," said Sanjita Auntie, and Archana sighed and went along with her to the buffet table.

"Hi, Auntie," she said, looking down at the vat of dal makhani with some resignation. "What can I do for you?"

"Ah, I can't come and say congratulations?" Sanjita Auntie said. "You should be very happy, beta, the family are very good." She meant Lupita's family, now applauding wildly at the close of Chandni's performance and looking thoughtfully determined as the first of the proper dance music came on. "And when the babies come it will be different, na? We will all help."

"With what?" Archana said absently, skipping over the whole babies thing and wondering if there might be dessert soon. *Indian after all,* murmured a voice in her head; she told it to get stuffed.

"Ah, beta, don't worry, you will learn Hindi before they come, and Chandni will teach them dancing, and your ma will—"

"Oh," Archana said, cutting her off, still half-thinking about fruit and ice cream and wishing very devoutly that those were the only things on her mind. "It's like that, is it?"

"Beta, don't get upset! I only say these things because--"

"Because you love me," Archana said, louder than she'd meant, "because you bloody love me"—and she was going to cry any minute, she thought. Thirty years old and she was going to start crying into a bowl of dal, like at every family party since the beginning of things. "You're going to fix me for the sake of my children. That's it, isn't it, Sanjita Auntie?"

"Archana, beta, why you say such things!" Sanjita Auntie said. "We all want to help you only."

"Thanks," Archana said, "but no thanks. Keep your goddamn help."

"Kya bath hain ye," Sanjita Auntie said, sniffing, and Archana looked over her shoulder at her mother bustling across the dance floor, deftly avoiding Lupita's whirligigging sisters; her father was coming in through the far door, with the quick eye for trouble you developed when running a six-day multiple-shindig event, and Archana thought it was still possible that she might make it through this without crying herself, but a good full-throated scream was coming up as an option— and then a quiet voice said:

"Step back."

"Chandni beta," Sanjita Auntie said, dabbing at her eyes with her dupatta, "this is grown-up talk, you just sit down and--"

"Auntie," Chandni said sweetly, "I am the deep-space exploratory mining vessel *Chandragrahan*. I have a top cruising speed of fourteen times the speed of light in a vacuum and enough standard armament to blow up an asteroid nine hundred and fifty kilometres in diameter. Step back from my sister before I make you."

From behind her, a woman's voice said, "Archana? Chandni sent a shuttle across. She said you needed me urgently."

Archana looked up and burst into tears.

~

"There, there," Lupita said, a while later. They were in one of the little anterooms off the function hall, where Chandni had provided soft lighting and Lily another bottle of bubbly. "Don't cry any more, it freaks me out."

"Sorry," Archana said, sniffling, and then took another chug of the wine and felt better. "Sorry, sorry, I'm ridiculous."

"Maybe you are," Lupita said, comfortably, "but your sister is soothing all your aunts and your mom and mine are comparing outfit notes and your friends from grad school are teaching my tía Marta how to do shots and we haven't even gotten married yet, so, you know."

Archana laughed a little and hiccupped. "We are married," she said. "We are in every way that matters.

This is just to"—she gestured—"keep my damned family happy."

"Is that so bad?" Lupita asked; Archana sighed.

"They want to change me," she said. "They want me to be a good, perfect, beautiful Indian girl. Like---"

"Me?" Chandni asked. She came in and sat cross-legged on the floor, pouring herself some champagne. There hadn't been a third glass a moment before, but that made no difference to her. "Archana-didi, I'm a *ship.*"

"Well, yeah"—Archana gestured—"but. . . ."

"But nothing. I won't get married. I won't give Mum grandchildren." She waved the drink around, a little unsteadily. "What, you think I'll meet a planetoid with prospects? Yes, I'm perfect. I'm a perfect *AI.*"

"Well," Lupita said, "what an interesting and complementary inferiority complex."

"You shut up, you're taking my didi away." Chandni folded her arms and glowered. Lupita grinned.

"Chandni," Archana said, meaning every word, "you're perfect and I love you"—and that time Lupita rolled her eyes.

"Good thing you brought me over," she said. "Clearly y'all need someone smart around."

Archana laughed a little at that, and Chandni smiled shyly, and Archana was thinking they might talk about it again, but not now, not yet. Lupita shook her head with amused resignation, then stopped short, looking at her feet. "Chandni," she said, after another moment, "where the *shit* are my shoes?"

Chandni looked expressionlessly at her. "I don't know what you're talking about."

"You've put them on a fucking asteroid, haven't you."

"Technically," Chandni was saying, as Archana stood up and walked back into the function hall, "Phobos is more of a moon"—and Archana kept on going, across the floor, to where her mother was standing back from the riotous dancing.

"Better, beta?" her mother asked, and Archana considered, then nodded. Her mother smiled wryly at her. "They do love you, you know," she added after a moment, and Archana didn't need to ask who she meant, following her mother's gaze to Dabbu Auntie and Manju Auntie flailing wildly and trying to persuade Lupita's abuela to join in.

"Yeah," Archana said, "I know."

"Why don't you and Lupita get ready together in the morning?" her mother said. "We can't send the poor girl back so late and Chandni can find another room to sleep in, I'm sure." She grinned. "She'll complain, but it's brides' prerogative."

Archana grinned back: she knew what her mother, in her own way, was trying to say. She thought that she might ask Lupita to dance with her, in a little while, and then maybe Chandni, or her dad; and after that, when Lupita's sisters got back from carrying Tía Marta to bed, it would be time for dessert.

# NINE THOUSAND HOURS

*(NB: like some of my other stories, this one is set among the people who call themselves Salt. But because this was the first, it has a different magic from the others. Think of it as a Salt alternate universe, or just an old tale retold.)*

While I was waiting to find out if I would be prosecuted, I went to see Cally by the sea. In those first few days you could only call people whose numbers you had by heart; she answered on the first ring, listened to me cry for a while and said, "I think you remember the way down"—which I did, of course, and then I thought that Commander Norwood would have said something very like that. He would have been just fine after the disaster: he spent his whole life using words as though each one were taxed. And then I was thinking of how they buried Commander Norwood on the hill, under a now-unmarked stone, and made an incoherent noise. Everyone was doing that a lot, back then: crying and laughing, shrieking and sighing, all sounds without words.

"About the disaster . . ."—Cally said that carefully; some people even then were already giving it the initial capital, the Disaster, but not her—"well." She was quiet for a while. "Here, things go on. Come home, Salt."

I went. There were no trains of course, and not many people on the roads, but I could drive—it was about the only thing I could do—so I got in the car and left London on one of those intense, luminous, bright blue days you only get in England at the turn of spring. At Weymouth I got the truth of what she'd been saying—although it wasn't any improvement in some ways, with road signs blank and shopfronts bare, everything was clear and dazzling so the puddles of seawater on the docks flashed sunlight, flashed sky. There were people hanging their nets, unloading their boats, with the fish sparkling in the water beneath them and the Salt flags flying above for luck. I'm of the people of the Salt. I took a deep, steadying breath when I saw the ensigns, and drove on up the hill to the lighthouse.

Cally came down to meet me, opened the car door and said, without preamble: "Where's your bar?"

I put a hand to my ear and mumbled something about it not feeling right, any more. Cally snarled—maybe literally, I don't know; I'd never seen her angry like she was in that single minute, ground down like a lens to a focus of fury—and said, "You have it with you, don't you?"

I had it with me, of course—it's never left my possession since I earned it, five years before that drive down to Weymouth in the sun—and Cally made me get down on my knees right there on the smooth cobblestones under the lighthouse, my hair still being whipped around my face by the wind, and pushed the bar through the tip of my ear without much concern for whether it hurt. It did hurt—my practitioner's bar is iron and rust, as befits a daughter of Salt—but once she was done I put my hand up and felt the flesh on both sides was warm, and healing around it. And that helped, too, like the bright light and the sea, which as my father and Commander Norwood both have said, at different times, need no words.

❧

Cally made tea and put biscuits on a plate; I didn't do too much of anything. Without even looking at me she got her phone out of her pocket, dialled a number and said, "Yes, this is Calliope Norwood. At the light, yes. Can you send up—mmm, cheese and pepperoni. Thanks."

I thought about that for a minute, and then said, "You know the pizza delivery phone number by heart?"

She ignored that. "Drink your tea."

I drank the tea and ate a couple of biscuits, and slowly the world came into a little better focus. When I was a child the kitchen in that house, with its cast-iron range and big white-painted rafters, seemed enormous: as enormous as the possibility of one day being grown up, of my being a practitioner of the Salt and Cally's being the lighthouse keeper. We knew, I think, that that's what Cally would be, some far-off day—but then Commander Norwood died suddenly, of a heart attack in the middle of the night, and that was that. My father still lived in the cottage in Weymouth where I was born, but he understood, more than anyone, why home was the house under the light: it was my father's people who built the tower.

On the table, stark against the stripped oak, were a handful of bare sheets of paper and a pen. I motioned towards them a little ruefully, and asked, "What did they used to be?"

"Tide tables," Cally said. "It's all right for me, I can remember them, mostly. But I tried to write them down for the others, and . . ."

"Yeah." I'd tried to write down lists of magical logarithms, and phone numbers, and then just my name, over and over. We all had. I picked up a pen and attempted to write "Amal" and then "Salt" on the page. My pen formed the letters, but a millimetre above the surface; when Cally took it from me and tried, she couldn't force it into the sweep of the C without it leaping from her hand. Above us, I noticed for the first time the neatly arrayed spice jars, now with blank labels, and the cookbooks on the shelf by the door with bare spines. "I really am sorry, Cally. I'm so sorry."

Cally glanced at me. "I guess you're apologising to a lot of people, right now."

I nodded. Having been right in the focus of the blast, I had been stumbling aphasic for a while, dimly fumbling through the confusion; after that cleared, sorry was the first word.

"Okay." Cally seemed to consider. "It's time to check on the light. Do you want to come up with me?"

I nodded and followed her up the spiral steps. "I thought it was lucky," I said, as we went round and round, round and around, "that the light magic can still be done."

"Yes," Cally said, "but luck has nothing to do with it."

I wasn't sure what she meant by that until we emerged into the lamp-room, greenish with daylight. And it was strange that I'd never seen it before, but then, perhaps I'd never really looked.

"Two power sources," Cally said, tapping the glass. "Magic, for when the power goes out, and electricity, for—well, for things like this."

I bowed my head. "I can still do it," I said. Because my magic comes from seawater and salt, it tends to the deep, wordless workings—heat and cold and calm and light. Not all the people of the Salt want to take time for the learning, the way I did—Cally was taught all she needed in primary school and then by Commander Norwood, for the upkeep of the light—but the power is in all of us, brought with us when life crawled out of the sea, or so I'm told.

Cally nodded. "I'll get you to help, then, when the time comes"—and then there came the ring of the bell from downstairs, so we finished up and went back down. Cally fetched in the pizza and paid for it over my protests—it's a good thing that sterling banknotes are different colours, because there wasn't a word on any of them—and set it down in front of me and watched while I ate it, and then I did help her with the light at dusk, and after that, went to bed before nine o'clock.

You must understand: there wasn't anything to do, at that time. You couldn't go online, or read a book. You couldn't check your email or read the news. You could sing if you knew the words; you couldn't do it for the first time unless you were doing it by ear. Offices and schools and universities were closed, waiting. So many people took up running that there were two London Marathons that year. And magic had become a primal thing—you could do it if you knew the working so well it was part of your body; you couldn't look it up. And I remember people didn't even do that: they were frightened, because of me, because of what I had done.

※

I woke up in the middle of the night and went down to see my father. Like me, he's an insomniac; there was a light burning in the kitchen window as I came up the garden path and let myself in with my old key. The hallway was shadowy and dim, comfortably familiar; I threw off my boots and went inside in socks. "Amal, is that you?" my father called, and when I pushed open the door, added, lovingly, "Salt."

"I'm not sure I deserve that right now," I said, honestly, touching my practitioner's bar. "Hi, Dad."

He pushed a chair out for me obligingly and waved at the steaming teapot. I poured cups for myself and him—there was a warming magic on the pot, I realised; it could have been sitting out for hours—and peered across the table with interest. "What is that?"

"Your grandfather was a dab hand with an abacus," my father said, pushing across some beads on the tiny rails. "I thought, now I can't catch up on my reading"—he glanced at me without reproach—"I'd give it a go. Of course, not being able to write down the answers is a bit of a bummer. Is Cally looking after you?"

I laughed a little at that. "Yes, of course."

"Commander Norwood would be proud of that girl." He pushed across another tiny bead and stared at it intensely, as though expecting it to yield some great truth. I got up, suddenly feeling restless, and looked out the picture window, down at the sea. Every few seconds, the great sweeping beam of the lighthouse crossed my vision, steady as a heartbeat. There were boats out there, still.

"People are managing," my father said, as though reading my mind. "Have you left Crayfish for good?"

"No," I said, a little surprised. Crayfish—which is a communications company, despite the name—at that time was based in south London, near where the river turns tidal (for the Salt practitioners, like me) with easy access to the estuary (for the Birds) and with a basement (for the Stone, not that London, built on its layer upon layer of clay soils, suits them particularly well anywhere in the boroughs). "I mean—we've done . . . whatever we've done. We're going to have to—well, you know. Fix it. If we can."

"Precisely." His gaze sharpened for a moment. "You know, the council sent people door to door to tell us that things would be better soon. I considered doing a working on the chap they sent to see if he were lying, but I thought it wouldn't solve anything if I knew."

I couldn't respond to that. "We are trying," I said. "The Salt faction within the government is coordinating the effort." *And financing it*, I added, silently; we protect our own, but that assistance in the event of disaster was a condition of my public liability insurance, I'm sure.

"Then I'll help, too." My father had a determined set to his jaw that I found, again, comfortingly familiar. "Shall I clear the junk out of your room, then? Or will you live at the light?"

"Neither," I said, a little surprised. "I'm not—ah, I'm not staying. Cally suggested I come and visit for a while."

"Ah," he said, after a moment. "I see."

"It's not like it was in the old days," I said, a little at a loss. "You don't have to be at the water's edge—I mean, I can do my work anywhere."

"I see," he said, again. Now, of course, I know why he said that, and why he called me Salt: not as endearment, or honorific, as at other times, but as a reminder.

"I'll stay a while," I said. "While we wait for . . . you know."

My father nodded; he knew. It might be the Court of the Tithebarn or it might be the Old Bailey, but I would be summonsed soon, and my father, born of Salt, would not try to save me from that. "Well, then, Amal," he said. "You should go to bed, you've plenty of work to do."

I hugged him, and promised I'd be back in daylight, and walked swiftly back up to the light.

In the morning, I was putting the dishes in the sink after breakfast—fried eggs and kippers: always Cally's favourite, even when we were children—when I said, over my shoulder, "I should go back to London tonight."

"London?" Cally repeated, and then there was a particularly fierce gust of wind across the harbour and a thud against the window. Cally opened it calmly and let in a stunned, but not dead, dove, who took a second to get its bearings before settling on my outstretched fingers. It hovered there for a long moment, and then I heard the soft, warm male voice at the edge of perception: *if you learn anything, send me back.*

"From Bird, one of my colleagues," I said. "Wants to know if I've made any progress, fixing this."

Cally got out a piece of bread for the dove, and pushed the window open a little further so the fresh air fluttered the curtains. "Well," she said, "have you?"

"I haven't . . ." I waved my hands. "I mean. I haven't started. I need to go back and start."

Cally sat at the kitchen table with her hands clasped in front of her and said, very calmly, "What were you trying to do?"

"It's difficult to explain," I said, but Cally merely looked at me.

(How to explain it? Those of you who are magic-users will be familiar with the Stone spells that allow near-instantaneous communication over distance, and those of you who use mobile telephones will be familiar with text messaging services. We were going to combine those two, so a practitioner's message would arrive as a text and a text message could be read on a palm. We were close, that morning at Crayfish; we were so close that I was going to light the metaphorical touchpaper, down under the building near the Thames estuary where the brackish water crept close. Only, when I shut my eyes and made the sign with my hands—the same geometric figure that rides out to sea on the Salt ensigns—there was a bright flash of light, bright like a nuclear explosion or the wrath of God, and a great internal cracking, like the marrow turning itself inside out in my bones. And then nothing but the burn of salt, and drowning. That's not how I explained it, over and over in those in-between days, but that's how it was.)

There was silence for a moment in the room. Then Cally asked, "Did you know about the risk?"

"Yes," I said. "We thought I had eliminated it, when planning the working."

"A risk like—like this," Cally said, waving at the rows of blank books. "Like *this*, and you assumed you could work it out."

"Yes," I said. I couldn't deny that. I hadn't denied any of it, at any point. "I did a risk assessment. I concluded that the chance was so slim, that the possible benefit so large, that it was worth it."

Of course now, looking back, I know that I never believed it could happen. Never believed anything I touched wouldn't turn to gold.

"I won't say anything about your arrogance," Cally said, suddenly. "Nor your"—she waved a hand again—"hubris. Nor anything about how you took all of our lives into your hands when you chose to do this."

Cally moved to stand by the window, looking out over the harbour. I waited.

"Four years ago," she said, after a little while. "After my father died. I thought—I wanted to do something for the light. Make it mine, if you like; take it into my own hands. I had the electrical supply put in, and

I didn't write and tell you, because I thought you'd see it. When you came home. You didn't come."

"I've been busy," I said, a little confused, "I'm always busy, Cally! My work is"—my whole life; it was then, and it is now—"all I have."

"No," Cally said, clipped, moving to the sink and filling the kettle with water, setting it down and hitting the switch. "You have me, and you have your father, and you have this house and you have the light, and you have the people of the Salt, and you went to London and you never came back."

"I had to," I said, helplessly. Commander Norwood had taught me magic, when I was young, more than my own father had been able to, and more than Cally had wanted to learn—but in the end, it wasn't enough. "I had to go."

Cally just shook her head. When we were younger she used to do this, and I loved her for it—she used to put the kettle on before the end of the fight, because she believes in tea and reconciliation—and the steam was rising behind her, but this time she walked out on me. I stood in the kitchen for a minute, quite still, looking around at the space, closely aware of all the changes wrought in it since I'd been a little girl, listening to the sound of her footsteps disappearing up the spiral staircase. It was difficult to work without benefit of notepad and pen, but I sat down and began.

꩜

I tried so many things, in those days, and I won't bore you with all of them. There were spells for healing, as though what we had done had created a wound in the world. When it didn't work, Bird wasn't surprised: in his message, he said that the world had existed, all the rocks and soil and rivers of it—and the flocks of birds, and the saltwater—long before any sign scratched into clay stood for anything other than itself. We tried spells of transformation, as though we could lift the world bodily back into what it had been, but my father was able to explain why that wouldn't work. None of us had changed, nor forgotten what we were; we were waiting, pens at the ready, to go on exactly where we left off. I walked down the coastal path in the mornings, tried to find some kind of understanding in the break of the waves against the rocks below, and then did Cally's grocery shopping in town, turned around and began again. And then one night on which it seemed quite hopeless, I was sitting at the kitchen table facing the windows when all the lights went out. Beyond the glass, the wave of darkness was spreading across the town below; from somewhere above, I heard a thump, and then a crash.

"Cally?" I said, but there was no answer. I got up without pausing to think about it, grabbed the torch Cally habitually left in a kitchen drawer, and started to make my slow torturous way up the stairs. "Cally," I was saying, over and over again, on each turn of the stair, and then in the pitch black lamp room: "Cally, are you—what . . ."

"Amal?" she said from somewhere near my feet, and I just about avoided walking straight into her on the lamp room floor. "Make yourself useful, will you?"

I overturned my palms, still unthinking, and then my vision whited out.

"Shit!" Cally said, still from somewhere below me. "Down, Amal!"

"Sorry," I said, "sorry, sorry"—and after a minute I pulled the light levels down to something usable rather than blinding. I had thrown power at it indiscriminately, in line with how things worked in London. I'd forgotten the salt in the air, here. "Sorry."

Through the blur of afterimages, I could make out Cally peering up at the roof; inside the narrow turret of the tower, the magical light had taken a globular form, hanging from the apex. "Can you hold that? For"—she motioned at the storm panes, at the sea beyond—"as long as we have to?"

"Yes." I sat down beside her on the floor, and concentrated on keeping the light steady. "I guess it's a power cut?"

"There's been a few," Cally said, thoughtfully, and I understood why: there was no real reason why we shouldn't have electricity, but if a thing went wrong at a generator, or a substation, or any such thing, they would have to send for the engineer who knew how to fix it from memory. Cally had pulled one of her boots off and was flexing her toes, experimentally; she grimaced when I raised an eyebrow. "I just walked straight into the mounting when the lights went out."

"I heard the crash."

She grimaced again, but said nothing. I checked the light again, and then said: "Is this why you didn't want me to go back to London? In case this happened?"

Cally sighed. "I couldn't have done *that*"—she motioned above her head to the luminous globe, now flickering at the edges as though it were made of luminiferous aether—"but I would have managed. No, Amal, that wasn't it. You overshot it first time, didn't you?"

I took a moment to understand, then nodded. "Less salt in London." I waved a hand and made the globe revolve slowly, largely to amuse her. But her eyes on me were serious.

"It's not just parlour tricks," she said, after a moment. "It's not just something to make our lives more convenient, or to make it easier to send text messages. It's not a game."

"I never said it was, or could be!" I snapped back, and I couldn't remember being so angry with her before: not since, at least, she was pulling my pigtails and taking too long of a turn on the rocking horse. "Are you saying this wouldn't have happened if I'd been here all along?"

Cally looked at me for a long minute. "What is it for, Salt magic?" she asked, at last. "Why do we have it?"

That brought me up short for a moment. "What do you mean?"

"Why are we the people of the Salt?" Cally asked, now sounding patient. "Lots of people can paint good pictures, lots of people can play the tuba. They don't organise themselves into tribal structures and then fly tuba flags over their boats."

When I didn't answer, she stood up and walked around the lamp room, picking up a cloth from the floor and absently polishing the storm panes.

"Your father's father built the tower," she said, "and my father and I have watched over the light. We do magic, or not. We use the technology available, or not. We keep it burning. That's what we're for."

"Sometimes," I argued, "you have to leave home, Cally. I know you never wanted to, and I—I understand that. But who's the light for, if no one leaves?"

"You could have carried it with you." Cally shrugged. "My father wouldn't have asked me to stay at the light, if I hadn't wanted to. Only to come back, sometimes, and only to remember. He taught you magic, and that's all he asked of you. Carry this place wherever you go."

"How do you know I didn't?" I asked, but then remembered the empty books in the kitchen, and leaned tiredly against the glass. "I'm sorry."

"I know." Cally was gentle, as kind as she'd always been. "I know you are."

I kept the light in the lamp room until well into dawn, burning and burning, burning and burning; when at last the power returned, the electric lights strange against the sunrise, Cally brought me breakfast. I was very tired, and everything tasted of salt.

I can't remember how many nights later it was that I came awake slowly with my face stuck to the kitchen table, Cally's hand on my shoulder. From the halfway-there look of the room, the blur of grey light filtering down the curved walls, it was a clouded early morning, and Cally's face was ghostlike in that dimness. "Amal, wake up. Amal!"

"What is it?" I said, at last, fighting a last shadow of aphasia into wakefulness.

"Look." She put a piece of paper in my hands, and I looked down and blinked and blinked again and realised I was not looking, but reading. My brain took a second to slot into that groove. On the sheet, Cally had written: *it is five o'clock in the morning on May 2nd. This is the Portland Light.*

Below, her signature, neat and perfect.

I want to say, at this remove of time, that I cried: but of course I didn't. Crying and tears, those were for before, when emotion with no content was all we had. Instead, I said, calmly, "Can I try?"

She gave me the pen, and I wrote, *Amal, daughter of Salt,* and watched the ink dry on the page, still with Cally's hand on my shoulder, watching the sea beyond the glass.

My father came up to the light before the sun had quite crept out from the horizon, holding another sheet of paper with words written at random. Down on the docks, I could see little movement, as though people had been distracted from putting out to sea with the dawn.

Cally was the one to figure it out. "Straight after the accident," she said, "you couldn't talk."

"You need words to think with, I think," I said, while my father inspected his own handwriting, and Cally sat on the edge of the table with her legs swinging. "It's funny, I never really realised that before, but without words you're just—pre-lingual, like a baby. All impulse and impression and feeling."

My father nodded. "Aphasia, you said. How long?"

I shook my head. "I don't know. You can't measure time when you're in that state. We all—all of us who were in that room—came around after a day or two, I think. People upstairs came out of it in a few hours."

"But you're okay now," Cally said, suddenly swinging to her feet. "Right?"

"Well, sure, it wore off," I said, and Cally glanced at my father, and he glanced back at her, and I'm an idiot and a fool: it took me a moment to get it. "It wore off," I said again, looking up at the books, and at Cally's blank tide tables. "Oh."

"I'll have to write them out again," she said, following my gaze, and it was strange, but until then I hadn't thought of it. I pulled down all the empty cookbooks and blank-labelled spice jars and laid them on the table; I booted up Cally's laptop for the first time in a month and watched the cursor flash and flash, waiting for input.

"So much to do," Cally said, watching me—and in the full light of day, I received a letter carried by a dove, bearing both the crest of the Crown Prosecution Service and the clerks of the Tithebarn. I was to return to London on the next train.

❧

What happened after that is a matter of—I say this advisedly, with gratitude—public record. First, there came the indictment, with all of us standing there in a row; there had been talk of raising corporate manslaughter charges against Crayfish and leaving us out of it, but in the end we all chose to stand for ourselves, alone. Then the coming of the Crown prosecutors, who had deliberated with care, and with no little kindness, over whether prosecution was appropriate in the first instance. The decision was made to try us in London in the ordinary criminal courts. (The Court of the Tithebarn sits in Liverpool with pomp and circumstance, its judges all with their practitioners' bars, but in the end it's only a thing of convenience, my old teachers used to say, like the Chancery or the Admiralty. In the end they brought us to the Old Bailey, where no magic has ever nor may ever be done, and left us there.)

Of the long, cold trial, I remember very little— only Cally and my father, in the front row of the public gallery (with a substitute keeper at the lighthouse as long as was needed; I was told later that the institutional compassion had spread even as far as Trinity House), and sometimes, on the edge of dreams, I remember the echoes in that ancient space, voices dissipating into susurrus—but I recall with saltwater precision the rising of the jury, the reading of the verdict, and the wordless silence that followed it.

I did not appeal. None of us did.

Here in Weymouth, the world goes on. Cally watches over the light; my father works on old magics and the abacus, and perhaps, finds better ways of doing things; the pizza delivery boy comes twice a week.

And I have been working out my time. Our counsel knew their business, and also something of how magic works, and what it is for. At least, I presume it was they who suggested my particular sentence while entering a plea in mitigation on my behalf: it may be that it was Cally, writing a letter to The Times.

Nine thousand hours is long enough to memorise the dictionary, or learn a musical instrument from scratch, or become proficient in a new language. It's enough to find yourself again. It's enough to fall in love. And it's enough time for a place to become your home, and not like it was before, either, but a new home, for the new person that you've become. It is not long enough to write down everything that has ever been written—there were eleven of us in that room beneath the earth and even eleven times over, it is not enough—but I have the magic I've always had, carried from the sea, and the willingness to try and reverse what I did. Word by word, step by step, we coax it back.

Nine thousand hours of community service has not yet brought all that was lost back into the world. But nowadays I see scribbled text on the Salt ensigns on the fishing boats putting out to sea, as if the act of writing is itself good luck; and on the other side of the hill, in the mornings as the light goes out over the water, you can read Commander Norwood's name in the stone.

# AKBAR'S HOLIDAY

You, too, will have quarrelled with your beloved over a share of your kambal, or the name of a favourite singer, or the phase of the moon. Akbar and her begum had fought over some such thing, and as is the way of youth and impetuousness, Akbar ordered her begum to leave the darbar.

Her begum could not but obey, because Akbar was her wife but also her emperor, and might not be gainsaid. So Akbar's begum went to her rooms in the palace at Fatehpur Sikri and began gathering her things into trunks, weeping all the time.

"What ails thee, sahiba?" asked Birbal, who liked the pretty, clever wife of her emperor, and loved Akbar well but was not blind to her faults.

The begum explained that Akbar was displeased with her and had said she must go away from the darbar. In the morning she would return to her father's house, which was on a world named Athāfi, fifty light years distant, and it grieved her greatly to go.

"Listen to me," Birbal said. "You must tell Akbar that you will depart in the morning as she wishes. You ask

## Akbar's holiday

only that you may take some dear thing, some token, to remember her by. Will you ask her for this?"

Akbar's begum was doubtful, but she sent this message to Akbar and received a reply that she might take whatever item she liked best from the palace, if she would only take it and get out. "That is very good," Birbal said, when she heard of this. "Sahiba, leave the rest to me."

Akbar's begum was still doubtful, because afterwards Birbal returned to her place among the navaratnas, carrying a glass of sharbat to her emperor. But the begum resolved to have faith. In the morning she took passage on a great ship bound for the stars. The journey was a long one over many hours, but at last they made orbit around Athāfi and the begum and her luggage took a shuttle to the surface of the planet below. When they reached the begum's father's house, he said, "Dear, I am so pleased to see you, but why have you come at such an odd time?"

"I will explain everything later," she said. "First we must make arrangements for the emperor's stay."

Akbar woke up not so very much later, with an aching head -- from the drugged sharbat Birbal had given her, and from the ship's jump into faster-than-lightspeed, which one should not experience while asleep for fear of just such an aching head. "Why, my wife," Akbar said, growling like an injured bear, "am I here in your father's house, on the world of Athāfi?"

"You sent me away," Akbar's begum said. "And you said I must take with me from the palace whatever was most dear to me. You are what is most dear to me, so you are what I brought."

Akbar was full of anger at having been made a fool of thus, and ready to make further edicts, perhaps exiling her begum from the empire altogether, or having her begum and her begum's father and all others in the household hanged from crosses.

But when she imagined the time it would take, and the inconvenience, the humour of the thing struck Akbar at last. When she had laughed and apologised to her begum for her foolish actions, she said, "Tell me, my wife, was this Rani Birbal's idea?"

The begum agreed that it was.

"Then let my clever Birbal handle the empire for a little while," Akbar said.

She called for a messenger to take a fast packet ship to Earth, to say that the navaratnas and deputies must tend to themselves for some short period. Akbar and her begum spent a pleasant time on Athāfi, and their journey back to Fatehpur Sikri was slow and meandering: for even an emperor may have a holiday, and Akbar had much apologising left to do.

# ALNWICK

"Queerness as the vanguard of transformation," the woman with the pink hair was saying, "that's what it's about. Whereas Deepika's latest is more about conformity with the establishment. She's this odd little government flunky. I'd think it were performance art if it weren't so sad. Meg, or Megan or something."

It was the fault of her shoes, Meg thought. Sensible ballet flats with soles that made no sound on the floor tiles. Or else the fault of the damn Victorian architect who'd built this house back in the year whatever and attached the bathroom to the kitchen, of all things, so you went off to hide from your girlfriend's tiresomely political friends and found yourself listening behind the door to their opinion of you.

"It's just" – that was Pink Hair again; Meg shut down the uncharitable interior voice wondering what profession allowed a thirty-five-year-old woman that particular shade of neon – "I never expected it of Deepika. Picket fences and homonormativity."

*And that, Deepika,* Meg thought, *is your cue to leap to my defence* – and perhaps it was for the best, that

that was when the message came, the crystal at her throat lighting up into magnesium brilliance. Meg put her hand to it, read the information scrolling across her retinas, and after that there was no choice: she strode into the kitchen on those silent footsteps and started hunting frantically for her handbag and keys.

"Meg!" Deepika turned from the other doorway. "Meg, what is it?"

"I have to go to work," Meg muttered, "my coat, where the hell is…"

"Here," Deepika said, holding it out for Meg to put her arms into it. "Meg, what is it? No, just wait," she added, as Meg started to pull away. "The last Tube has gone, I'll call you a taxi. What happened?"

"It was a train," Meg said, her eyes blurring. "There's been a derailment on the east coast line near Alnwick. One of my ship's engineers was on board."

"Shit," Deepika said, feelingly, and picked up the phone. "I'd like a taxi as soon as you can – just across from Belsize Park. Yes, please. Thank you."

"Where's Alnwick?" Pink Hair asked, looking at the whole scene with interest. She had put her wineglass down on the table laden with party nibbles and was chewing her hair. Meg wanted to strangle her. She resisted the urge and threw off her shoes, looking for proper winter boots.

"In Northumberland," Deepika answered, while Meg peered at the data scrolling across her pad, waiting for the woman to ask, *where's Northumberland?*

"Your ship?" – that was another one of Deepika's friends, Anna or Annelise or something. "You have a ship?"

"Halley," Meg said, lacing up her boots, thinking, *odd little government flunky*. "The faster-than-light deep space exploration craft *Halley*. Perhaps you've heard of it?"

"Halley," Anna-or-Annelise said, in wonderment. "Halley. Deepika, you never said…"

*I've told them all about you*, Deepika had said. Meg touched the crystal at her throat so it returned to its dormant state, picked up her bag and went out. "The taxi will honk," Deepika said.

"I'd rather wait on the pavement," Meg said, but Deepika grabbed her arm.

"We'll talk later," she promised, her eyes fierce, and then gestured. "Meg. You said, Alnwick. Does that mean—"

"Yes," Meg said, flatly, and when she stamped down the front path the taxi was waiting. "Whitehall," she said softly to the driver, and they set off. Meg clenched her hands into fists, breathed, and watched the lights of the city slip past the windows.

※

The security guard on duty gave Meg a sympathetic look at the door, which probably said everything she needed to know about what was going on inside. In the department, the main lights were still off – civil service energy-saving measure, clearly – so all work was being done by anglepoise lamps and LEDs. The rapidly moving shadows of her people made it look faux-spooky, like a sleepover or children's party. Meg slammed her handbag down on her desk, and noticed for the first time she was wearing a Halley ID badge over a pink party dress and a pair of snow boots. London had turned cold in the last week, so the newspapers had made jokes about the Halley crew seeking better climes. "Right," she said, her voice carrying. "What the hell happened?"

The room fell silent for a moment, and then Adrienne – Meg's closest friend and colleague here in Interstellar Science and Exploration – sighed and angled a lamp towards them both. "Well," she said, with a studied calm, "it sort of fell out of the sky."

Meg's heart hit her ribcage. "*Halley?*"

"No, for heaven's sake. A supply pod." Adrienne snapped her fingers and the holograph appeared at Meg's eye level; Adrienne twisted her wrist and rotated the image, showing Meg the fluid lines of the thing, pyramid-shaped but with no sharp points. "It's about the size of a transit van, I suppose. Something happened – we don't know what – and instead of going up from Leith to Halley, it, er. Came back down."

Meg's mouth was open. "On top of the *train?*"

"Not on top of the train," Adrienne said patiently. "But pretty close, hard enough to jolt the track. The train derailed maybe another half-mile down the line, near Alnwick."

Meg sat down on the edge of her desk. "Okay. I'm calm. Look at me, I'm exceptionally calm. What have you done about the pod?"

"A team of investigators are flying out at dawn. It was an unmanned shuttle – they'll get the flight recorder and recover what they can of the cargo."

"Okay, good." Meg took a breath. "What do we know about" – she picked up the sheaf of notes presumably being prepared for the minister – "Campbell? The boy on board the train."

"He's a light-field engineer, one of the core team," Adrienne said, shrugging. "They're all on furlough, you know – three weeks till launch preparations begin in earnest. It was the King's Cross to Edinburgh train, we think he was visiting his parents."

"Oh, God," Meg said, picturing them waiting for him at the station, then lifted her head. "The last Friday train, due in – midnight, I suppose?" She glanced at her watch; it was coming up on two in the morning, and Saturday, now. "Adrienne, get a team and a report together, what happens if we have to do this launch without him, what are our options, that kind of thing."

"We can't," Adrienne said, "not in three weeks – the training alone would be prohibitive, and the Halley light field, it's attuned to the minds of the particular—"

Meg waved her silent. "Just do it, Adrienne, please? Best options no matter how bad they are. In the meantime – what's that?"

*That* slowly resolved itself into an image, blurred on the white projection wall. "Ms Tripathi, is that you? Good evening."

"Good evening, Minister," Meg said, and bit down the hysterical laugh. Apparently Her Majesty's Secretary of State for Interstellar Science and Exploration chose to sleep in natty blue-and-white striped pyjamas. As though reading her mind, he glanced down at himself on the screen, then lifted his hand. "Transparency in government is everything, Ms Tripathi."

"Yes, Minister." Meg allowed herself a very quick smile; it seemed like there might not be many in her immediate future.

"What can you tell me so far?" he asked.

Meg counted off on her fingers. "One. It was an unmanned shuttle accident that caused the derailment. Two. One of Halley's launch crew was definitely on board, a Scottish light-field engineer named Leonard Ansari-Campbell, who may be injured, or" – she hesitated – "worse. Three. The train derailed near Alnwick."

"Has anyone else been hurt?" the minister asked, and Meg sighed for their collective human decency; she ought to have asked Adrienne that first. "We don't know, Minister. Although I suspect our paucity of news is good news."

"Is it possible that I'm closer to the site than you are?" the minister asked.

"Closer in distance but not in time," Meg said, shaking her head. The minister's constituency was on the Sefton coast, not far from Camell Laird where Halley had been built. "It's a direct route up from London. In fact" – she made the decision – "I'll go up there myself."

"You don't want to attract media attention," Adrienne said from beside her, but Meg was thinking of that already.

"I'll take the first scheduled service up," he said. I believe the line is open as far as Morpeth."

"Good luck, Meg," the minister said. "Keep me informed. And let's try and keep this from the newspapers as long as we can, please? Particularly" – his expression stilled for a moment, becoming unreadable – "the issue of the Alnwick coroner's sinecure."

Too late, Meg realised why he had been asking about other deaths. "Yes, Minister," she said, and was grateful for the cup of coffee Adrienne placed straight into her hands.

The first scheduled service of the day from King's Cross turned out to be at 5.15am. Meg called for another taxi and went home to dress more suitably for her day, discarding the pink-sequinned dress in the bathroom. "About last night," Deepika tried, perched on the counter top, but Meg shook her off.

"Not now," she said. "I have to go up north. I don't know when I'll be back."

"To Alnwick," Deepika said, and Meg nodded, taking a minute to stand still in the quiet kitchen. Deepika had clearly been awake since Meg's departure; it was clean and tidy in here now, with dishes gleaming in the rack, and no other sign of the party.

Meg sighed, relaxing a little. "I need to see my engineer, and perhaps" – she gestured – "keep it a little quiet, if I can. Try and avoid any inquiries into the sinecure list."

"That sounds ridiculous," Deepika said, and Meg took a deep breath.

"If it gets out," she said clearly, "if some journalist figures out the right sort of questions to ask, and why wouldn't they, about Halley and Campbell and Alnwick, then there won't be a launch whether or not we have a full complement of light-field engineers. The scandal will kill us. So don't tell me it sounds ridiculous."

"Oh, not at all," Deepika said, with a crackle of anger, "not at all ridiculous, nor political. Meg, for what it's worth, I'm sorry you had to overhear those things last night. And I'm sorry if" – she overturned her palms – "it turns out the mission, everything you've worked for…"

She trailed off, but Meg softened at her obvious sincerity. "Yeah. That's why I've got to go."

Deepika nodded, then said, "You won't have time to get breakfast at the station. Let me make you something."

By the time yet another taxi arrived, she'd done two rounds of ham and cheese with chutney and a little sprig of parsley, the way Meg liked it. Meg kissed her goodbye and meant it, and ate the sandwiches three hours later as the train crossed the Tyne, feeling fragile and exhausted in the dawn light.

There were train carriages strewn in the fields. From her perch on the bonnet of a jeep, Meg counted five of them, some still coupled, others strange islands in the burnt-off stalks and snow. It made Meg's stomach turn horribly to see them like that, at perpendicular angles to how the world ought to be. "Can I help, or will I be in the way?" she asked, watching as ambulances drove down the farm tracks, wheels spinning in the mud.

"Wait till they get through the side, miss, it won't be long," said the voice from next to her, warm and Geordie. Meg had arrived at Morpeth to find the tiny station hushed and intensely active, passengers being herded away from the misty platforms, and had not wanted to interrupt. But the first of the local constabulary she met had recognised the crystal at her throat, and not very long after that she had been brought up here along the route of the old Great North Road, the snow vivid on the trees. "It won't be long," PC Throckley said again. "That carriage is the last one they got to. In the dark, you know."

"Oh," Meg said, a little weakly, trying to imagine what it had been like for the passengers waiting for hours in the pitch rural blackness, while distant lights flickered across the landscape and emergency response vehicles fought through the snow and mud. Down on the railway line, a group of emergency workers were using a cutting torch on a train carriage as though it were a tin-opener. The noise stopped, a paramedic in green and high-visibility yellow shouted into the crack, "You're all right, you're going to be all right!" before cutting began again.

"You're here from the ship and all," Throckley said, in wonderment, and Meg turned to him sharply.

"From London, actually," she said, anxious to correct his misconception. "I'm just a civil servant, I'm here to report back to my department. I'm not that exciting, really."

"No, it's grand," Throckley said, gesturing upwards, "it's exciting all right" – and then with a welcome, harsh sound, the torch cut through the metal. Throckley started forwards and Meg scrambled to her feet to follow him, slipping and sliding on the mud on the way downhill, and as they reached the flat ground, one of the rescue workers reached inside the hole and yelled:

"Five to come out!"

It took a few more minutes, but the hole was enlarged, paramedics rushed down to the site and started unfolding stretchers, and a first passenger – ambulatory, Meg noted with some relief – was helped out. The second one had to be carried. Meg reached out to steady a paramedic skidding in the mud, and helped him unfold the stretcher. Up the hill there were vehicles disgorging more people, and for the first time, Meg realised that some of the workers were wearing dressing-gowns under the high-vis. "Leave the inside to the professionals, miss," Throckley said to her, but when the remaining passengers were brought out from that jagged-edged hole in the railway carriage, Meg got a whiff of musty air and darkly organic smells, dissipating fast in the metallic tang of snow. The last passenger to be brought out was a young man with curly hair, on his side on another stretcher, and Meg watched as a rescue worker squeezed his hand on the journey up to the waiting ambulances.

"All right," she said, turning to Throckley. "Constable, if that's everyone, and there were" – her voice betrayed hope and trepidation – "no fatalities?"

"No. At least" – there was an echo of that hopefulness in Throckley's voice – "not yet."

Meg nodded. "I'd be grateful if you'd give me a lift to Alnwick or wherever the injured have been taken."

"So you're here to make sure they still go up into space?" Throckley said, still hopefully, as the wheels bounced beneath them in the rutted ground. "*Will* they still go, after this?"

"Perhaps," Meg said, remembering suddenly why she'd come in the first place, and the coroner in Alnwick.

It seemed a petty concern out here in the snow. "What is that?"

Her attention had been caught by a point in the sky above the supply pod wreckage, keeping pace with them like a star but bright and visible even against the morning light.

Throckley chuckled. "That's your ship, miss," he said, taking a hand off the steering wheel to wave at it, and Meg remembered his earlier gesture upwards. "You've never seen it?"

"Yes," Meg said, discomfited, "but I'd forgotten" – and cut herself off by yawning hugely. She meant to keep her eye on the bright star all the long drive down to the town, and would have done, if she hadn't fallen asleep embarrassingly against the window, her lips leaving condensation kisses on the glass.

"Excuse me, may I come in?"

The figure in the bed turned over, and Meg had his file to hand, knew every biographical detail about him including his date of birth, but was still surprised at the degree of youth in his face. "Oh, hello," he said, with mild surprise. "Who are you?"

"I've come from London," Meg said, suddenly awkward, "from Whitehall, you know" – and in lieu of any better way to express it, touched the Halley crystal at her collarbones.

"Oh," he said, "I'd hoped to meet my first representative of the department while wearing trousers"

– and Meg laughed, grateful for the release in tension, and sat down in the chair next to the bed.

"It's a pleasure to meet you, Dr Ansari-Campbell," she said, reaching out a hand and then thinking better of it. There was a drip running into his arm and a suggestion that his skin was not usually so washed out and distant from brown, but nothing glazed about his expression.

"Firstly," he said, "I don't actually have my doctorate yet. Secondly" – this with a weary resignation – "call me Leonard, I meant it about the trousers."

"Meghna Tripathi," she said. "I'm one of the civil servants from Interstellar Exploration. How are you, Leonard?"

"I've been better." He rolled over again, and then something seemed to occur to him; Meg watched the look of dread appear from nowhere on his face. "You're not here to tell me I'm being replaced?"

Meg shifted in the chair. "I'd rather not have to do that." She hesitated, then asked, "Can you tell me how you are? I mean, really."

"Apparently," Leonard said, "I was in that train carriage for eight hours before they got me out of there. I don't remember it. They tell me I hit my head and had a seizure of some sort."

"Oh, my goodness." Meg leaned back in her chair, and wondered if he had been the passenger she had seen rescued from the last carriage. "I'm so sorry."

He looked at her levelly. "Well?"

Meg let out a breath. "We don't *want* to replace you," she said. "It will be easier to delay the launch than replace you."

"You'd do that for me?" He looked hopeful, Meg realised suddenly; he tried to sit up for a minute, then thought better of it. "I mean – I'm not dead. I can be treated. I can get over this. I will get over this. Can I still…"

He trailed off, and Meg pushed away the urge to reach out and take his hand again, this time out of compassion rather than formality.

"Perhaps," she said. "I don't want to say for certain that you *will* go to the ball, you understand? But I've had a note from my team in London, and they say it will take so long to train another light-field engineer, and the circuitry in the ship is designed with your particular neurology in mind, and – well." She paused. "I don't pretend to understand the technical detail. But yes. It might be easier to delay."

"Thank you," he said, fervent and with eyes shining, "thank you, Ms Tripathi, you won't regret this."

She shook her head, not knowing how to respond. "Is there anything else you need?" she asked after a moment, awkward. "Anything I can do for you?"

"Actually, there is." He looked up at her, frowning. "My parents are my next of kin – they're coming down soon. But there's a couple of people – I don't want them to hear from the news outlets, they'll think the worst, you know?" He made a confused gesture. "You know what I mean."

"Of course," Meg said. "Let me have their names, my department will take care of it."

"Thanks," he said, scribbling on the tablet she offered from her bag. "There's Pen – she's my roommate, she'd worry. And my, er, partner up in Leith."

"Your, er, partner?" Meg said, with a slightly unprofessional flash of humour.

"Three weeks of furlough." Leonard gestured. "But after that he and I have – a termination agreement. Faster-than-light communication not being, ah, at its technological zenith." He grinned. "I'm allowed to say that, I'm gonna be the one actually pushing the boat. Ah, inshallah."

Meg smiled back. "I'll make sure he's informed as soon as possible. And" – she hesitated, then went on – "I'm sorry. I suppose we all must make personal sacrifices, for the mission, but I... I didn't think."

He shrugged. "It's a sacrifice, sure. But I get to go into space. I get to push a ship through space faster than light with my head." He laughed a little, as though at his own foolishness. "I'm a light-field engineer. It's what I'm here to do."

"Yes," Meg said, softly. "Thank you, Leonard. I'll leave my card on the table. We'll be in touch."

She let herself out, very quietly, and when she looked back he was still staring after her, his eyes bright.

"And so," Meg said, in conclusion, "that's my formal recommendation. Delay the launch by – say, a fortnight if we can. Adrienne has put together some second-best scenarios if Campbell isn't fit to fly by then, but we'll hope that he is. In either case, we're working out how to deal with the press. Thankfully, there were no other serious injuries."

The minister nodded, and yawned. "Apologies, Ms Tripathi," he said, and Meg couldn't blame him; it was evening now, the city lights bright around them, and neither of them had slept since the first call had come about the accident. Meg looked across the Holyrood grounds and spotted the small shuttle waiting for them both, and up above her head at the bright lights of geostationary spacedock. "What about the supply pod?" the minister asked. "I ask this out of pure academic interest and not in the slightest bit because we're about to trust our lives to one of the damn things."

"It's a different model of pod," Meg said, amused, "and this one has a crew. Adrienne will let us have the report when it's done."

"Good," the minister said, and said nothing while they were guided on board the small craft, the flight crew disappearing into the cockpit and the straps descending from the ceiling. Meg secured herself in her seat, next to the window, and wondered not for the first time why the minister had called her up to Edinburgh to begin with. She'd been investigating train times southbound when she received the message, and had come up with all due alacrity and increasing mystification.

"Now, Meghna," the minister said, finally, twisting round to speak to her from his seat in front. "That was your formal recommendation. What is your informal one?"

Meg hesitated, and in that moment of silence, the shuttle left the ground, moving straight up as though hung from a cable, rapidly enough to make her ears pop. The city receded beneath then, becoming a jewellery box of shining lights. "I don't like to say, Minister," she said, at last, and to her surprise, he smiled as though he'd been expecting her response.

"I won't push," he said. "Oh, one more bit of shop-talk: I suppose it's all lost beyond recovery, but what was the cargo in the pod?"

"Tins, sir."

"Tins?"

"Tins." Meg spread her hands. "There's going to be hydroponics and food reclamation on board, but it's a long way to Barnard's Star. It was thought the crew might like – well. Tinned pineapple. Cream of tomato soup."

"Tinned pineapple," the minister said, faintly.

"But it's all right," Meg added. "Heinz and the other suppliers have offered to replace everything free of cost. I pushed them into it because they need it for their advertising, you know – *enjoyed all the way out to the stars!* and all that nonsense."

"Meg," the minister said, chuckling, "you are a marvel. How's your young lady?"

"She's well," Meg said, amused at the phrasing. "Thank you for asking."

He caught something of her amusement, and shrugged apology. "Forgive me. When I was your age they used to ask, how's your *friend*. Sometimes, *special friend*. Wink wink, nudge, nudge. It grew tiresome. Though, of course" – he smiled, wistfully – "friends do grow special, over the years. Meg, it's time we come clean."

"About what?"

"About the sinecures list."

"Alnwick," Meg said, automatically, and then: "We'll need to take legal advice. And, sir – politically speaking…"

"Not your bailiwick, Meg," he said, a little stern. "It's time. Thirty years ago this was the only way we could do this. Halley is… well, it's remarkable what's been done. Crown prerogatives will do that."

"If the prerogative money is withdrawn," Meg said, "we become a government department like any other. We'll need to be funded by way of legislation. We'll have to go before Parliament."

"And so we should, and so we will." The minister glanced at her. "Meg – thirty years ago, I'm sure the people in your position thought the Alnwick loophole was a gift from heaven. So inimitably British, of course. Some unknown prerogative post with unlimited executive funding! Our own Civil List! And all we have to do is make sure no one ever finds out that we're funding a faster-than-light interstellar space programme through a twelfth-century Northumberland sinecure, administered through the coroner's office."

"When you put it like that," Meg said, with regret for her brusqueness with Deepika, "it sounds ridiculous."

The minister nodded, and Meg suddenly realised she'd been too distracted by his conversation to notice the rapid fall of the earth. Beyond the window glass she could make out the Firth of Forth laid out in the patterns of its own cartography, dusted with wisps of cloud. When Meg turned back from the view the minister gave her a small, secretive smile. "Tell me," he said, "was that going to be your informal recommendation?"

Meg thought for a minute. "You know," she said at last, "I met a man in Morpeth who thought my job was *exciting*. That it was wonderful, to do what I do, in my office in London. Leonard Ansari-Campbell was trapped for hours in the freezing cold and dark three weeks before he goes out into space, into the freezing cold and the dark, and his greatest fear is that I'll take that away from him."

"If we delay the launch," the minister said, low and careful, "perhaps you will not have to do that."

"And, well." Meg paused, and brought a hand to her throat. "I thought we wore these little Halley ID crystals as a publicity stunt. I mean, we could use tablets like everyone else, you know? We're not crew. We're only logistics."

The minister nodded. "I won't say it wasn't thought of in those terms, at least to begin with."

"But, maybe," Meg said, hesitated again, and then said it. "Maybe something of us goes out there with them."

The minister smiled at her. "Maybe it does." He motioned beneath him at Scotland, now bright in its entirety; then at the lights gleaming out on the North Sea, and in the far distance, the terminator creeping over the earth's surface. "Now hold onto that thought and step back. Think about the greater picture. Ask yourself why we're not at the heart of government. Why we, of all people, and of all things, should not be funded. Ask yourself why three pence in the pound cannot go to carrying citizens into the great unknown."

"Minister," Meg said gently, "there's no need for a speech. I'm not your public."

He glanced at her sidelong. "Did you vote for this government?"

Meg grinned. "Yes, Minister."

"Then call it *your* three pence in the pound." He shrugged again, and overturned his hands. "Are you ready for this?"

"It's what I'm here for," Meg said, and watched Halley curve into view above, like a paper aeroplane made glorious and enormous, sharp and silver. Beyond it, there was nothing but the inky blackness of space. "Except," she added, "I don't know why I'm *here*. Why did you ask me to come up?"

At the sound of the docking clamps, and the pressure beginning to equalise, the minister looked at her as though it were obvious. "This is the ship we built, Meg. Let's take a look."

⁓

Back in London, on a Sunday morning hushed with snow, Meg curled up under a blanket on the sofa and let Deepika bring her tea. "Masala chai, just how you like it," she said, and Meg smiled up at her, breathing it in.

"You know," she said, idly worrying a loose thread on the blanket, "I don't like your friends. Especially Pink Hair. She's a twit."

Deepika blinked. "She has a name, Meg."

"So do I," Meg said. "It's Meg. Meghna. Clouds, you know? That's what it means. Like, up in the sky, though I suppose the Magellanic Clouds would also count."

"Meg, is there a point to this?"

"I'm getting to it," Meg said. "I didn't like what's-her-name, Annelise, either. I'm sorry I ran out on your party but I'm not sorry I was rude to them."

"You were rather rude," Deepika agreed. "Maybe I should trade you in for a better model."

"Maybe you should make new friends."

"Maybe I should," Deepika said, easily, and Meg was comforted by it. "Maybe I'd do worse things than that for you, you grumpy hidebound Luddite. Is your engineer okay? Did you let his family know?"

"I spoke to them myself," Meg said, "and I think he's doing all right. I mean" – she smiled at the thought – "I think he'll get to go where he needs to go. Deepika, don't make new friends."

"Oh, really?" Deepika said, fetching her own tea and taking a sip. "Have you come round to queerness as political, then?"

"I'm just a civil servant," Meg said. "No, that's not it."

"You're not just anything, Meg," Deepika said. "Well?"

Meg leaned back into the sofa, resisting the urge to fall asleep. One day, and then it would begin: one day before the legislative reveal; one day before the department went before Parliament and all around them a change in the weather. "Turns out she was right. I just saw some queers at the vanguard of transformation."

"Idiot," Deepika said, fondly, and went to fetch a plate of biscuits.

# EIGHT CITIES

They've done some rough arithmetic, some ABCs and ka-kha-ga. Then Kim's Game – given a tray of objects and one minute to look, how many could they write down and remember – and now the children are dropping things over the edge of the boat.

"Which falls faster?" Nagin asks, her bare feet stirring the water. "The big stone, or the small one?"

"The big one," says the nearest child, puffed up with its own cleverness. Nagin never learns their names, but they love hers, calling, *Nagin, Nagin*, when they see a snake slide through the murk.

"No," Nagin says, gentle. "Look. Look."

The two pebbles leave her cupped hands and hit the water at exactly the same time. The impacts shatter her reflection, each scattered droplet carrying its own load of sunlight. Nagin is breathless, broadsided by the beauty of it, her ears ringing, the hair on the back of her neck prickling despite the noonday sun. The child mutters to a friend; the friend mutters knowingly back.

Nagin waits for it to pass and says, "You see. You don't need to guess, or believe. You only have to look."

They all look at her, caught between understanding and doubt. One of them picks two more pebbles out of the bucket provided and drops them in the water. Nagin smiles.

And then another child – who might have been there before and might not; to Nagin the children are indistinguishable, but inevitable as the weather – is bouncing along from boat to boat, making them all rock gently in their ropes, the floating lanterns slipping in and out of line. "Naginji! Raonaid-auntie is here!"

It's delighted to be the bearer of good news. Nagin turns, ready to tell the child that it must be mistaken, that Raonaid left two months ago and can't be back so soon, and then remembers her own advice and looks up.

"They told me you've run mad," Raonaid says, disapproving. Rather than wade, she has come out to the raat-bazaar in a small courier boat, the pole creeping silently through the water.

"I have not run mad," Nagin says. "And that's not what they told you."

"She keeps crying all the time," pipes up the herald-child. Nagin sighs and throws another pebble into the water, listening for the splash.

"Is that so," Raonaid murmurs. She still sounds disapproving, the light washing her skin through to harsh bones. Nagin wonders what is going undelivered because of Raonaid's precipitate return; how many people are watching the horizon, waiting for news. Raonaid was once a diplomatic messenger, carrying the great messages of state. These days she carries the state itself.

"What did they tell you really?" Nagin asks, wishing for a moment that she had never spoken of it to anyone, and then she's just happy, again, joy like pain cracking open her bones.

"That you've found God," Raonaid says, worry and disbelief in her voice, and Nagin doesn't doubt that she heard and dropped everything, because she thought Nagin needed her.

~

Dilli-raat-bazaar-ki, Delhi of the night markets. They climb out of the courier boat as the water becomes too shallow for it, and Nagin considers if she and this city she was born in are undergoing transformation together. When she was born, it was the most populous metropolitan conurbation in the world, frenetic, smoky, desert-dry. As Raonaid leads the way through quiet streets, cheery with sun-faded paint, Nagin feels the great stillness of a place she never knew in youth.

"Well?" Raonaid says, at last. "Have you really... found religion, Nagin?"

Nagin hesitates over her answer, her attention caught elsewhere. A boy is taking his bath by the pump, a striped plastic mug in hand. He ought to move swiftly in the crisp, luminous chill, but he reaches into a gulmohar tree for the pleasure of touching its leaves. The branch springs away from his grip and he lets the water splash on his head, gleaming on polished skin. Nagin's father taught her of Brahman, the unknowable creator, of atman, the imperishable within all life, and after all these years she is stilled by it, the tenable divine.

"Yes," she says, her voice cracking. Raonaid gives her an exasperated look. "I'm fine."

"Nagin," Raonaid says, and spits in annoyance at the gutter at the name. "I wish you wouldn't let them call you that. It's insulting."

It's not meant as insult, Nagin is sure; cobras are quick and clever. The raat-bazaar-wallas give her the name for the striped hood she often wears, and her eyes, the irises nearly black. "I like it."

"You would," Raonaid says. "Nagin, for God's sake, do you never come home?"

They claimed this space after the city was drained of people. There are bare lightbulbs wired across the ceiling, thick blankets on the jhula hanging over the verandah. But in these days of Raonaid's absence and her own becoming, Nagin has preferred the rock of the boats beneath her feet, and the dust here is thick. She says nothing, unwilling to attract further ire. Raonaid moves to wipe down the jhula and sets it in vicious motion instead, the ropes twisting above. She hooks it out of the way and tips the contents of her canvas bag on the floor. Nagin looks without comment at Raonaid's talismans and shibboleths. An old two-anna coin, amid the shrapnel of more recent currency. A ration book. A bound volume of the last Government of India Act. A gazette in scrappy printing with a modern seal. All the things she carries to the remote places, the villages which have not seen a stranger in her lifetime.

At the bottom of the bag is the hand-crank radio. Raonaid winds it with a sound like a mosquito whining and flicks the switch.

"One, two, three, four," says a voice distorted by static. Something quickens in Nagin's heart at the sound. "One, two, three, four."

"It'll be on longwave soon," Raonaid says. "And I ought to be out there above the plains, telling people so. Instead I'm here, chasing after you."

Nagin lets that pass, sitting cross-legged on the floor, listening to the test signal. *One, two, three, four.* She lets it run several more times before she asks, "Why are you so angry with me?"

"I need you to be what you are," Raonaid says, fretful.

"What's that?"

"A scientist," Raonaid says. "Especially now, Nagin. This" – she gestures at the radio – "will change everything."

"Some things," Nagin says. It won't reverse the inundation. She may live a thousand lives, or just this one. The uncertainty doesn't concern her. But however the hereafter, she won't ever forget the weight of water, the snowmelt overwhelming the banks of the Yamuna. "It will change us, perhaps."

"Yes!" Raonaid looks like she wants to spit again. "And I thought I could rely on you. I go out there and tell people, there's nothing to be afraid of! What happened wasn't a judgement on us."

"There is nothing to be afraid of," Nagin says. "We had our faiths before the flood. We were more than—"

Ash and dust, she thinks, remembering the God of Raonaid's upbringing, who brought hellfire and vengeance. Nagin thinks she might cry again, waiting for that overwhelmed feeling, but it doesn't come. She's steady and calm, aware of what transcends the mundane in herself and in Raonaid; in the city of Delhi; in all other living things.

"More than what we can see," Nagin says.

"It's superstitious nonsense!" Raonaid says. "Wish-fulfilment, for those who need to believe it."

"I see," Nagin murmurs, delicately. "Like your pahari."

It's a calculated remark. *Pahari*, hill-folk, an old-fashioned pejorative – but Raonaid came from such people, a lifetime and half a world away. Nagin walks out after that, clambering down the crumbling stones beneath the neem trees, back to the bazaar.

※

Some people are concerned by the new lights at the top of the hill, visible for miles around. Nagin sits at the edge of a boat where by day they sell spices, breathing in dal-chinni, elaichi, and hing, and points up towards the high ground. She has taken the children up there to see the radio transmitter up close. Some were fearful of it; others wanted to climb to the top and find out how far they could see. She had hoped they might carry their new knowledge home to their parents, but none really understood its purpose.

"Invisible waves," Nagin says, again, pointing upwards, but the children who attend the night classes are unimpressed. Until today, they had never heard a recording of a human voice.

"They don't believe in what they can't see," Raonaid says, softly, jumping from the nearest boat. She's carrying chameli from the far edge markets, the scent luscious in the saturated air. Around them, the raat-bazaar bustles with laughter, music, people calling their wares. The long lines of floating lanterns clank together, clank apart.

"It's not my area of specialism," Nagin says, the academic's phrasing rising complete from the depths of her mind. It's true: Nagin's post-doctoral research concerned the chemistry of the noble gases.

"I suppose not," Raonaid says, tentative. Nagin has been dozing afloat, rather than going home. Until now, she was unsure if Raonaid had set out for the north again. "But you're trying."

"I will find a way of explaining it to them."

"Yes, you will," Raonaid says. Nagin wonders if it's an apology, and then Raonaid hands her the armful of flowers, and she knows it is.

"Rachel," she says, and Raonaid looks at her sharply. She keeps her name in her own tongue, disliking it in English. But Nagin values the old language, and in particular its impersonal consonants, permissive of distance from what is spoken of.

"This is something new," she says, meaning whatever it is that's happening inside her, this coming of faith or consciousness of the ineffable, or merely a recognition, in the twilight of a frantic life, that she has come to where she ought to be. "And so are the longwave transmissions. But you're right. There's nothing to be afraid of."

Raonaid nods, slowly. "They'll be calling you panditji," she says, not as though this is a thing to be welcomed.

"They called my father that," Nagin says, lightly, as Raonaid puts a flower in her hair. "All right, my children. Once more."

She hits the switch on the radio. Around her, the children start at the sound. *One, two, three, four* – and they begin again.

Panditji means scholar, as well as priest. If it comes to pass, it will do.

❧

"You could come with me," Raonaid says, the morning she leaves, the long road stretching ahead beneath the open sky.

"I will," Nagin says. "Some day."

Perhaps some day they won't have to go on foot. Perhaps they will in any case, step by step, across the soil of this land that's still theirs. On her way back across the water, Nagin rows past a cobra in a neon sign, curled snugly around the loop of an R. Like her, it's content to be where it is. Nagin doesn't disturb.

# UR

The mali came in the morning to talk about their plans for the garden. "Flowers, madam," he said, firmly. "We must have flowers."

"Flowers?" Mrs Mukhopadhyaya said, amused at his determination, and he faltered for a moment, as though remembering whom he was speaking to. "Tell me," she added, gently, looking at the sweat gathering on his forehead, the firm grip of his knuckles on the spade.

"Flowers," the mali said, more softly this time. "I know the minister sahib would wish that we grew vegetables—"

"Not just the minister," Mrs Mukhopadhyaya said. "We take the first steps towards ourselves, here." She was quoting a governmental slogan; it had been drafted here, in this garden, produced on massive sheets in Devanagari calligraphy so beautiful that it had been drawn rather than written. "That means, self-sufficiency: that means, growing our own food."

"But you love flowers, madam," the mali said, and Mrs Mukhopadhyaya laughed and said,

"Perhaps."

She called for tea and Leila brought it, and Mrs Mukhopadhyaya and the mali took careful sips, looking out the light rising over the garden. Sunrises in Ur were pink, not the orange-red-pinks of home but true fuchsia, like the azaleas of her childhood window boxes. They watched it with reverence.

"How is Chotu doing in the new school?" Mrs Mukhopadhyaya asked, when the light had wholly diffused over the bare garden.

The mali nodded. "He is doing well, madam. He had a good result in his exam."

"I'm sure you helped him study," Mrs Mukhopadhyaya said, and the mali shook his head.

"They did not teach this language when I was in school."

Mrs Mukhopadhyaya smiled. "Not in my school, either."

※

The minister came home for lunch, and he and Mrs Mukhopadhyaya sat on the verandah to eat. The government contributed some money to the running of the house, which they spent on wages for Leila, the girl who helped with the cooking and the cleaning and other matters of the household, and spent her evenings taking classes in the local college that had been purpose-built close by. The minister had learned the Xi Lyr language on Earth, at night classes in Meerut, impatient with being set homework and drills like a boy; Mrs Mukhopadhyaya had learned over his shoulder at that time, picking up his books from where he had thrown them down in frustration. Leila was learning from the same books. At least, Mrs Mukhopadhyaya thought they were the same the ones she had seen on Earth, but it could just be that they were the same as first books everywhere, brightly-coloured like the ABC and ka-kha-ga of her childhood. But when Leila spoke to the minister in words from those pages, her eyes seemed to flash with intense and unholy light.

"Leila," the minister said, stiffly, over aloo paratha and imli, "I would prefer that we spoke in English. Or Hindi," he added, as a vague afterthought, and Mrs Mukhopadhyaya hid her smile. Every mention of Ur had driven him to sarcastic irritation back on Earth: every verb in the new language, every fresh decree regarding his new role. She was wondering if this were a twilight of that rage, that ultimately impotent railing against a world under water.

"That's fine," Leila said, in English, then again in Hindi, perhaps for emphasis, or just absent-minded repetition; Mrs Mukhopadhyaya wasn't sure.

Before they all rose, Leila to return to the kitchen; the minister to the legislative assembly building that was a shady five-minute walk down the winding old street; and Mrs Mukhopadhyaya to her garden, she said, "I was thinking of some flowers, with the vegetables."

"Mmm?" said the minister, looking into his bag for his papers and data pad and stylus.

"Flowers," said Mrs Mukhopadhyaya, with sudden confidence. "The other people grow vegetables underground, like carrots or parsnips, and above there are flowers. Perhaps we could grow those, to keep the garden beautiful."

"Underground," the minister said, and then repeated himself absent-mindedly in Hindi; Mrs Mukhopadhyaya was struck by it, so soon after Leila had done the same thing. "Beneath the ground. My dear…" – and he looked up at her, with a kind condescension that turned, as his eyes rested on her face, into only kindness – "you're speaking of things that root, yes? Things that burrow deep down."

"Yes," she said, a little confused, "yes."

"Bide a little time," he said, gently, "before you put down roots. Be sure someone will be here for the harvest."

She didn't reply to that, and he picked up his papers, his fingers sliding automatically over his pad to see the afternoon's legislative agenda. She said nothing as he left the house. As he left through the garden gate, Mrs Mukhopadhyaya realised that she had forgotten about the vote.

※

The mali went home just as the sun was dipping beneath the horizon, leaving his tools polished and gleaming with just a tenacious trace of Ur dirt. Without asking, Leila brought tea to Mrs Mukhopadhyaya, who was sitting in the garden as the evening breezes began to lift. From the smell, a few of their valuable Earth spices had been added to the blend. Mrs Mukhopadhyaya sipped it and listened to Leila humming as she closed the shutters. For a moment she allowed herself to imagine the possibility of a vote to withdraw – the possibility of packing up this house, and leaving this garden – until the steam from her cup reminded her of the care with which Leila had made the tea, and that it would be proper to drink it before it cooled. But the glass cup slipped unaccountably from her grip, bounced off a rock the mali had dug out of the ground earlier, and smashed into fragments in the grass.

"Oh," she said, because life here was like life had been when she was young – things broken could not easily be replaced – and then she thought about the mali bringing Chotu to play in the garden, his little hands perhaps being cut, and she got down on her knees and tried to pick up the shards.

From behind her, a voice like thunder and bells said, "Madam, may I offer sahayatha?"

"Sahayatha," Mrs Mukhopadhyaya said, stupidly, and looked up. On the other side of the garden gate stood a person who was made of glass. Their body gleamed with iridescence, giving off an impression of deliberate restraint, as though an abstract sculpture had come to life and was eager for motion.

"You seemed distressed," said the person, in English, and Mrs Mukhopadhyaya clambered to her feet and opened the gate.

"The cup," she said, still stupid and uncertain, and the person drifted through the gate and began, effortlessly, to pick pieces of glass from the grass and lay them carefully on the table. Mrs Mukhopadhyaya realised that they could do so easily: their long pincers would grip, without being cut.

"Thank you," she said in Hindi, "thank you." And then, because after they had finished placing the glass in rows, they carried on standing there, looking at her and her garden with curious, warm interest, she added, "Sahayatha is Hindi."

The person shook their great, lambent head. Mrs Mukhopadhyaya was not sure where their voice emanated from, or if it were a product of their body at all or something achieved mechanically. The minister would know. "I do not understand."

"You asked me," Mrs Mukhopadhyaya said, "if I needed sahayatha. You asked me in English, but sahayatha is Hindi."

"Another language," said the person, and again, Mrs Mukhopadhyaya had the impression of blinking, of blurred but clearing understanding. "I see. Thank you for this education."

"I cannot" – Mrs Mukhopadhyaya hesitated, then went on – "speak your language. Not well."

"We are all learning," said the person, brightly, and that, Mrs Mukhopadhyaya thought, at least, was true.

"May I bring you some hot tea?" she asked. It grew cool quickly in Ur in the evenings; the ground was baked solid from long-ago desert, letting the heat out at twilight. Mrs Mukhopadhyaya had once seen that dim night haze from space. Her hands were getting cold, away from the little steaming cup on the table.

"I could not drink it," said her friend. "It is not for my body. But thank you."

"Oh," Mrs Mukhopadhyaya said. In English, she knew she should say, *you're welcome*. Not in Hindi, and now she thought of it, perhaps not in English either, not after thanks for a gift not given. When the person drifted on, down the path beyond the gate that led to the house next door, she watched them go with sunset catching pink and fiery in the crevices of their body, and thought, *neighbour* – and wished she had had something else to offer.

❦

In the morning the legislative debates were broadcast, in Ur and on Earth, with each speaker choosing their language shortly before rising and trailing a comet's tail of subtitles at the base of the screen. Mrs Mukhopadhyaya had lifted a trowel and was going out to help the mali; Leila was washing pans and stockpots with a piece of steel wool; but they both paused, set down their tools and looked up at the screen.

"DEBATES: ALIEN CITY VOTE", said the headline above the subtitles, and that was what the first speaker said, as he rose and walked slowly to the podium. Although some of the representatives and delegates were on Earth and some in Ur, the technology worked seamlessly, so everyone watching felt themselves addressed, intimately and personally, from just a few feet away.

"The experiment," he said, hesitating – his name was Patrick Adeyemi, said the text – "the aliens who run the experiment."

Mrs Mukhopadhyaya said, with a vehemence that surprised her, "They are people."

"With respect to my learned friend," a new voice was saying, from the front bench, "the people of Earth and the other people of Xi Lyr are the people of Ur, together."

It was the minister. Leila and Mrs Mukhopadhyaya exchanged smiles.

"I grant that," said Adeyemi, uncomfortably. "I grant that they are people. But for eighteen months, Earth time" – a year in Ur, Mrs Mukhopadhyaya was thinking; a year, so it was time now to think of planting – "we have left our people be. We have left them in this foreign city, of which we know nothing. It is the ruin of an ancient civilisation, say the other people, and we have chosen to believe them: it is on another world, they say, but it will be safe, and we have believed it. We have sent money and seeds and equipment and more money and asked no questions. Now is the time to assess whether the, ah, experiment in xenoanthropology, is over."

There was a hubbub, then, as those who had put hard work into the city bristled, and others laughed with not a little derision. Leila said something to herself which Mrs Mukhopadhyaya didn't understand, in the other people's language, but she noticed that the steel wool by Leila's hand shone a little, as though touched by spark and fire.

"It is foreign to all," the minister said, above the throng. He had risen to speak, this time; the screen identified him as *vithra mantri*, the Ur minister of resources. Mrs Mukhopadhyaya noticed he had chosen to speak in Hindi, which was unusual; he was often ineloquent in it. "We are all foreigners, here. It is not their experiment, nor ours, but ours. We stand and fall together."

It was strange, Mrs Mukhopadhyaya was thinking, but he looked surprised: as though until that moment, he had not known that that was what he was going to say.

Some people came to the garden, the following day: some women Mrs Mukhopadhyaya had known from the party grassroots back on Earth, and some of their children and partners, and some of the others. The women came into the house and helped carry stacks of steel tumblers and tea urns out onto the grass, and the other people stayed in the garden, their bodies catching the sunlight in prismatic splendour. They helped put out the cups and jugs, although they themselves drank only from saucers; their upper bodies could not uncurl enough to grip cups.

"Thank you," said Mrs Mukhopadhyaya, in their language; that was a word she had been careful to learn. And then, because the nearest person to her was waiting patiently, as though expecting her to say something else, she added, "You drink water. Can you drink tea?"

"No," they said, ponderous. "Tea has no meaning for us."

Mrs Mukhopadhyaya smiled; she suspected they meant *taste*. "Is there something else I could bring for you?" she asked, and they made a gesture that seemed to indicate a negative.

"No," they said, and quickly. "Water is fine and suitable."

"I know," Mrs Mukhopadhyaya said, "but you have been kind, and I wanted to be kind in return."

The person made a gesture that might indicate resignation, or approval, and drifted quietly away. On the open space of grass, children were making large banners out of old sheets: *Ur says YES*, *Ur hamara hai*. In the language of the other people, affirmation could not be conveyed concisely enough for an old bedsheet, so one of the children was busy with a stylised depiction, an economy of black brushstrokes somehow conveying the impression of one of those great glass bodies, making a gesture that again might indicate resignation, or approval. Mrs Mukhopadhyaya thought that if perhaps someday she attended a class with Leila, she would understand it a little better.

"I suppose it doesn't matter either way to you," said one of the women who had helped with the tea. Her name was Shanti; Mrs Mukhopadhyaya had known her vaguely on Earth. "I know the minister sahib will be glad to get home. Although your garden here is beautiful," she added, as though those two statements had some connection Mrs Mukhopadhyaya did not quite understand.

"I suppose," Mrs Mukhopadhyaya said. The words had made her uncomfortable.

"The kids love the banners," Shanti continued, seemingly oblivious to Mrs Mukhopadhyaya's discomfort. "Not that they'll do much here, not with all the voters back on Earth! But maybe the news feeds will pick them up in the background, the kids will like that."

Mrs Mukhopadhyaya was not really listening; she was looking up at the tree at the bottom of the garden, and she had had an idea.

❦

The minister left for the evening session just as the mali came down from the tree. For a minute it seemed as though he would hurry past without asking any questions, but then the mali's spectacles caught the sun and with it the minister's attention; he appeared to take the whole scene in for the first time, stopped, and asked, "What are you all doing?"

"We're fruit-picking," Mrs Mukhopadhyaya said, amused.

"I can see that!" The minister waved an impatient hand at Leila, who had been good-humoured about catching the fruit in her skirt, laughing as the juice spread and stained. "What on earth for?"

No one corrected his idiom. "For our neighbour," Mrs Mukhopadhyaya said gently, and when he still looked confused, added, "Parosi."

"I know what a neighbour is!" the minister said, irritated. "Why?"

"So we can offer them something to eat," Mrs Mukhopadhyaya explained, and the minister gave an impatient shrug, as though casting off the whole affair, and went through the gate.

After he had gone, Leila began closing the shutters again, and lit the lamps. There were people in the city who had come from northern latitudes, on Earth or on the other people's home world of Xi Lyr, and found the snapshot-short twilight eerie, as though the way the days neither grew nor shortened were a constraint on their consciousness. Mrs Mukhopadhyaya found it familiar, and a comfort: it made her think about long-ago twilights in bigger cities than this, listening to the tuk-tuks and the low hum of the generators.

In the kitchen they chopped and sliced the spiky red fruit into neat slices, each as large as a human could eat in a bite, so when their neighbour came past the gate at the same time that they had the day before, Mrs Mukhopadhyaya called them back. "Please," she said, stumbling a little with their language, pointing to the plate of fruit slices balanced on the flat surface of the gatepost, "if you would like."

"You can eat also?" asked the neighbour in English, and the fruit was an acquired taste for humans, sour and strange but not poison, so they ate together, careful of the plate. After a while Leila came hurrying out of the house, trailing a long chiffon scarf and wearing fresh lipstick; Mrs Mukhopadhyaya had wondered before if there was someone at the evening class whom Leila thought was beautiful. "I'll be back late, I left the door to the verandah open," she said, a little out of breath, and paused, looking at the plate.

"Eat before you go," Mrs Mukhopadhyaya said, and then, remembering when her mother had done the same for her, she picked up a slice of fruit and placed it directly into Leila's mouth, as not to smudge the perfect lines of her lips.

"Thank you," Leila said, muffled and grateful, and said something polite to Mrs Mukhopadhyaya's friend in their own language, so her eyes glowed like embers for a moment before she scurried away down the street.

Mrs Mukhopadhyaya said, curiously, "I know a very few words, and so does the minister sahib – but that does not happen, when we speak."

"It is a language," said her friend, and although they had no expression, only the petals of iridescence blossoming along the crystal lines of their body, Mrs Mukhopadhyaya could read that pause before speaking as the tentativeness of considered thought, "that lives in its speakers."

Mrs Mukhopadhyaya considered it in her turn. "But we learned from books."

"Yes." They paused, and continued, "You might yet speak it so."

Mrs Mukhopadhyaya nodded, thinking about what it would be like to see her eyes glow in the mirror. "What do you call the city?" she asked, in Hindi, remembering lessons in school of Ur, and Mohenjo-Daro.

The answer was more thunderclap and bells than word, but Mrs Mukhopadhyaya thought it was probably like Ur, too – a real, old place, from long ago, on that other world that she might someday see.

Much later, after the lamps Leila had lit had been turned off for the night, Mrs Mukhopadhyaya heard a banging sound from the kitchen. She moved through the house animated by curiosity, letting herself quietly inside. The outside door to the verandah was banging in the evening breeze; she sat silently on a wooden chair, waiting for her eyes to adjust, while the minister stumbled from object to object in the dark, muttering about food, using the same curses his mother had used.

"What do you need?" she asked, in Hindi; he startled so badly he hit the hard work surface with his knee, and almost fell, so she had to steady him, and bring him to her chair. He sat for a moment breathing heavily, and said, "You foolish woman" – but in Hindi, lovingly, and reached for the nearest, softest light.

After that he said nothing more, so she found the last of the fruit the neighbour had brought, placed it in a bowl and brought it to him; he ate it hungrily, licking the juice from his fingers, then looked up. There was a look of apology in his dark eyes that she did not try to decipher.

"I thought," she said, carefully, "that you did not want to come. That when we came, you did not want to stay."

He offered her his overturned palms, his hands still smeared with red. It would have looked like blood, were it not for the pomegranate tint of the juice, made pinkish by the dimness. Mrs Mukhopadhyaya was reminded, in that colour, of the sunsets that had seemed so alien.

"If we can get past this," he said, in his impatient, blunt way, "then I will no longer sit in the chamber alongside the worthy men, the naysayers, the delegates from Earth who have come to help us keep an open mind." In his voice was the bitterness of the fruit, she thought. "If we stay, then they will come. The others, from Xi Lyr. They will sit in that chamber alongside us. Or perhaps we shall go to their places of meeting. We can meet in either place; we will be *we*."

He paused, his hands wringing, a little helplessly; as though he understood he had not answered her question, but could offer nothing better. He had fallen into Hindi again, just for the last sentence. Mrs Mukhopadhyaya found it a comfort.

# Ur

The mali had come into the kitchen to drink some water – the day was turning hot – and to ask what Chotu should call the neighbour.

"They do not have names," Leila said. "They are the others. What does he call the minister sahib?"

"Uncle," Mrs Mukhopadhyaya said, and Leila nodded. The mali drained his glass, thanked them and went back into the garden; Mrs Mukhopadhyaya could hear him telling Chotu to say namaste, politely, and the distant chiming of the neighbour's pincers.

"It is not only this," the minister was saying, carefully. In English, Mrs Mukhopadhyaya noticed, looking up at the screen, and Leila put down the dish she was washing. "Certainly, it is this. Perhaps twelve or twenty or two hundred years from now, there will be no city on Earth worth living in. Perhaps the waters will have engulfed them all, perhaps the politicians of the day will read back the record of today's debates and answer the question definitively. But there is more to it. Ur is the great experiment. Ur is the first time two sentient species have lived in the same city; have lived as one people; broken of each other's bread."

There was a murmur in the gallery; Mrs Mukhopadhyaya nodded. The phrase was calculated, for those in the ranks who came from Jewish and Christian backgrounds. English, she thought again. The view depicted on the screen tipped back slightly, to show the whole chamber, all homogenous old stone like every building in Ur, as though the city had been hewn out of the rock as the world was forming.

169

"We live in the remains of an ancient civilisation," the minister continued, and Mrs Mukhopadhyaya smiled, a little foolishly, as though he had looked into the house through the other side of the screen and seen the thought in her mind. "We more than anyone should live in the shadow of *memento mori*; remember you must die. Who built the stones on which we stand? We may never know, though there are xenoarchaeologists arriving every six months with the transports. But we will never know – we will never know what might have been, if we are not brave enough to see what will be. To say, we go on."

He paused, and looked at the assembled ranks with an expression of contempt, and in that look, Mrs Mukhopadhyaya saw years of frustration as the waters rose, moulded by pressure and anger into diamond. "Honourable delegates from Earth. If you have come in fear, go in fear. We will remain."

He had spoken his last words in Hindi. When he sat down, the chamber was hushed, and across the millions of miles of space there was another silence, as though all the Earth were quiet. The minister gave a small, inarticulate cry as he moved to sit, shattering that soundlessness; his eyes were shining with a bright white light.

※

The legislature went into recess that day and the next for the polls to be conducted and votes counted. There was a complex system of eligibility for voting on Earth, and high tempers and barricades around polling stations. On Ur, Mrs Mukhopadhyaya, the mali and Leila went together through the cool of the morning and voted in the foyer of the legislative building. The people from Xi Lyr were not voting – the colony would continue with or without the people of Earth – but they seemed to understand the gravity of the situation, and stepped back to let the humans past.

On the second day, the Speaker sent a message: the outcome was to be announced before lunchtime the day after. She would bring them the result shortly before planet-wide broadcast. Mrs Mukhopadhyaya was grateful for that short reprieve, at least. When morning came none of them had slept more than a little; the mali took Chotu to school and returned dazed and distracted. "The other parents were asking," he told Mrs Mukhopadhyaya, "but I said there was no answer. Not yet. Not yet."

Their neighbour arrived not long after that, body made pinkish with the late sunrise, and paused at the gate as though waiting for something. Mrs Mukhopadhyaya recognised that tentativeness as a refusal to enter uninvited, and lifted the latch.

"Have water," Mrs Mukhopadhyaya said to them in their own language, and they took it from her with gratitude, in a saucer. Mrs Mukhopadhyaya saw them start abortively towards the minister, then step back. He was sitting on one of the verandah chairs, quite still. During the course of their most of a lifetime together, she had seen him work days and work nights, reading reports two at a time with one in each hand; she had seen him at family weddings, checking his messages every five minutes; every morning she saw him reach for his data pad before his spectacles. She had rarely, if ever, seen this stillness in him; and never that light in his eyes.

"What happened to him?" she found herself asking, wondering after she had spoken if the neighbour would understand; but they did, with no further explanation.

They said, "He spoke in a language of Ur" – and Mrs Mukhopadhyaya wanted to say, no, that was Hindi. But they might all be here after this, she remembered. They might all be here, speaking Hindi and English and the language of Xi Lyr, and they would all be the people of Ur.

"Will you eat?" she asked, and when her friend nodded, she made up a tray of tea, coffee, water, fruit and pastries for all of them. The minister ate a bread roll when she handed it to him, although his mind was elsewhere. Perhaps not elsewhere, she thought: perhaps as much present, here in this garden in this city, as it had ever been. The mali refused food; he had begun work, planting out perennials not out of certainty, he said, but of hope. Mrs Mukhopadhyaya nodded and poured water into his glass. He had reached the end of a row and paused, leaning on his spade and sweating in the sun, when the gate latch creaked. It was the Speaker, holding an envelope.

"The vote," she said, her voice carrying cross the garden, "the result has come" – and the minister and Mrs Mukhopadhyaya, Leila and the mali and their neighbour, turned to hear it.

"We stay," the Speaker said, and sat down heavily on the grass.

# AKBAR LEARNS TO READ AND WRITE

You may wonder how it was that Akbar – whose strategising had taken battalions to the stars; who took poets as well as generals on galactic campaign; and who loved the art and literature of her people with a passionate, critical love -- came to be illiterate. And you may wonder how she remained so, even after she had led armies, conquered worlds, and ordered their libraries be catalogued and copied.

I am afraid I do not know the reason for this. It may be that the child Akbar was disobedient, and could not be stilled long enough to study. She was heard to say to her tutors that the letters were unruly: *alif* and *meem* unravelled like string in front of her eyes, and perhaps it was more difficult for her than the other children. After the wars were over, I suspect it was because she was ashamed of her lack. When she resolved that she must learn, for the sake of her people as well as herself, she asked that it might be kept a private matter. Birbal, who loved her well, arranged that it should be so.

(You must remember how young Akbar was then, and how prideful. In the dignity of her later years she read well but slowly, and would encourage the children of her navaratnas to come to the dais and lead her through the obfuscations of the court economists. But that is another story.)

The tutor that Birbal found was a brisk and kind woman. "Jahanpanah," she said, "we learn at any age."

She had taught grown men who had played truant during their schooling and gone on to regret it. She had taught soldiers who had spent their lives on Akbar's campaigns, and come home knowing only the scripts of other worlds. She had taught a woman whose father's house had been a petty tyranny, whose freedom to learn had come with her marriage. There were always reasons, which were not important. What was important was the student's application.

So Akbar settled down to her studies, and in due course *alif* and *meem* ceased to dance around the page and came obediently from her pen. On a day of rain, some months after Akbar had begun her lessons, she noticed that her teacher seemed listless.

"What troubles you, adhyapika-sahiba?" Akbar asked.

(Does it surprise you, that Akbar addressed her thus? Akbar accorded her advisers respect, and her teachers too.)

The teacher did not at first wish to speak of it, but the afternoon was cool and pleasant, and Akbar a willing listener. It seemed that there was to be a sitar recital in the darbar that day, given by a well-respected man, known throughout the kingdom for his talent. He was the brother of Akbar's tutor, and although she was pleased to see him perform to such acclaim, he brought to mind a secret sorrow. She had had talent of her own in her childhood, but she had been lazy about studying the instrument, and squandered her opportunity to play alongside him.

Akbar said, "Adhyapika-sahiba, we learn at any age."

After the lesson was over she went to Birbal and asked if someone might be found who could teach the sitar to a beginner, privately, with consideration for a long-ago regret.

Birbal said, "It shall be done, huzoor."

The darbar was full of musicians and those who loved music, and they directed Birbal to a man who had been a flagship musician during the campaigns, and who lived in a quiet retirement in Agra. He was happy to take Akbar's tutor as his pupil and teach her the music he loved.

Now, this man was a widower. His wife had died from a sudden illness soon after their return to Earth, and his grief had been all the more terrible for its being unexpected. When the first cloud of it had passed, he found that his ten-year-old son, who had been the apple of his mother's eye, now looked at his father as though he were a stranger. "A good boy," he told Birbal. "A good, obedient boy, who works hard at his studies. But I know nothing of him."

"What does he enjoy, this good boy of yours?" Birbal asked. "If you give him a little money to spend and a day free of study, what does he do?"

The sitar player did not know. He went home and gave his son a coin and said he should do with it as he pleased. He came back to Birbal to say he had seen his son and his friends on the curve of hillside above the palace, flying their kites in the spring breezes.

"Well, sahib," Birbal said, "we must teach you how to fly a pathang."

The sitar player agreed that perhaps this would bring him closer to his son, but he was apprehensive. How, he asked, does a man who is nearly forty years old, who was always consumed by his art and never by the joys of his schoolfriends, learn to unroll a string and catch a wind?

For once, it was Akbar who said, "It shall be done, my friend."

You will recall that Akbar had a son, Jahangir, who had been born on campaign. Back on Earth he was unruly, as Akbar herself had been, and more inclined towards playing carrom and roaming the hills than working at his lessons. Akbar had seen him flying kites above the battlements, and she meant to promise him some sweetmeat or trinket, if he would teach the sitar player how to do the same.

But then she remembered Jahangir's tutors had said he was shiftless, that he took no responsibility, and it occurred to her that to take responsibility one must have responsibility. She told him of the sitar player's son, her tutor's regrets, and though it troubled her to speak of it, her own illiteracy. "I owe this man a debt," she said. "You must discharge it for me."

Jahangir said, "Amma, I will try."

# Akbar learns to read and write

Birbal was one of Jahangir's tutors who believed he was lacking in application, but she trusted Akbar's judgement, and she was not wrong to do so. On breezy mornings when Birbal breakfasted with Akbar on the verandah, they would see Jahangir climbing up to the battlements with the sitar player, and from the voices carried in the wind they learned that Jahangir was a patient teacher.

"You see, Birbal," Akbar said. "I cannot teach him to read and write, nor to play the sitar. I cannot teach him geography or history or languages. I can teach him to take care of his people, and that only."

"It is not a little thing, huzoor," said Birbal.

After that Jahangir gave his tutors less trouble, and Akbar, too, studied hard. Reading remained a chore for her -- she always preferred to hear the poets recite and the musicians sing – but she could make her way through a dispatch from her frontiers, and through a column of figures, and was content. Among her musicians was her tutor, who struggled with her technique no matter how hard she practised, but she was persistent and Akbar liked to hear her.

Grief is a terrible thing, and it did not lift easily from the sitar player and his son. But they walked the hills together with their brightly-coloured kites, and it came to pass that they found contentment again.

And as you will have learned in school, dear reader, Jahangir became the fourth emperor of the greatest empire ever seen. But that, too, is another story.

# QUARTER DAYS

*(i) Candlemas*

On the Monday, Grace put the advertisement for the new apprentice on the door of their chambers; on the Tuesday, she had a couple of interested, and uninteresting, respondents; and on Wednesday, it was the seven hundred and thirty-first Candlemas of the City of London, so Grace went out with all the other Salt practitioners and raised the year's magic for the City's lamps, lighting Ned's as well as her own; and then on Thursday, a little after five o'clock in the morning, Ned knocked on her bedroom door and shouted, "Grace! Wake up!"

They'd been raising light magic in the gardens till dusk, and afterwards they had watched the tapers burn away the night into the small hours. If she only had an apprentice, Grace thought ignobly, she could send *them* to see what was wanted. Then Ned knocked again, and she was on her feet looking for her dressing gown and slippers.

"What is it?" she shouted through the door, thinking reflexively of Zeppelins, and then shaking her head to clear it of that sudden image, of fire in the dark.

"A boy came from the station," Ned was saying, as Grace stepped out of her door, casting more light as she went, hanging a luminous globe off the roof. Ned was fully dressed with his battered Virgil closed on his thumb; he didn't sleep at night, now. "They're asking for every practitioner — there's been an accident on the railway bridge."

Grace breathed in sharply. "Thanet?"

Ned shook his head as they went downstairs. "Not here. Said something about a girl over the water. Grace, this may be our fault"-- and before Grace could respond, they were through their chambers and on Middle Temple Lane, standing on cobbles gleaming with last night's rain.

There was no light in the sky yet and no stars, but across the water, Grace could make out the orange glow on the bridge by St Paul's. "Come on," she called to Ned, who was rarely outside these days and catching his breath. They hurried through the deserted gardens, down towards the Embankment. There were some carriages and motorcars on the roadway, though not many at this hour, and over them Grace could hear the distant shouting and the crackling of flames. Looking over her shoulder, she could see the lights coming on throughout the chambers surrounding the gardens, and other figures in flapping mishmashes of hastily-grabbed clothing.

At the entrance to the station, they came up short at a police cordon. The constable looked askance at

Grace's dressing gown - and at the darkness of her skin, no doubt - and then at Ned's general unkempt air. Reflexively, they both dipped their heads so their practitioners' bars were visible at their ears.

"We're Salt," Ned said. "I worked on the signalling systems for the railway."

"Thank goodness," the constable said, with unexpected fervour. "You're to go through."

On the other side, all was heat and light. Grace realised at once that the cordon had been a magical one, made of both Salt and tape: because suddenly the smoke was choking and the heat a vivid presence, the surface of the platform warm beneath her feet. A half-dozen practitioners had raised their lights and she could see the spilled railway carriages as great sinister bulks looming out of the darkness. Running the debris patterns backwards in her mind, she imagined the accident: a train run straight into the back of another, but the one in front made of stronger stuff so it had stayed upright, its engine and carriages still standing straight on the bridge, with the other train on the station's landward side, now spilled behind it like confetti. Out of those strewn islands the flames were rising, and in the gloom beneath, there was the shadowy suggestion of movement, of limbs.

"Oh," she said, stricken by it, and felt rather than heard Ned step forwards in the dark beside her. His presence was comforting and close, and Grace dismissed the protective instinct telling her to push him back behind the cordon.

"Are you the magical folk?" called another policeman, and without waiting for an answer, "This way, ma'am, please."

Closer-to, Grace could make out people being helped from the shattered carriages by way of splintered doors and windows; others were banging inside, waiting for the rescuers to come. Grace saw Ned look unhappily up and down the track, towards the signalling wires.

"Can't do anything about that now," he said, and using his cane to balance, jumped heavily down onto the trackside.

As Grace watched, he leant down beside a woman just pulled from a carriage, and helped her drink some water from a canteen. Without even thinking about it, Grace had begun work herself: she was casting spells for cooling and healing, of things as well as people, drawing water up from the river, dumping it on the flames, then beginning again. As light appeared in the sky and brightened, more and more Salt folk arrived from Temple: they worked in concert where they could, as to make better use of whatever power they had, and around them the flames burned blue-white with gas. By the time the sun was clipping the horizon Grace was exhausted, her eyes blurred with smoke and tiredness. Brought to herself by the ash burning in her throat, she looked around her at the chilled dawn in the east along the river, and the bleak aspect it gave to the passengers and the practitioners, their bedroom slippers incongruous in the light. The fires were still burning low and bright beneath the wooden railway carriages.

"Grace." Ned was leaning against the platform edge below her, looking up. "Use me, if you must," he said, with his right hand on his heart; Grace checked he was fully supported against the edge before she reached into him and did it. It wasn't good practice to take the heart out of a layman, but Ned's qualification as such was dubious, and her doubts were eclipsed by gratitude as she felt the strength of it.

Then, somehow, it was morning: the light had risen sufficiently for her to make out the opposite bank of the river, and the slow progress of the injured being taken across the bridge. It was only then, as that Grace noticed the flock of starlings fluttering above her, making a neat, low circle about the station. Their wings were soaked through and raining down water, damping the very last of the flames. Grace wheeled around and called out, "Thanet? Is that you? Thanet!"

"Grace!" Thanet called, hobbling across the platform, having ducked out from behind one of the shelters. He might have been there all the time, Grace thought; the three of them in their familiar formation, all unknowing. "Grace, I'm here!"

Below them, Ned turned sharply, recognisable more by his gait than anything else, his face and hair smeared with ash. "Thanet? Oh, thank goodness."

He leaned against the platform edge again, tipping his head back. Under the starling rain, the fire had died down to smoke, billowing and dissipating across the water. Grace looked down at Ned and up at the remains of the wreckage, and said, "Shall we?"

Between them, Grace and Thanet got Ned back up to platform level, they paid their respects to the also exhausted police constables lining the bridge, and the three of them walked quietly along the Embankment, watching the first of the day's trams rattle past.

"We were afraid," Ned said to Thanet, as Grace rummaged for the keys to chambers, "that you might have been on the train."

"I was late coming back," Thanet said, his voice hoarse. "It was a girl in trouble, you understand? Didn't want the neighbours to see. I was walking across the road bridge when I saw the crash. And then, you know, I thought..." He paused, looking pale in the rising light. "Ned, did we do this? I mean - if, say, the signals were faulty, and the train..."

"There will be an investigation," Ned said heavily. "We'll find out."

"The door's unlocked," Grace said, opening it. "After you, Ned. We left in rather a hurry."

Thanet chuckled grimly as they went inside their sitting-room and opened the curtains, which did little to address the dimness. To make light was properly Salt magic, but Thanet did it regardless. "You know," he said, "we should think about electricity."

"We don't need electricity, we have magic," Grace said, then smiled a little. "I suppose they said the same thing about the wheel, once upon a time. Tea for all of us, I think."

She used the gas rather than magic to heat the kettle, handed steaming sweet cups to both Thanet and Ned, and said nothing for a few minutes. Thanet was methodically picking ashes and burnt fragments out of his hair, and Ned was sitting on the ottoman by the fireplace, his hands shaking violently around the cup. Grace watched them both, and wondered. She had run the practice mostly alone from 1916; after that the nature of Ned's war service had been mysterious, while Thanet's had involved driving ambulances around unexploded shells. "If you want to get some sleep," she said, after a moment, "I won't open up yet."

They both nodded, and Grace picked up the loop of heavy keys in time to hear the knock from the other side of the oak door. Normally their housekeeper, Mrs Throckley, would have answered it, but there was silence. Knowing her, Grace thought, she had probably gone to the station to see how she could help.

Grace opened the door and looked down at the girl waiting beyond it, perhaps twelve or thirteen, with perfect braids over both shoulders and a neat dress and coat.

"Hello," said the girl, peering back at Grace, who was still in her dressing-gown and all-over ash, blood and grit. "I saw your advertisement. I want to learn magic."

❦

## (ii) Lady Day

"Now, before the inquest there's a libel listed," Grace said, and was amused to note the slightly hectoring note in her voice. She thought of the old Salt practitioner, Mrs Macomber, who'd taught her in Liverpool when she was a girl of ten, and silently apologised through time. "I'm a practitioner *ad litem* on the case. You remember what that means?"

Kira, whose braids were done up in blue bows today, looked up at her seriously. "It means," she said, "that you help the, er. The plaintiff-or-defendant. On a magical case. If they don't know about it already, I mean. Magic."

Grace waited, and they advanced a few steps through the Temple gardens, but there was nothing else forthcoming. "I suppose that'll do," she said. "And after that, there's the coroner's inquest into the rail crash. It may be rather upsetting," she added, severely. "Talk of dead bodies and suchlike. Are you sure you'll be able to sit through it?"

Kira nodded. *Sotto voce,* Thanet murmured: "Still trying to put her off, are you?"

"Kira, we're early," Grace said, looking over at the gardens at junior counsel bolting their breakfast in the sun. "Take sixpence and get some rolls for us from the baker's, there's a good girl."

"For you as well, Miss Thanet?" Kira asked.

Thanet nodded. "Thank you, dear," she said, and Kira ran off.

Not so long ago, Grace thought, they wouldn't have had to fetch their own breakfast. Grace's father - and Mrs Macomber too, for that matter - would no doubt credit the imminent triumph of the revolutionary proletariat with that particular change in the weather. "Not putting her off," Grace said. "At least, not for the reasons you're thinking. I said I'd let her follow me about and see how she goes, but I'd half-decided to take the notice down before she turned up. Perhaps we don't need an apprentice, not now."

"Why is that?" Thanet asked, turning on the spot, and Grace understood what she was trying to say: it was busy and beautiful here now, after the quiet of the last few years. Stallholders sold trinkets for the holding of

Bird charms, and tinderboxes full of magical heart's energy; Salt practitioners unrolled great blueprints out on the grass, to get their colleagues' advice; up in the barristers' chambers and the practitioners', the curtains were pulled back and the plaques and signboards were dusted off, ready for custom. And there were children here: practitioners' children, who'd never known anything but the Temple gardens and the riverbank, laughing and playing, throwing sparks and bright firecrackers up at the sky (despite the sign: "No Recreational Magic In The Gardens, By Order"). Grace had grown up around the Court of the Tithebarn, the High Court for magical matters up in Liverpool; Ned had grown up here at Temple; and though Grace didn't like to pry into Thanet's past too much, there was warmth in her eyes here, surrounded by all the artefacts of their practice.

"Because." Grace spread her hands. "Because she's a sweet girl, and maybe she really does want to learn magic with us, or thinks she does. But with the future of the practice uncertain—" She trailed off. "*You* know, Thanet. With Ned - how he is, now, and the world so changed. Training an apprentice is a serious business and I don't know how prepared we are for it."

"She wants what she wants." Thanet shrugged. "And in the meantime" - a pause, as they both watched Kira make her way back across the gardens, carrying a basket of bread rolls - "if you want to warn her off, don't think the dead bodies will do it."

"I'll take it under advisement," Grace said, amused. "Are you ready for the inquest?"

Thanet looked uncomfortable for a moment; she and Ned had both been summonsed to appear after the Board of Trade investigation. "First I'm going with Ned to see the Registrar," she said. "We need to - well, to sort things out, before Ned can address the court. It's Lady Day, you know."

Grace nodded, pushing her braids out of her eyes. Registration day for practitioners was the first of the quarter days, the old Roman new year. For her part, she'd have to make a decision about Kira today. "I'll see you afterwards, then."

Thanet shook her head. "I've another girl to go and see. I can't be late, she said if I came this afternoon her mother would be out."

Grace nodded again, understanding. "Good luck."

Thanet smiled and made her own determined way across the gardens, while Grace accepted a bread roll from Kira. "Now remember," she said. "You're not my apprentice."

"Yet." Kira looked up and didn't smile, eating her own bread roll; she was entirely serious.

"That's as well as may be," Grace said, one of Mrs Macomber's set phrases to the letter. "But in the meantime you'll sit in the public gallery and you'll behave."

"Yes, Miss May," Kira said, still calm. Grace shook her head and led the way through out of Temple, up the terraces and stone steps set amidst the greenery, and back into the noisy space of the world outside.

※

Among the ceremonial morass of the City, the Worshipful Companies of Salt and Birds-in-Flight were, as they put it, outside the precedence: for them, no tussling over orders of procession and entitlements in the manner of the Skinners and the Merchant Taylors and suchlike, but a dignified existence elsewhere. Which might explain the clerk, Thanet thought: he'd wanted a better position, with more gilt-edging and less dust.

On the other hand, perhaps nothing explained the clerk.

"What kind of a name is 'Thanet', anyway?" he asked after a minute, lifting his pen in irritation so it spattered a long trail of ink over his page. He glared at it, and then up at Thanet, as if it were her fault.

"Perfectly respectable name," Thanet told him. "I believe there's an entire region of Kent that goes by it. In fact, I know there is, I spent some time there as a young man."

"As a..." The clerk trailed off, and seemed to give up. Carefully screwing the lid back onto his fountain pen, he went through to the internal door, knocked and put his head around it. "Registrar, there are some" - he turned back, glared again for good measure - "*people* here to see you. A Miss Thanet, and..."

He trailed off again. It had been quite some time since Thanet had heard Ned laugh, but he did so now, and there seemed real mirth in it despite a twist of irony to his smile. "As you forgot to ask," he said, "here's my card. You might remind the Registrar of the apples and cheese I gave him in the schoolroom, his mother having neglected to provide him with same."

"Edward Devlin," the clerk said, reading off the card; he must be new, Thanet thought. If so he was the only such person or thing around here; the bomb damage to the building and the piecemeal repair work seemed more apparent than ever. The Salt Guildhall had been the first place in London to be bombed.

After a moment the Registrar came out, holding a fountain pen of his own. "I suppose you'd better come inside," he said, querulously, and then, raising his eyes to the heavens: "Apples and cheese, Ned, really? Are you able to come up?"

Ned nodded - there were only a few steps - and they followed the Registrar, Thanet careful to keep pace with Ned. "Well," the Registrar said, sitting in ungentlemanly fashion on the edge of his carved mahogany desk, "I can't say as I don't know what this is about. Miss Thanet, are you here for some particular reason?"

"I wouldn't let him come without me, sir," Thanet said, smartly bringing her heels together, also in ungentlemanly - unladylike - fashion. Ned looked embarrassed. From above them, the spring sunlight filtered through the room, making the dust on the books and papers more obvious than usual.

"Right enough," the Registrar said. "State your case, Ned. Think of it as advocacy *in camera.*"

Thanet might have been a little thrown by that, but Ned did not seem to be; she remembered from before that it had always been his habit to pace up and down when addressing a judge in chambers, and his discomfort seemed centred on the fact this was no longer possible. He put the cane down with a nearly voiceless sound of frustration and leaned on the back of a chair. "Sir," he said, "as you are aware, I am a Salt practitioner."

"One of two in a class of six children," the Registrar said, with some wryness. "Do skip ahead."

"I am a Salt practitioner," Ned said, stubbornly, still leaning forwards with his hands on the chair back. "I was apprenticed and educated at Temple and Wadham College, Oxford, following which I was a practitioner *ad litem*, in service of the District Court of Farringdon Without. In the spring of 1916 I was asked to fulfil a certain office for the Crown, the details of which I am not able to divulge."

"Skip ahead, Ned," the Registrar said.

"Although I remain a trained practitioner" - Ned's hand went up to the metal bar driven through the flesh of his ear; Thanet put a hand to her own - "I can no longer, ah. Sir, you will be aware I can no longer do magic." Ned's hand came down in a gesture of defeat. In that gleam of overhead sunlight, Thanet could see the lack of tarnish on his practitioner's bar: Salt, like salt, had a tendency to rust. "And I do not ask to remain registered as though I could. However, I humbly request that my registration *ad litem* be allowed to remain. I can still advise defendants and plaintiffs on Salt magic, its history and practice. I merely, cannot... ah."

He stopped, and this time made no effort to continue. Thanet held a breath for a moment. The Registrar straightened up, his hands clasped. "Ned," he said, very softly, "I'm sorry."

"You're not." Thanet took a step forwards, her heels tapping sharply. "You can't possibly—"

"Thanet, hush." Ned held up one hand. "Sir?"

"I knew you'd come today," the Registrar said.

"Did you?" Thanet asked; she had wondered if Ned would ever return to practice.

The Registrar gave her a sharp look. "I heard about the inquest."

"I've been asked to appear before it," Ned said. "We both have. I will have to stand and give my name, and my... calling. My nature."

"I can't take what you are from you, Ned," the Registrar said, still softly. "And neither can the District Court. But the rules require that you raise a light, at Candlemas. I can't renew your registration."

"Oh, no," Thanet said, involuntarily, and Ned said nothing at all. "Registrar, in the circumstances, surely you understand..."

"Miss Thanet," the Registrar said, and then changed his mind, addressing Ned instead. "Remember those apples and cheese," he said. "Remember your lady mother and her kindnesses. Think about the kind of accusation that you and I would be open to, if I were... less rigorous."

"No good deed goes unpunished," Ned said, after a long moment.

"Ned, I'm sorry. I— " The Registrar waved a vague hand, swinging to his feet - "I wish things were different."

"So do I." Ned bowed his head, then reached for his cane. "Thank you, Registrar. Thanet and I will be late for our appointment, if we don't hurry."

At the threshold, the Registrar called them back. "Ned," he said, quick and a little embarrassed. "Go on as you are for the remaining quarter days. I'll smooth things over if there's trouble."

Ned stopped and turned around. "As a kindness?" he asked, standing quite still and straight, his cane gripped loosely in one hand.

"Yes," said the Registrar, sounding defeated. "Yes."

"Thank you." Ned bowed his head again, and Thanet kept step with him, *tap-tap-tap*, as they went out.

☙

The libel went as well as expected. Grace's learned friend for the defence called her forth and the jury listened with all semblance of focused attention, though as she turned away from the lectern she heard a juror murmur "negress". *A country jury*, Grace thought, then brought herself short for unfairness: city folk could be just as bad. The judge quelled the murmurs with a look. It was Justice Devlin presiding and Grace was grateful, but it rankled regardless. And then the matter was adjourned to the Chancery and the court's usual business finished for the morning.

"Next," called the usher. "The coroner's preliminary inquest in the St Paul's and Blackfriars railway crash of the third day of February in this year of our Lord 1919. With gratitude to the District Court of Farringdon Without for postponing its docket, we reconvene at noon."

As Grace made her way into the public gallery, there was a hand on her arm. "Excuse me, dear - a quick word?"

"Of course," Grace said, with a gesture behind her back to encourage Kira to stand up. Justice Devlin was taking off her horsehair wig and bundling it away, but she had quite enough force of personality without it, in Grace's experience. "What can I do for you, your ladyship?" she asked, then turned to her side. "Kira, this is the Honourable Mrs Justice Devlin."

Kira looked alarmed at the title, and Justice Devlin smiled. "A pleasure to meet you, little one," she said. "It's good to see you taking on an apprentice, Grace." She waved away Grace's attempt to correct her with something about a *trial period*. "Speaking of, I must visit and have a conversation with you about your practice soon."

Grace nodded, her heart sinking; she had an idea what such a conversation might involve. "Of course, my lady."

"Good, good. And how are your parents? I hear there's been unsettled news from Liverpool."

"The riots were bad," Grace said, thinking of her father's understated letters on the subject. "But they've been all right, so far."

"I'm glad to hear it. Oh, also" - she paused, on the point of turning - "how's my boy?"

Grace hesitated, and Justice Devlin shook her head. "Still refusing to emerge for anything short of major railway disasters, I see. A bientôt, dear."

Grace smiled to herself, feeling rather like a hurricane had passed through, and sat down next to Kira in the gallery pews. "Justice Devlin is Ned's mother," she explained. "She used to practise from the same chambers as we do."

Kira nodded, and then shuffled forwards, trying to see through the gaps in the railings. ""What's a libel?" she asked, when it became clear nothing was yet happening in the court below.

"It's when you write something about someone else that's not true," Grace told her, "but everyone believes it anyway."

"And you were telling them if they're true or not?"

"No," Grace said. "I told them the pamphlets were made by magic. That makes it a magical crime, you see? And that's a different thing."

Kira was apparently turning that over in her mind. "And what's a knocking shop?" she demanded, loudly enough for the couple of railway men who were just filing in to turn and look. "And what's a Bolshevik one?"

Grace surprised herself by laughing. "Hush, little one," she said. "It's a libel case, the knocking-shops are only allegedly Bolshevik - and I will explain it all to you later. Sit down now and be quiet."

Despite the grave faces of the people coming into the public gallery for the inquest, Grace was still smiling as the usher closed the doors. When silence had fallen, the coroner stepped out and said, "Ladies and gentlemen and Birds-in-Flight, thank you for coming to this preliminary inquest into the recent tragic events at Blackfriars Bridge. It is my unfortunate duty to inform you that of the seventy people known to have been aboard the rear train, the 5.01 service from Moorgate, thirty-five of them were killed as a result of the accident. Happily, if such a word may be used in this circumstance, the forward train bore only freight, and its driver was uninjured. However, the driver of the overturned train, a

Mr Ferguson, was killed at the site of the crash, and his apprentice, a man named Roberts, has been taken to St Bartholomew's Hospital and is quite unable to give testimony.

"I don't propose to undertake a detailed hearing of the evidence this morning. But from what I understand from the Company" – he nodded at two dour-looking gentlemen on the front bench – "the railway's magic practitioners are holding the bodies charmed against corruption. In the interests of releasing them for burial as soon possible, let us make a beginning."

The jury were sworn, and then the coroner called his first witness, a woman with dark skin and heavy curls. Her voice was low but not faltering: she spoke of how the journey had been unremarkable; that she took the early train every day. "I was near-sleeping," she said, apologetically, "we're all always half-dead on that train. The witches at the riverside had lit the lamps afresh, I remember. Before that night they'd been dimming to nothing. And then we stopped."

"At the signal?" the coroner asked, then paused. "I apologise, I understand you would have no way of knowing. What happened next?"

"We went on." The woman unfolded her hands. "Silent, like. I mean the train made no noise but I saw the lights get further away, if you follow me? And then we were going a decent clip at the bridge, and then..." She trailed off, and the coroner's sympathy was evident.

"That will do fine," he said. "Next, please, I call the two practitioners who were originally responsible for the signalling system, Edward Devlin and" - the coroner consulted his notes - "Thanet. Thank you."

Ned and Thanet took the stand together. To Grace's eyes, they both looked insubstantial, washed-out by the slice of daylight falling through the window. "Before I speak any further," Ned said, abruptly. "Sir, I am no longer permitted to address the court *ad litem*. I come as a private citizen."

"Thank you for informing me," the coroner said, and Grace thought, as her heart was sinking again, that he had probably understood all that was meant by that, and needed to ask no more questions. Once they had confirmed their names for the record, Ned took on the burden of the explanation.

"The connection between the signal box and the train cab is automatic," he said. "A silver bell is mounted above each driver's head, in his cab. Should a signalman wish to raise an alert to every train within a fixed number of chains, all he need do is ring his own bell. Every other bell should ring at the same or almost the same moment, and each driver is well-trained to bring his train to an immediate standstill at the sound of the bell, which is itself designed to carry clearly through the sound of the train in motion."

"I see," the coroner said, after a moment. "So what went wrong?"

"In my view, nothing," Ned said. "The system has been extensively checked by my colleague and by the railway's magical practitioners, and they believe it was working perfectly on the night of the accident."

"Did you not undertake a review of it yourself?"

"No. I'm not able to assist in that kind of work any longer."

"I see," the coroner said again. "Is it possible that your current... ah, state, may have influenced your previous work?"

"No, sir." Ned was calm, though Grace could see his hands gripping tightly on the edge of the stand. "Magic once done is done."

"Excuse me, sir," Thanet interrupted, "it's by no means clear that there was any fault in the signalling system at all. It might have been a mechanical fault in the train. It might have been an error on the part of the driver."

"The Board of Trade is investigating those possibilities," the coroner said, repressively. "Mr Devlin, where were you on the night of the accident?"

"At home, above my chambers at Temple," Ned said. "And then at the station, assisting with the rescue effort."

"Thank you. Miss Thanet, and you?"

"On a professional call south of the river," Thanet said, blandly, and the coroner paused.

"An odd time of day for a call," he said, curiosity animating his voice. It was not the place of the coroner to cross-examine. "Could you care to elaborate?"

"No," Thanet said, still blandly. "My client's case is confidential and unrelated to the matter at hand."

"I see," the coroner said. "Before we conclude this preliminary inquiry, I'd like to hear from Mr Williams, solicitor to the Company."

One of the dour-faced men took the stand, removing his hat as he did so. "Yes, sir."

"Perhaps you'll give us some information about the driver of the train, Mr Ferguson. Was he a man of good character?"

"Yes, sir," said Mr Williams, and polished his spectacles before going on; Grace, who had a lifetime's experience of old, solemn lawyers, hid her smile. "He was a hardworking man, not taken to drink. Certainly he was of good character."

"Was he recently demobilised?" asked the coroner.

"Yes, sir," said Mr Williams, this time with some confusion as though referring to some alien condition. He'd been too old to be conscripted, of course, and it was true that these days the average age of the male lawyers and practitioners at Temple had taken a great leap upwards. "Mr Ferguson returned to his employment with the Southwestern Railway in January of this year."

"Was he of a magical family?"

"No, sir." The solicitor was quite definite on the point. "It is a matter of policy at the Southwestern that no driver may be of the Salt or Birds-in-Flight. The risk of interaction with the magical control and signalling systems is too high."

The coroner nodded. "Was Mr Ferguson's war service a hard one? Was he injured?"

"I am afraid I am not cognisant..." the solicitor said, and the coroner waved a hand.

"We will leave the matter for the full inquest," he said, conciliatory. "In the meantime, however, I will issue interim recommendations to the Birds-in-Flight and Salt Worshipful Companies. Ladies and gentlemen of the jury, that is as long as I propose to keep you. We adjourn until further notice."

There was a small murmur from the public gallery, and then the sound of people getting to their feet. Below, Grace noticed Thanet being waylaid by someone she didn't recognise, a Birds-in-Flight practitioner judging from the bar through their ear, and from Thanet's aura of deference, perhaps a senior one. After a moment, the coroner and his clerk joined them. The conversation seemed heated, and Grace looked on with interest, before Kira plucked her sleeve and they followed the crowds down out of court, back to Temple. Ned was nowhere to be seen.

※

Earlier, Mrs Throckley had been talking about collecting together their ration books, for scones; now, as Grace and Kira let themselves back into chambers, the scent of baking was drifting comfortingly through the house. Kira scuttled down to the kitchen, and in the study, Grace thought about how the quality of the silence in this room had changed from the war years, when Ned and Thanet had been so palpably *away*, rather than just elsewhere. When she looked up, Kira was standing in the doorway, as though afraid to come further.

"Come in," Grace said.

Kira seemed to steel herself to it, and took a step inside. "Are the others not here?" she asked, looking around nervously.

"Not yet," Grace said. "Thanet has a client, I believe. Kira, come here. Come and sit down in front of me."

Still looking apprehensive, Kira did so, so they were facing each other over the bench, like client and retainer.

Grace leaned back. "I said I'd give you a fair trial before I make any decision about taking you on, and that's what we're going to do. Let's start with this: who are you?"

"My name's Kira, I told you when I first came," Kira said, with a flash of irritation; Grace hid another smile.

"It's not as easy as it sounds," she said. "Names are a funny thing, in magic - they tend to stick. Take me, for example." She gestured. "I'm Margaret Grace, actually. When I was your age my mother called me Margaret. But for magic I was Grace, because that was the name I called myself, in my head."

Kira appeared to consider that. "So I can't change my name, ever?"

"Not never," Grace said, thinking of Thanet, "but not easily, and perhaps not soon. You don't want to make life difficult for yourself when you're just starting out.

"Next - what calls you?"

From the look on her face, Kira understood the question. "I don't know," she said, tentative, and Grace remembered the same lacuna on the subject when Kira had introduced herself on the step. Too much information, perhaps, with which to begin their acquaintance.

"Your mum's something, your dad's something else?" she guessed; Kira looked unhappy, but nodded. "So what do you think you are?"

"Salt," Kira said. "Like - well, like Mum."

"And me," Grace said, gently, "and Ned, too."

"But I don't know," Kira said, very quietly. "Dad was like the Birds, you know? And sometimes I can do the things he used to do."

"You're young, you haven't settled," Grace said, with more authority than she felt - she was sure the girl knew that a mixed magical parentage was rare - "and if it turns out you're with the Birds, well. Then if I take you on - *if*," she added, sternly. "If I do, then Thanet will have the majority of your magical teaching, and Ned and I will look after you in other ways."

"All right," Kira said, looking up with her eyes fierce and determined again. "What comes next?"

"What do you give?" Grace said, giving the words the resonance of a quotation, though in truth, she did not know - and perhaps, no one did - where the recitation had come from. Perhaps with the Salt itself, from the sea.

"Is this like," Kira said, shaking her head so her braids bounced, "when Mum makes the cakes?"

"Cakes?"

"When she's baking she keeps one aside, sometimes, and then it's not there any more after but the others taste better."

Grace laughed, but not too much. It wasn't her place to comment on another woman's practice, but the neatness of the trick amused her. "Something like that. Magic always has a price. Not money," she added, at the confused look on Kira's face, "though it could be, I suppose. No reason why not." Working quickly in her mind, she raised a light, a tiny globe suspended off the tips of her fingers. "I did that just with the gift of my own energy," she said, as Kira looked at the light with wide-eyed, unalloyed joy. It had not been difficult at any point to understand why the girl wanted to learn. "Just my energy," Grace said again. "So I'm a little more tired than I was. But what if I wanted to light a whole building for a month? Or the whole City for a year?"

"Something bigger?" Kira guessed.

Grace nodded. "That's right. So what might we do?"

"I've seen," Kira said, again hesitantly, "out in the parks sometimes, they burn rubbish."

"That's certainly one way," Grace said. "You can sacrifice the flames to magic, if you're careful. There are other things, too." She hesitated, trying to put it in terms that Kira would understand. "I might give up something I'd made, like your mother and her cakes. Long ago in the Middle Ages people used to give up their arms and legs."

"Really?" Kira said, sounding fascinated; Grace hurried on.

"And finally. What do you ask for?"

"Light," Kira said, grinning, pointing at the one still hanging off Grace's fingers, and Grace grinned in return at her joy.

"Yes," she said. "Yes, exactly."

"Will I have to do that whole thing every time?" Kira asked, suddenly dubious. "You didn't have to, when you made your light."

"Eventually," Grace explained, "it'll come to you quick as thinking. Quicker than that, it'll come to you like breathing. But it'll be the same in your head, even so: your name, your calling, your gift and your asking. That's how magic works."

"Right." Kira put her little hands together. "Well, my name is Kira."

"Good," Grace said, reserved. "That's good."

Kira looked at her, her eyes still wide with hope, and Grace was saved from facing them by the ring of the outer bell and footsteps in the passage.

"Ned?" she called, thinking suddenly that Ned and Thanet would be *Mr Devlin* and *Miss Thanet* to any apprentice of hers, and wondering at where the years had gone for the three of them. "Thanet? What is it?"

Thanet was shaking off her coat with far more violence than necessary. "Damn their eyes and damn them all to hell," she said, caught sight of Kira and gave Grace a quick, miserable look of apology.

"What happened?" Suddenly, Grace thought the worst, imagining an abortifacient gone wrong, and blood tainted with failed magic; she'd seen that before. "The girl - your client..."

"I never got to see her." Thanet threw herself down into a chair and put her face in her hands. "I've just been barred."

Grace looked at her in confusion. "You mean, Ned..."

"Not me," Ned said, throwing his hat on a hook as he came in and landing heavily in his own chair. "It seems the coroner's interim recommendation was to bar Thanet from practice until, and I quote, it becomes clear, or otherwise, that her work has not been grossly defective, negligent, or otherwise reprehensible. The Birds-in-Flight Registrar rolled over and agreed."

"That bloody coroner." Thanet lifted her head and looked straight at Grace. "Where were you on the night of the accident? Bit of an odd time of day, wasn't it? And now if I don't get my act together, if I can't be trusted to work a simple signalling magic—"

"It wasn't remotely simple," Grace said. It had been the last major project Ned and Thanet had worked on before the war, and had involved months of effort and planning, but most of all Grace remembered the joy they had both taken in it, filling their study with tinkling silver bells, ringing out a different complex melody with each combination of signals. "Thanet, what exactly did they say?"

"They said, as my work is under suspicion of having caused a railway accident..."

"It *isn't*."

"I'm suspended until further notice. I can't practise until the situation is resolved." Thanet pulled a letter from her coat pocket and threw it down on the table. "Bastards."

Kira was looking on with wide eyes, but Grace found she wasn't concerned about the effect of profanity on the girl's morals. "Thanet," she said, firmly, "we'll talk to them."

"I tried," Ned said, spreading his hands. "I tried telling them the signals were working perfectly on the night of the accident - and by the way, the Board of Trade report has come back. They didn't find a scrap of evidence that anything had gone wrong."

"Damn it," Thanet said, again. "It's nothing to do with the signals and you know it, Ned. It's the girls in trouble. It's always girls in trouble." With a noise of frustration, she stood up. "I'm going downstairs. I need a drink."

The door slammed behind her, and Ned looked up at Grace. "I even tried telling them that only I designed the signals." His eyes flashed with something, not humour. "That Thanet wasn't involved. After all, they can't take my registration from me *again*."

"I'm sorry, Ned," Grace said, softly. Ned shrugged, put his head in his hands, then looked up again.

"And now what?" he said, with more bitterness than Grace had ever heard from him. "Jesus Christ, Grace, it's not - it's not just a job, or a livelihood! It's my *life*. It's all I've ever known."

"Ned..."

"And now what, for those already half-destroyed?"

"Ned," Grace said, sharply, "you're scaring Kira."

She wasn't sure if that were true: Kira was still staring wide-eyed at them, but whether in fear or interest, Grace couldn't be sure. Ned hesitated, and then buried his head in his hands again. "Little one," he said, and Grace took a second to realise he was addressing Kira. "I apologise, and may you be spared the sins of your fathers."

From her expression, Kira had no idea what to make of that. A minute passed and Thanet did not return, although Grace could hear her voice rise and fall in the distance, and guessed she was relating a version of the morning's events to Mrs Throckley.

Surprisingly, it was Kira who broke the long silence, getting to her feet and stepping out into the space of the room. "What happened to you?" she asked Ned, with-- yes, Grace thought, with interest. Ned seemed taken aback, lifting his head. To Grace's amazement, he laughed, hoarsely, rubbing his eyes with the heels of his hands.

"No one's ever told you," he said, after a moment, "that there are some questions you don't ask, have they?"

"You don't have to answer," Kira said, composedly. "You can say you don't want to. Do you not want to?"

Ned paused, then again to Grace's surprise, patted the edge of his own workbench. "Why don't you sit down, so I don't have to look up at you?"

For the first time, Kira looked a little abashed, but she sat on the edge of the bench; Ned leaned back in his desk chair. "It's a long story," he said, after a moment. "But the short version is that I was in the wrong place at the wrong time. The Salt Guildhall – perhaps you've seen it, or what's left of it? I happened to be on the premises when the first bomb fell. I'm very lucky," he added, turning to look at her properly. "I didn't die and I was pulled out after not too long. But I was hurt quite badly and that's why I walk with a cane. Does that answer your question?"

"Yes," Kira said. "Thank you. It's just you tap your cane like my granny does, and she's *blind*."

"The reason for that," Ned said, "is an even longer story, and one I don't always enjoy telling. So I think I'm going to have to take advantage of your get-out clause, if that's acceptable?"

"Yeah," Kira said. "I mean, yes."

"Kira," Grace said. "Run along down to the kitchen. If you're lucky the scones will be done."

Kira stood not upon the order of her going. Grace walked around the open space of chambers for a moment, taking in the old-fashioned beauty of this space she had always shared with Ned, its high ancient roof and weathered beams. She walked two circuits, then tapped her fingernail on the side of their kettle, using a little magic to make it steam. "Tea, Ned?"

"Thank you," he said, sounding almost normal, and Grace felt a rush of gratitude for him: for the years of their friendship, for his quiet, reliable presence, though the world had changed around them both.

When the tea was poured out, she asked, "Why *do* you tap your cane?" She held up her hands before he could respond. "If you really don't want to talk about it..."

Ned shook his head and took a sip of tea. "It's a little beyond the grasp of a twelve-year-old, that's all. It's because of" – he gestured vaguely – "the other thing. Without any awareness of the salt in my own bones, I'm less aware of where I am, relative to everything else. Proprioception, I'm told it's called. The cane is grounding."

"I had no idea," Grace said.

"It's little-studied," Ned said. "Due to a lack of experimental subjects."

"Quite," Grace said, with affection. "No, Ned, I hadn't noticed that you were tapping the cane on purpose, not in all this time. I didn't notice, but *she* did."

"Quite," Ned echoed. "You've time to write to the girl's mother, before the last post goes."

Grace smiled at him, tentative. "It'll be lively," she said, "to have an apprentice about the place. Like the old days."

Ned nodded. "Grace," he said, after a minute. "what can I do now?"

"Help Thanet," Grace said, with wrenching, inarticulable sympathy. "Help her clear her name."

Ned nodded again. "Yes. And apart from that?"

"Scones," Grace said, holding out a hand to him. He took it, pulled himself up to standing, and they walked down to the dark-timbered space of the kitchen, lit only with pavement lights and gas. Mrs Throckley didn't hold with magic around food. Grace helped Ned get along, down the steps, and he carried the tea.

※

*(iii) Midsummer*

Their first visitor of the day was a messenger bird made of light and rainwater, already soft-edged as it landed on Thanet's hand and said its few words before becoming a puddle at her feet. "That's a beautiful piece of magic," Grace said, admiringly, as Thanet reached down to mop up the water.

"Not good news, though," Thanet said. "I've a client up by the docks. I was going to see her, but –" She shrugged, looking frustrated. "I shouldn't – I mean, I must go by the Guildhall today and talk about my suspension, maybe I shouldn't—"

Grace nodded. "I can drop in, if you'd like?" she said tentatively. "I can't do your kind of magic, but I'm going up there anyway – "

"Would you really?" Thanet's face lit up.

"It's no trouble," Grace said, and led the way down the steps. "Kira," she called down to the kitchen, "ready to go in five minutes."

"Thanks so much," Thanet said, and gave Grace an impulsive kiss on the cheek. "Just let her know I've not forgotten."

Grace smiled and went through to the study, which was colder than it had been a few minutes earlier. Ned looked up at the sight of her and turned away listlessly.

"Oh, Ned, look what a mess you've made of the fire." Grace got down on her knees on the hearthrug, trying to find a speck of red in the embers; it was hard to make out in the sunlight. Strange to want a fire on a day as brilliant and bright as this one, but there was an unseasonal chill in the air. "If you're going to sit here, make yourself of use. Don't just poke the fire because you can't think of anything better to do."

Ned was wearing fingerless gloves, poker in hand. He laid it down, perhaps as some sort of apology. "What would you have me do instead?" he asked.

Grace straightened up, brushing the dust from her skirts, and looked at him with some irritation. "You could look over the accounts," she said. "You could work out how we're going to pay the rent next month. You could drum up some business for us."

Ned looked like he might say something sharp, but then the idea seemed to catch on his fancy. "I could wear a crinoline and feathers and parade along the Temple gardens, advertising our services?"

Grace chuckled. "That's my boy."

"Love potions and murders a speciality, of course."

"Of course." Grace held up a hand. "You'd be drummed out of respectable practice but I'm sure you'd look very fetching. Now get up so I can measure you for a sandwich board."

Ned laughed a little but stood up. "I'll do the accounts," he said. "Will that do?"

"That's my boy," Grace said again, lovingly. "I have to be out this morning, I'm calling on Kira's mother, so it's just you holding the fort."

"Ave atque vale, then."

Grace gave him the look she reserved for idiots and the classically educated, gathered up her apprentice and the address Thanet had left, and went out.

∾

The accounts were not immensely thrilling, but, as Ned remarked to the kettle when making the tea, the problem of the rent did tend to focus the mind. He lifted his head from Grace's immaculate figures at the sound of the bell, and was surprised to find no heat in the teacup next to his hand. Mrs Throckley must be out, he decided, picked up his cane and went to answer the door. "May I help you?"

The woman on the threshold seemed nervous about coming any further inside. She was tall, with hair pulled back from her face. "Are you a witch?" she asked.

Ned smiled, and said, "You'd best come in. It's this way, Mrs-"

"Ferguson."

"Well, Mrs Ferguson," Ned said, busying himself with the kettle again. "I have a colleague here, a Miss May, who will be able to help you with whatever you require. She's out at present but I can get you some tea if you're willing to wait."

Mrs Ferguson sat on the chair he indicated, but unwillingly. "*You're* a witch, ain't you?" she said, pointing to the bar through his ear. "And you're here already."

"Miss May is very good," Ned assured her, picking up the sugar tongs. "I'm sure you'll find her helpful. Or Thanet, she's – wait." He tipped his head back and called. "Thanet, are you in? She or he?"

Thanet peered around the door, the trim of her hat providing the answer. "She," she said, crossly. "I've got to go out, Ned, more registration nonsense. I'll see you this afternoon."

She disappeared as swiftly as she'd appeared. "Well," Ned said, bringing his hands together. "Milk and sugar, Mrs Ferguson?"

Once the essentials had been furnished, Ned went through the next couple of lines of Grace's meticulous record-keeping. He checked the figures, wrote a note, and then looked up at the unmistakable sensation of eyes boring into him. "You *are* a witch," Mrs Ferguson said, a little belligerently. "I've seen you before."

"You know," Ned said, mildly, "the first time I met a northerner, I quite enjoyed being called a witch. It sounded much more exotic than being a common-and-garden practitioner. You're from Cumberland, then?"

"The north Lakes," Mrs Ferguson said. "I came to London when I was a girl. So you'll help me?"

Ned laid down his pen and sighed. "Mrs Ferguson, my colleague will be here shortly and in the meantime I have work to do. So if you don't mind…"

She stared at him over the rim of her cup, but said nothing. Ned wrote another couple of numbers in a column and somehow wasn't surprised when she said, "Let me tell you about my trouble. My husband…"

"Mrs Ferguson," Ned said, controlling his temper. "Yes, I am a witch. A Salt practitioner. I am also about to lose my registration permanently and I haven't done any magic for around six months. If you, or your husband, are in trouble, I'm very sorry to hear it, and if you would just *wait*—"

"What did you do?"

"Excuse me?" Ned stared at her, thrown by the interruption.

"What did you do, for them to take away your registration?"

Ned put the pen down again. "You don't give up, do you?"

Mrs Ferguson shook her head, moving slightly into the light, and Ned realised she was younger than he had originally thought; her face was drawn, dimmed by the black she wore, but not lined. "No. Mum used to say I was worse than a donkey at the seaside for going where I pleased."

Ned chuckled and leaned back in his chair. "Well, Mrs Ferguson, it isn't what I did, so much as what was done to me." He paused on that thought. "But I'm sure you understand why I think you should go with Miss May – she's a northerner like yourself, she's a skilled Salt practitioner, and she's not under the sword of Damocles."

"No," Mrs Ferguson said, thoughtfully clasping her hands. "I'll take you."

Ned shook his head. "Mrs Ferguson, I'm not sure you understand-"

"I understand just fine." She gestured at the room, at the books and papers and spread of mess. "You'll do."

Ned gave in. Getting to his feet, he closed the door firmly, and settled back in his chair. "Let's begin at the beginning," he said. "What happened to your husband?"

～

Thanet's client turned out to be an Indian woman who spoke little English but smiled at Grace, put her hand on her heart, and said, "Kamala." Above her head, flocks of messenger birds glowed, iridescent and luminous, forming out of dispersed water and then filtering off to nothingness. Grace remembered the birds were being used by the union men on the docks in the general strikes, and liked thought of them taking flight from here, keeping the movement alive from these unassuming rooms above a whelk shop. Kamala's husband seemed to understand a little more, when Grace explained her errand.

"We'll send someone else about your trouble," she promised. "Even if Thanet can't come."

He looked at Kamala, and smiled. Kira was busy, feeding the messenger birds with ice chips from her hands. Grace beckoned and she came reluctantly.

Kira's mother lived by the old West India quays, on the industrial edge of the City. Grace had assumed Kira's father must work on the docks, but when asked, Kira said, "He died when I was little."

Subsequent questioning had revealed that *when I was little* meant the summer of 1916. Ned had found that difficult to bear.

"Don't wander off," Grace said, as Kira darted away, distracted by the trams rattling noisily past towards Victoria. Services had been restored after the crash, but the railwaymen were striking and the streets were crowded with the overspill. When they left the towpath, Kira seemed reluctant again. "It's a bit cramped," she said, in tones of apology, and Grace followed her through the little door, opening on a set of steps that led up to rooms behind an ironmonger's.

"You'll be Miss May, I suppose," said the severe-looking woman who met them at the top, wearing a spotless apron and with hair kept in braids very like her daughter's. "Come in and have some tea."

Grace sat in the indicated chair and accepted the teacup, feeling herself appraised. "Sugar?" the woman asked, and turned to get it without waiting for an answer.

"Thank you for your hospitality," Grace said, formally, and set down to business. "Mrs James," she said. "I'm here, on behalf of the Worshipful Company of Salt practitioners, to propose your daughter enter Salt apprenticeship. She's spent some time with me over the last few months, and I would be honoured to take her on."

"Salt, then," Mrs James murmured, and Grace read something in her expression – something like irritation or distrust.

"Excuse me," she said. "I was under the impression Kira had said – well, if I've overstepped, I apologise."

"Miss May," Mrs James said, interrupting firmly, "what's done is done. Kira, honey, get your old mum some biscuits. And your –" She paused, her expression becoming still. "Principal."

At that word, Grace relaxed a little. "Mrs James," she said. "Are you quite happy for Kira to train with me?"

Mrs James looked at her seriously, but without hostility. "Kira's father was a white man," she said. "If he'd been living, things would be different."

"I'm sorry for your loss," Grace said, automatic, and Mrs James acknowledged her with a nod.

"Her father wanted her trained, and I'm going along with his wishes," she said after a moment. "If he was around still – but then she went to you and you've been kind enough and things are how they are. You from Jamaica?"

Grace smiled briefly. "My grandparents were," she said. "I was born and brought up in Liverpool, myself."

"That's no matter." Mrs James regarded her. "Better with you than anyone else. And a woman is right and proper. You don't know where the men have been."

Grace smiled again at that. "In which case I should mention my two colleagues, Ned and Thanet."

"Thanet a man, is he?"

"Sometimes," Grace said, and Mrs James raised an eyebrow. "Birds-in-Flight," Grace added, "not Salt."

"Thought they weren't like that any more?" Mrs James said, and then seemed to recollect herself. "No offence meant to your friend. Just you don't see them too much now."

"Thanet persists," Grace said, with a grin. "In any case, she – or he, depending – would be teaching your daughter as well as Ned and myself. Would that be a concern for you?"

"Not if you'll vouch for them," Mrs James said, and Grace sighed again and sat back in her chair: it was time to be truthful.

"Mrs James," she said. "I'm a practitioner in good standing. But Thanet – Thanet's registration has been withdrawn for conduct reasons by the Company of Birds-in-Flight. And Ned was a practitioner like myself, raised at Temple. But he's unwell, presently, and it's unclear what his future in Salt practice will be."

Mrs James nodded. "Conduct reasons," she said, suddenly. "Does that mean, helping people they're not supposed to help?"

"Something like that." Grace kept her expression even.

"And the other." Mrs James paused. "Shell-shock?"

"Not exactly," Grace said. "But it's very similar."

"He was an officer, then," said Mrs James with a grim humour. Grace understood that – officers came home with neurasthenia, not shell-shock, and she didn't bother to correct the misconception.

"But I have the utmost trust in them," Grace went on, "and we will all do our best for Kira. She can stay here or she can lodge in chambers – it's for her to decide, if you're willing."

"I'll come with you," Kira said, her little voice clear and bright. She was standing on the threshold with the plate of biscuits held in both hands. "I mean – if I can."

She was looking at her mother, then at Grace. Grace read fear and excitement and amazement in her face, and regret too. On glancing around, Grace noted the room was sparse but clean and tidy, with books and brightly-coloured ornaments, and photographs on the mantel, and suspected this had been as happy as a home as it could be, for those who were left.

"Miss May," Mrs James said. "I know the way of things. You people look after your own."

"Of course we do," Grace said, startled by her tone. "Ned and Thanet and I look after each other, and we'll look after her."

Mrs James nodded. "And in the end, you'll be her family, more than her flesh and blood."

"We already are her flesh and blood," Grace said, suddenly snapping to anger. "She's already one of us. She's Salt, and so am I, so is Ned. She's a sister and a daughter."

"A white man, raised at Temple? You call him your brother?" Mrs James said, then put her hands up, as though holding Grace's words away from her.

"You'll show her a world for than this," she said, quieter now. She pointed out of the window at the street outside, at the dusty road traffic, the stallholders, the dock-workers eating sandwiches one-handed from greaseproof paper, at men with trays around their necks hawking trinkets. "She'll become – not like you, but almost, and she won't ever come back here and see it the way she sees it now."

Grace nodded. "That's true," she said, honestly. "Temple is my home. It will be Kira's."

"Is it the best thing?"

"We will look after her," Grace said, knowing she wasn't answering the question, knowing it wasn't for her to answer. She held still for a moment, letting the moment take its time in passing. "Shall she come with me?"

"Yes," Mrs James said, finally. "Yes."

Kira made a small wordless noise of joy. "Kira, you should say your goodbyes to your mother properly," Grace said. "We'll come back for your things this evening, if that's suitable?"

"Yes, Miss May," Kira said with an obedience that Grace suspected wouldn't last. She nodded respectfully to Kira's mother.

"Good luck," Mrs James said, perhaps deliberately making it unclear which of them she was talking to, and Grace grinned. As they walked down back towards Embankment, Kira seemed a girl enchanted, quiet, with luminous eyes. Of the two of them, only Grace turned to look back – and that was when the rock hit her in the side of the head.

※

"My husband is dead," Mrs Ferguson said, flatly. "Nothing to be done for him now."

"I don't –" Ned began, then sat back. "Your husband was driving the train at St Paul's."

"They're going to make out it was suicide," Mrs Ferguson said, fiercely. "They've been round asking. Was he shell-shocked? Was he drinking? They don't want it to be their fault is all. And my widow's pension – well." Her expression darkened. "I need you to show it wasn't his fault. All that signalling and that, that's magic."

"I know," Ned said, sharply. "I was the one who designed it."

"Then go and find out what went wrong." She glared at him, and Ned thought that he might be the first focus for her anger she had had, since the accident. "If you designed it, then who's right to do it but you?"

Ned brought his hands together, fingers lacing and interlacing. "My colleague," he said, "may lose her own registration over this."

"All the more reason for you to get to the bottom of it, then."

Ned nodded. "With all due respect, Mrs Ferguson," he said. "Why are you so sure it wasn't – what they say it was? Sometimes" —he hesitated —"a man won't speak of what's on his mind, until speaking does no good."

Mrs Ferguson gave him an unreadable look. "Because of this," she said.

She pulled a card from her bag and handed it to Ned, who took it without thinking. Ostensibly handwritten, it had been reproduced by a form of Salt magic with which he was very familiar, and the letters spelled out an invitation to a wedding in Penrith three weeks hence. "The bride is your sister-in-law?" he guessed, from the name.

Mrs Ferguson nodded. "It's a good family. Alfie was right proud. He was going to make them a proper present – maybe proper silverware, he said, like we never had when we were first married. And we were going to go up for it on the railwaymen's specials."

Ned could feel a headache starting. "Mrs Ferguson, I'm afraid I still don't quite understand—"

"He had the money for the present on him," she said. "He was going straight after his shift. Why would he have – if he was going to—"

"Ah," Ned said, understanding. "I see." He paused. "*Was* your husband shell-shocked, Mrs Ferguson?"

She half-stood up, and Ned thought for a mad moment that she would take a swing at him. As he held his ground, his own hands damnably shaking, the moment filtered away into silence. Mrs Ferguson sank bank into her chair and took a moment before she rose again, this time with dignity. "He didn't return the same as he went," she said, voice clear. "But did anyone?"

"Not in my experience," Ned said, with a calm he did not quite feel. "I'll write to you in respect of my retention."

"Thank you," she said, nodding, and gave Ned no look of pity as he took the usual length of time to get to the door and open it for her. "You'll do," she said, again, on the threshold, and departed.

Ned turned to go inside, then paused, aware of the sounds of the city, rattling trains and distant crowds, and of the soft, comforting heat of the summer air. The morning chill had quite dissipated. He sat down on the front step, pulled a battered paperback from his pocket, and began to read.

※

When Grace opened her eyes she was lying in the dirt, the sky darkening into azure in a narrow slice between the rooftops. "Kira," she said, blearily. "Kira, where –"

"I'm here!" Kira sounded terrified, her voice high-pitched. "I'm here, the man helped me."

Grace forced herself into a sitting position, her head spinning sickly. Her hair rained down street dirt onto her shoulders. She'd been dragged here. "The man?" she asked, turning around.

The sudden movement prompted another bout of nausea. Grace put a hand to her head and felt her fingers come away sticky.

"Here," said a male voice, and someone handed her a handkerchief.

Grace pressed it to her head gratefully and took him in: a man in the rough trousers and jacket of a dock worker, his sleeves dark with dirt and oil. "Kamala's husband?" she said, stupidly.

"Amir," he said, nodding, beckoning her to follow.

Grace breathed, willing the dizziness to pass, and got gingerly to her feet. From their shadowy hiding-place in this alley, the street seemed an unknowable mass of people howling forwards. It had been so quiet, before, and the sky so many shades brighter. "How long was I..."

"I don't know," Kira said, her little hand creeping into Grace's; Grace squeezed tight. "These men were throwing stones. They got you, they didn't get me but they tried, then so many people, shouting – " She looked up. "Bad words. Then the nice man came running down, he helped."

"Thank you," Grace said to him. Out on the street she could hear those 'bad words,' perhaps worse than Kira knew; she could make out the scrape of metal on metal, and the howl of the mob.

Amir nodded. "Come," he said, and Grace and Kira both followed.

Further into the shadows the alley grew narrower until they reached a timbered door hanging wildly off its hinges. As Amir led the way in, Grace's vision adjusted to the half-darkness, and she realised there were others inside: men dressed like sailors and labourers and dockers, with bright eyes in dark faces, and in their voices she heard India again. They were frightened, holding back; she heard the word "coloured", and then: "*mitti attar*".

"Salt," she said, understanding that at least. She lifted her hand to the bar in her ear. "What do you want?"

"Can you help us escape from here?" asked one of the men, stepping forwards. Grace could make out blood on his hands, scraped and raw, and the recent tears in his clothes. "They think they come from war, and we have taken their jobs, their women. They come wanting blood for it. The Musulmans also, and the ones like you."

There was bitterness as well as fear in his accented, assured English. Grace wondered how long they'd been hiding and if, in coming to find her, Amir had put himself at risk. "Is Kamala all right?" she asked.

He nodded, and Grace was grateful. "We should wait this out," she said.

"They will find us," said the other man. "But if you help us get out—"

"They'll destroy me," Grace said, then pulled herself together. "Listen, are any of you like me?"

A murmur, in the darkness, and Amir stepped forwards, bringing another man with him. Grace couldn't make out how many had taken refuge here, and could barely make out what sort of a space it was. A warehouse, perhaps, long abandoned.

"This is Raj," Amir said. He gestured to his friend's ear, where it was a clear a metal bar had been dragged forcibly out of the flesh. Grace shivered. "He is like you. Not you. The others."

"The Birds-in-Flight," Grace said, but to her surprise Amir shook his head.

"No," he said, frustrated. "the others."

He said something in his own language to his companion. "The others," he said, again but Grace didn't understand.

"All right," she said, after a minute. "You two, me, and my apprentice. We'll have to work together. Kira, you'll listen to me and do exactly what I say, do you understand? All our lives will depend on it."

"What," Amir said. "What you need?"

Grace turned. "Sir," she said to Amir, "may I borrow your handkerchief again? Thank you."

She showed it to Kira with some disgust, the brightness of her own blood dimming to dark brown. "Old-fashioned magic," she said, wearily, "and not done any more for a reason. Come now."

"The gift," Kira said, "The blood –"

Grace nodded, not surprised; Kira learned quickly.

"Come on," Grace said again, to all of them. Still holding the handkerchief in one hand, wishing the world wouldn't spin so much, she led the way to the bottleneck of the alley, where the mob milled and shouted in the street. At this distance she could feel the heat of all those bodies massed together, the animal anger.

"I need you both to be ready," she said, with more determination than she felt. "I'm going to take your heart – your power," she amended, not knowing how common the idiom might be. "Your magical power, you understand? You have to let me take it, I can't if you don't."

Amir and Kira nodded, both looking scared but determined. After a moment, Raj stepped forward, took the handkerchief out of Grace's hands, and said something under his breath Grace didn't catch, but she felt the change in the air: the charge of magic rising, fizzing in her teeth. He caught her eye and Grace decided she had no choice but to trust in whatever he'd done. Out on the street, the crowds seemed to be moving with greater focus, and Grace pictured a black or brown body under that mob, and shivered.

"Ready?" she said, and they all nodded.

Grace held herself still, setting her mind on the clear, quiet image of the last time she'd done this kind of magic: Ned on the station platform at St Paul's, saying, *use me, if you must.* At once she became more than herself, hearing scraps of what must be Hindustani in her mind, and seeing the flash of Kira's memories, brightened at the edges by the intensity of childhood. Then Grace stepped into the street, into the mob, thinking of who she was and what called her, of what it was to be Salt, of her own and Kira's and these strangers' gifts, and threw a great wave of energy into the air around them.

In another second the mob's thrown missiles glanced off that invisible surface, as though deflected by a shield; rocks and stones tumbled away, weapons turned on the surface, and even the noise of the screaming, howling mob dimmed and blurred. The mob had been moving haphazardly, dispensing directionless violence, but they had a target now and the noise grew louder. Within the shield, Amir and Raj called the others out from within the alleyway and the men came out from hiding and fanned out, splitting off in every direction. Kira whimpered and Grace thought mad thoughts about covering her eyes, so she wouldn't have to see the mob of white men in pulled-down caps brandishing domestic, devastating weapons: boat hooks and tools and cleavers, and whatever they'd brought home from their wars. The barrier was dissipating, burning off their magic: through it she could hear chanting, mostly indistinct, although with the occasional word that rose with clarity above the general roar. Those words, Grace thought, with a return of the nausea, ought not to be spoken, not so close to home. And then she took a steadying breath, poured the last of her own energy into the shield, and grabbed Kira with both arms.

"Run!" she shouted, into the blackening sky above, and didn't look back.

༅

"Ned," Grace said, because when she finally stopped running Ned was on the doorstep, as though he had been waiting for her. "Ned – Kira..."

"Thanet's got her," Ned said. He took Grace in on his arm as though escorting her to a ball – which he had done often, in those ridiculous pre-war days – and sat her in the consulting room with her feet on an ottoman.

Thanet took over after that, knitting the wound in Grace's scalp with magic as strong and light as gossamer. Ned was talking to Kira, asking her short, simple questions, and Grace was grateful that she would not have to tell the story, not tonight.

"Kira," Ned said, finally, standing up. "Would you like anything? Mrs Throckley can get you a cup of hot milk, if you'd like."

Dumbly, Kira shook her head. She looked so scared, Grace thought, dimly: this girl who had lived through a war, just as much as any of them.

"Then to bed with you." Ned's tone was still gentle, and Grace remembered.

"I forgot," she said, dismayed. "I thought…"

She trailed off, too tired to articulate the thought. She had planned to take Kira back to her mother's this evening, for one last night at home before apprenticeship – and, in the way of the Temple folk, adulthood – and to make arrangements for her here tomorrow.

But Mrs Throckley was at the door holding the tin cup of hot milk, apparently set upon on someone drinking it, even if not Kira; the look on her face rested halfway between kindness and defiance. "I hope you'll forgive me," she said, "but it's been so quiet since you all came home. I did hope as the little one was staying… come with me, both of you."

She pointed up the stairs, so Grace had no choice but to follow, with Kira trailing behind. Mrs Throckley went round several turns of the staircase, holding up a kerosene lamp and opened the door on the attic room beneath the eaves, with the porthole light. It had been shut up since the war, accumulating dust. Grace looked around at the room, aired and cleaned, now with a little truckle bed and a lamp beside it, with a pretty bedspread and neat frilled curtains. Despite everything, Kira looked delighted.

"Mrs Throckley," Grace said. "It's perfect. Thank you."

Strangely, it was that act of kindness that did her in. She waited to make sure Kira got to bed safely, thanked Mrs Throckley again, and meant to pour a cup of water in the kitchen before retreating to her own bed, but somehow she burst into tears between there and the staircase.

"Come," Ned said, taking her arm again. "Let's take a moment."

Out on their front step, the air was still and heated, carrying the distant sounds of shouting across the river toward them and then away again. Ned lit a cigarette and offered it to Grace, blowing smoke. She took a drag and passed it back. They sat in silence for some time, the glowing tip of the lit cigarette the only light other than the City's lamps and the waxing moon. Neither she nor Ned had smoked before the war.

Finally, Ned threw the cigarette end onto the cobbles and watched it smoulder. "Tell me," he said.

"We're falling apart," she said.

Ned glanced at her, then away. "Grace..."

"What are we here for?" she said, suddenly angry. "We're Salt, Ned. We're here to serve. When people ask for our help, we give it."

"With contributions to our minor expenses," Ned murmured. "Such as the holding together of body and soul."

Grace didn't smile. "Those men in the alley came for me because of the bar in my ear. They thought I could save them."

"And you did," Ned said, mildly. "Didn't you?"

"I went out into that alleyway yelling and throwing shields and fireballs about," Grace said. "But I didn't even look back. I picked up Kira and ran. They could have been knocked over where they stood right behind me and I wouldn't know."

"Getting yourself killed wouldn't have helped anyone," Ned said, with an edge to his voice. "Least of all Kira, and she's your first responsibility. You did exactly the right thing."

"Did I?" Grace asked, bleakly. "I told Kira's mother – today, even, it was only this morning – that we could give her the training she needs and deserves. That *we* could, you and me and Thanet. But Thanet's being drummed out of practice and you're – oh, God, Ned, I don't know what they did to you, but you know what I mean by it – and now Kira and I are being chased down the streets by a howling mob."

"Yes." Ned sighed. "Grace – she's a sweet enough girl and she deserves training. But does it have to be by us?" He paused. "By *you*?"

Looking at his familiar face, his grey eyes reflecting the light of the cigarette still smouldering on the cobbles, Grace was reminded of what she had said to Kira's mother about Kira, and about Ned and herself: a sister, a brother, a daughter.

"Yes," she said helplessly. "Yes, it had to be us. I'm not sure I can make you understand."

"All right." Ned shrugged, taking it philosophically. "I'll accept that. But you're not to blame for fools and animals," he added. "And we'll clear Thanet's name."

"What if we can't?" Grace asked. "What if Thanet's right, and it's really about the people she helps? What if it's really about what she is?"

"Thanet is part of an honourable tradition among Birds-in-Flight practitioners," Ned said. "It's a magical practice built on organic fluidity, for heaven's sake! They'll come to their senses."

"What if they don't?" Grace asked.

Ned shook his head. "This is Temple, Grace. That's not how things are here."

"Even if that's so," Grace said, sadly, "we have to leave it sometimes. It can't be the only place in the world for people like us." She paused and shook her head. "Listen to me, talking as though we're the ones who need protecting. When did we become such sorry shadows of ourselves, Ned? When were we so bowed and so – broken?"

Ned shook his head again, and she knew there was no answer.

"Arma virumque cano," he said lightly, and Grace was glad that he still found such comfort in his books. "We came away from Troy, and into greater exile."

"Speaking of exile," Grace said. "Your mother is planning to pay us a visit."

"She'll have heard," Ned said. "She won't come, not now."

"Not yet," Grace corrected. "But once all this blows over, there's the spectre of the rent. Ned, how much longer can we go on? I don't intend to be melodramatic. I really mean it."

"It would be," Ned said, with some difficulty, "grievous, for us to have fought so hard for what is ours. And then, after everything—"

Grace nodded, allowing him the time to finish that sentence, or choose not to. Ned lit another cigarette, and she waited, thinking of how she had kept the practice running even when the windows were blacked-up with crepe and Salt magic was as strictly regulated as sugar and petrol. She had written letters to Ned about it, and had them returned with "Not known" written on the envelopes, by order of the War Office, but in Ned's own familiar hand. They had laughed about it, afterwards.

"We go on," Ned said, breathing out smoke. "Like we did before. We just go on."

"Go on," Grace echoed, and then fell silent, watching Ned's hands move to his mouth, and the cigarette tip glowing in the darkness.

❧

### (iv) Michaelmas

The Temple gardens were turning over into autumn by the time the coroner set the date for the full inquest, and perhaps by then, Ned thought, the revolutionary fervour would have dimmed a little in the streets.

"November," Grace said, looking up from her letters.

"We'll know by then, one way or the other," Thanet remarked. He had taken up needlework, to fill the time, and when that palled, carried tea to the workers on strike.

"Oh, Ned," Grace added. "Mrs Ferguson was by, earlier. She said that the fireman on the train – not the fireman, the other man in the cab, anyway – he's come around. He's still at Bart's, but he's well enough to speak to someone. I can go with Kira this afternoon."

"No," Ned said, quietly. "If you can spare Kira, she can come with me."

Grace looked at him for a long moment, and then smiled. "It's good," she said. "To see you out and about again."

Ned returned a tentative smile. "Don't count your chickens. Wait and see if I make it back alive."

She didn't castigate him for being overly dramatic, which Ned was pleased about. In the months since the Armistice, he had begun to wonder if his mental condition were infirmity or melodrama, but he was shamefully grateful for Kira's presence through the noisy, crowded streets, and then for the clean antiseptic quiet of the hospital corridors.

The railwayman's name was Jack Roberts, he explained, although the nurses called him John, which put him in mind of school and childhood visits from elderly relatives. "But who're you?" he asked after a moment, belatedly surprised at a visit from a stranger.

"My name is Ned Devlin," said Ned, putting a hand to his ear and dipping his head. The man's eyes widened with recognition. Salt practitioners were usually called to layings-out, and Ned couldn't blame him for being apprehensive. "I've been retained by the wife of your driver – your friend, Mr Ferguson."

That the men had been friends was a shot in the dark, but it paid off; Roberts smiled a little, and something eased in his face. "You're in the pay of Mistress Ferguson?" he said, rubbing at his eyes; Ned suspected that in ordinary life he wore spectacles. "Better you than me, mate."

Ned laughed a little and sat down in the hard wooden chair closest to the bed, waving to Kira to keep close to him. The man in the bed blinked at the movement, trying to follow it with his head. "That your kid?"

"My apprentice."

"Tell her to have a grape, everyone's been that kind, but I've no hope of eating them all. So she's got you to find out the truth of what happened, has she?"

Ned nodded. "Something of that order. I'm wondering, Mr Roberts, if you can tell me exactly what happened in the cab, before the accident. If we can get to the bottom of this, your friend's wife may take her widow's pension from the Southwestern, after all."

"If I can help I will," Roberts said. "Alf was a good mate. They told me he went straight off – didn't feel any pain?"

It wasn't the first time that a young man had asked Ned that question. "I'm told that's so. You had known each other some time, then?"

"Oh, yeah. I'd been a lampman on the railway before the war, and since I got back I'd taken a fancy to driving. Alf said he'd take me along, show me how it was done, so I went down to Moorgate in a 'bus bright and early. Alf was telling me something about his sister up north somewhere. Getting married in a month and it was going to be quite a do. His wife was sending him out for a present, straight after his shift."

"When was that?" Ned asked. "Towards the beginning of the journey, or closer to the bridge?"

Roberts paused. "Later – oh, towards the bridge, I recall seeing the lights up across the river. We were at the signal. I said to him, it'll be a fine morning, no doubt, and he said, if we only could get this train into depot a little quicker! And I said something about how fast they'd let you go, what with the freight trains ploughing out at night, and he said I'd have to sit down and study it all in a book before they'd let me train to be a driver. And then…" Roberts paused again. "The train moved. I said to him, Alf, should we be – and that's when the other train came out of the dark. I thought the end of the world had come."

Ned nodded. "I see. Thank you, Mr Roberts, you've been very helpful."

"Don't see how, but I suppose you folk are a rule to yourselves," Roberts said. "You'll do your best for Mrs Ferguson, won't you?"

"I will," Ned promised. "Kira, come along. Thank you again for your time, Mr Roberts."

"Wasn't any bother. Take some more grapes."

Kira did, and was eating them industriously as she followed Ned out of the ward and through the long hallways, into the brilliant sunshine outside. "Well," he said. "What did we learn from that?"

Kira inclined her head. "I don't know."

"Me neither, little one. Do you feel up to another errand before we return?"

Kira looked at him with all the perspicacity of twelve years old, and all the kindness: she did not turn the question back around on him.

"Come, then," Ned said. "Let's go and take a look at the railway line. Besides, I could do with someone to help me up if I fall flat on my face in the undergrowth."

It wasn't quite a joke, but Kira smiled, and they went on past Temple towards Blackfriars.

"Can't take you across the picket lines," Ned remarked. "Your principal would have my head."

"Really?" Kira asked, seemingly more intrigued than anything else by the prospect of Ned's possible decapitation.

"Really," Ned said, and true to his word, took Kira around the back of the station, away from the strikers, and through the rusted gates. In another life, he would have been able to break any lock. As it was, he was grateful for some railwayman's carelessness. With a crack, the fencing shifted to allow them through.

"Watch yourself," he warned Kira, motioning to the thick layers of scrub and weeds where it would be easy to catch a foot. "I thought we might take a look alongside the track where the crash happened, while the strike's on."

"So no trains are going to come through," Kira said, sounding rather disappointed, and Ned smiled to himself; he suspected that aged twelve, he too would have liked to see a train go past from a foot away. "What are you looking for?"

"I might know it when I see it." Ned paused, tapping the rail with his cane, then leaning forwards to investigate it more closely. "Onwards."

Kira nodded and they pushed on for a while, boots kicking up dead grass and gravel. "Were you in France in the war?" she asked, suddenly looking straight at him. "If he'd come back, would my dad have come back like you?"

Given some experience of it, Ned had come to find Kira's directness refreshing: rather like the cool, pleasant autumn air, after so long spent inside. "I can't say as to your father, little one," he said, "but yes, I was. Now, what do we have here?"

With some difficulty, he got down to his knees, laying the cane beside him. The track was sun-warmed and smooth under his hands, then metallic and chilled in the shadows.

"See, Kira," he said. "What do you think this is?"

Kira investigated it, lip curling. "It's like icing on a cake," she said, after a minute, and Ned was pleased with the analogy; the metallic layer on top of the track surface had spread just like melted chocolate, weatherbeaten in places but mostly smooth. "It's – yellow? Under the dirt I mean."

"Yellow," Ned said, pushing his thumbnail into the battered surface, unsurprised to find it left a mark. "Gold, in fact. A splash of gold on the railway track, just where the accident happened. Now isn't that interesting?"

"Why is it there?" Kira asked.

"I don't know." Ned glanced up along the track, then down. "I think we'll have to find out. Shall we?"

Kira helped him up, and kept pace with him back to the gap in the railings. She didn't speak, but Ned thought something of the tension had gone from her, and from him, too, here in the mid-afternoon sun and birdsong. As they emerged from the trackside behind the station, Ned caught himself looking up and down to avoid railwaymen or the local constabulary and any associated difficult questions. The ridiculous furtiveness lifted his mood, as though he were Kira's age, on an adventure.

"Off you go, Kira," he said, once steady on his feet again, rummaging in his pocket for tuppence. "Go down to the station and get yourself a chocolate bar or a comic or something else you'd like. Don't cross the line," he added, firmly. "Quickly now."

Ned took the few minutes she was gone to catch his breath and collect himself. The walk had been long enough for him to be in pain, though still appreciative of the sunlight and clear air. He expected Kira to come back with a comic – sweets were still rationed for the most part – but it was bright Cadbury's purple in her hands when she returned. They walked down the Embankment in comfortable silence, Kira munching happily. To Ned's surprise, she broke off a piece and gave it to him without comment, and he ate it in the spirit given.

"You know," he said hesitantly. "Chocolate was in my rations, when I was in France. But they never sent it all in the right place and time, so you'd get it all at once or not at all. I used to give it all away to the men."

Kira turned. "You used to give it all away?" she asked, aghast, and Ned chuckled.

"Yes," he said, still laughing. "That was the great sacrifice I made in the war."

But Kira was looking up at him as he spoke, her eyes serious. Ned knew even before she said it that this was the question she had been gathering the courage to ask.

"Do you think you might have met my dad?" she said. "In the war I mean."

"I didn't always ask men their names," Ned said, very gently. "Sometimes there wasn't time even for that."

"So you might have? And not known it?"

"I might have," Ned said, still gently, "yes."

Kira seemed contented, unwrapping another piece of chocolate and handing it over. She'd learned the habit from Grace of keeping in step with him, and Ned walked along thinking over the puzzle on the railway, breathing in his own contentment in between the taps of his cane.

～

That evening there was a knock at the door, just before nightfall; Grace was the one who set down her tea to answer it.

"You're the chaps who did the work," said the man on the other side, pulling off a London Underground hat to reveal a forehead slick with sweat. He turned around and charged across the cobbles as though expecting Grace to immediately follow.

"Excuse me?" she called, and he shook his head impatiently and gestured for her to hurry up.

"Come on, you're needed." He was looking over her shoulder at Ned, Grace realised. "Signal failures on the bridge and at St Paul's. Everything's at a standstill. Come on!"

"Kira!" Grace shouted over her shoulder. "Come on, we're wanted! Thanet—"

"I'm not registered," Thanet was saying, but Grace waved him quiet.

The man from the Underground – his name badge announced "WHITWORTH, A." – led the way down Middle Temple Lane seemingly unsurprised by the extent of his entourage. As they scurried down the Embankment, Grace could see the strangeness on the bridge at Blackfriars – two trains held massively still, like dragons turned to stone – and then they were in the station itself, past the passengers being herded into the street. Whitworth called a lift and pushed the doors open with a shove, gesturing all of them inside, and it was only when the lift was descending silently to the lower levels that he spoke any further.

"At about six o'clock this evening a train was signalled clear through the southbound platform to go on to Waterloo," he said, expressionless. Grace glanced at her watch; it was coming up on half past six. "There was already a train at the platform."

Grace inhaled sharply. "Did—"

"No," Whitworth said, severely. "The signalwoman on duty realised something was amiss and manually altered the signals. At 6:10pm, the same thing happened on the northbound side. The train driver jammed on the brakes in time."

"That can't happen," Ned said, sounding disbelieving. "That absolutely – that can't happen."

Whitworth continued, inexorable. "At 6:15pm, every train on this part of the network was halted at the nearest station. I was asked by the control room here at Blackfriars to track down a Mr Devlin, who had originally set up the Salt system of magic that prevents collisions between trains on the Underground. I believe, sir, that that's yourself."

"Yes," Ned said, "but you should know—"

His voice was lost in the screech of the doors pulling back: the lift had reached the platform levels, and dusty tiles proclaimed "To The Trains". Whitworth strode forth and Grace brought up the rearguard, pausing for a moment to peer down the single flight of steps to the deserted platform below. Stray litter skittered across the edge, but otherwise the silence was absolute. Whitworth led them through a door gleaming with Salt magic at its edges, sealed against fire or flood, and into the dim control room beyond.

"Got them," he announced.

It took Grace's eyes a second to adjust, to take in the two signalwomen sitting at the long benches, the large train operating charts spread out across the walls, and the rows and rows of silver bells, gleaming as though with some inner light. The hum of Salt magic underpinned everything, invisible but inescapable, like the Tube itself beneath London.

"This is Devlin," said Whitworth, and then, confusedly: "And some others."

"Grace May," Grace said. "That's Thanet, and that's my apprentice. Ned—"

Ned wasn't listening to her. With his cane, he had waved the two operators away from the panels. "You hit the killing bell," he said.

One of the two signalwomen looked cowed at his tone; the other stood up straighter. "Yes," she said, clearly. "I didn't trust the system, I shut everything down."

Ned nodded. "Run it all past me," he said, and Grace startled at the imperious note in his voice. "Tell me exactly what happened, every detail."

"We control most of the City from here," said the signal operator to Ned. "When things started going wrong, the bells rang." She reached out to a bell halfway along the second row, her finger stopping just sort of its surface. "This one, then" – another bell, just above it – "this one. That was the train northbound. And then…" – she pointed at the one below – "that's the kill bell." She gestured at it, as Ned had done: it was the largest bell on the assembly, held at a seemingly unsupported angle.

Ned nodded again, more to Thanet than the signal operator. "You remember the emergency signal," he said. "A red smoke rises in the window of the train cab, and every driver knows they're to stop at once. Miss – what's your name?"

"Miss Lynley, sir."

"Miss Lynley. What did you – what's that noise?"

The noise had been bothering Grace for a moment or two, and judging from the way she drew closer, Kira, too: a rumbling sound, like something very heavy beginning to move. "Can't be a train," Ned said, unnecessarily. "Not if they're all stopped. I suppose they *have* all stopped." He reached out and deliberately struck a bell. Miss Lynley and Whitworth flinched; Ned smiled a little dangerously and said, "It's my system, Miss Lynley. Trust me."

Thanet stepped through the door and Grace realised he had gone down to the platforms to check. "They've stopped," he said, authoritatively. "Ned – all right, what the hell is that?"

*That* was the noise, getting louder now, but losing none of its low resonances and layers, as though whatever it was was at the bottom of a well. Something deeper even than this, Grace thought, and shivered.

"Damn it," Ned said, making an abortive motion with one hand, holding short of the bells. "Ring one bell, the matching train bell rings, instantaneous or close-as. The drivers aren't colluding to play Greensleeves for the signal operators' amusement, I suppose. This doesn't make sense."

"What happened to your hand?" Grace asked, suddenly distracted. Thanet had stepped out of the light so Miss Lynley's left hand, cradled to her and roughly bandaged, was visible.

"That was my fault," said a soft voice, and Grace looked at the other signal operator, peering shyly through her long brown hair. "I asked Alice to open my lemonade bottle for me."

"Silly thing went right into my fingers," Miss Lynley said, pointing to a discarded bottle opener, together with the remains of some sandwiches.

"Thanet will look after that for you," Grace said, a little amused at herself despite everything. Kira was hiding behind her skirts; Grace seemed to have taken on the role of mother hen and principal to the entire world. Thanet grinned and nodded.

"Just give that here," he said, cheerfully, already raising some healing magic into the air, when Ned spoke.

"Stop."

"Ned?" Grace said, but he held up a hand.

"Stop. All of you, stop. Don't touch anything." Ned stepped forward. "I've been an idiot and a fool. Grace – when you were in the alley, with those dockers –"

Grace hesitated, thrown by the non sequitur. "What about it?"

"You had a bloodied handkerchief."

"Yes," Grace said, surprised. "Yes, I told you that – Ned, what is it?"

"And the inquest." Ned was pacing up and down, though everyone else had taken his advice to heart and stood quite still. "The woman on the train said that it stopped, then moved again. Is that right? It stopped, *then* moved."

"Yes," Kira said, with unexpected clarity. "She said it moved again so quietly she almost didn't notice it."

"That's my girl," Ned said, half-exultant.

"Ned, blood magic is superstitious nonsense," Thanet said, comfortingly trenchant to Grace's ears. "You know it."

"Perhaps we've been wrong about that," Ned said, running his hands through his hair. "Magic is Salt, or Birds. Living things, or just things. But the world has changed so much." He waved his hands, a little helplessly, as though trying to indicate the city above them. "What passing-bells, for those who die as cattle? People becoming things, and things" – he gestured again, at the train operating panels, and the bells – "coming alive."

"Ned," Thanet said conversationally, "get to the point before I insert that cane in your ear."

Ned spread his palms. "Salt, Birds, and iron. Not blood. *Iron.*"

"A new form of magic?" Grace said. "Ned, that's... I don't know. Are you sure?"

"Ferguson, on the bridge," Ned said. "He brings the train to a stop at a signal. He remarks to Roberts, perhaps laughing, that he wishes the train would move faster. With his pockets full of metal, and those passing bells in his recent memory, and all around him a locomotive made out of—"

"Iron," said Grace, with reverence. "So the train moved, to take him home. Miss Lynley, what exactly were you saying to your friend, before the signal failure?"

Miss Lynley looked miserable. "There's a dance tonight, down in Clerkenwell," she murmured. "I was just saying to Cara – I wish everything would hurry up, the last hour of the shift always drags."

"But what about the gift?" Thanet said. "Do you think Ferguson cut his hand on the controls?"

"Ferguson had the money for his sister's wedding on him," Ned said. "It wasn't burnt away, it was *given*. Kira and I found the remains of it, the sovereigns, on the railway track."

"Overpayment?" Thanet asked, and then nodded to himself. "He wouldn't have been trained – he wouldn't know how much—"

"He wouldn't have known he was doing magic at all," Grace said, a little excited. "Ned, the Indian man who helped me in the alley. He said he wasn't like me, but he wasn't like the others. Not Salt, not Birds, but —"

She turned her head.

Whitworth cleared his throat again; he was standing was at the door to the control room, the magical light from its seal soft on his face.

"Excuse me," he said. "Miss May, Mr Devlin, if I could have your attention, just for a moment." He pointed out into the tunnel.

Grace and Ned exchanged glances and followed him out, leaving Thanet to look after Miss Lynley's hand.

"Once," Whitworth said, without turning, "long ago, they were going to terminate the line here, and not cross the river. Bit of a crush for the trains, though." He waved casually down at the platforms as he spoke, and the rumble rose again, making Grace shiver again, involuntary and deep in her bones. "Bit of a palaver. So they built a turning loop, under the river. Quite a miracle of engineering, in its day. Then of course Parliament came through for them. Straight line extension across the Thames. So they built that" – he pointed down into the tunnel, the Salt lights within flickering eerily – "and they sealed the old loop off."

They were climbing a small staircase, dusty and slick with oil; Ned's cane slipped and Grace reached out to steady him.

"Can't bury a thing time out of mind," Whitworth said. "It'll rust to nothing some day, but in the meantime we keep an eye. Here's the door."

Grace looked up. The door was small, human-sized, and sealed with enough Salt magic to hold down an inferno. "Behind that door," she ventured tentatively. "Underneath the river –"

Mr Whitworth took the keys from his pockets and opened the door. Grace felt the small piece of magic raised, as the door opened onto a wall of black earth.

"It's not a tunnel," Grace said, surprised. "It's not there!"

"It was yesterday," Whitworth said, calmly. "It was this morning."

Though the words were delivered with utmost calm, something seemed to enter beneath Grace's skin and begin to crawl.

"The tunnel should be there, miss," Whitworth said. If it's not" – and then the rumbling came again, almost too loud to bear, reverberating in Grace's very being – "it's shifted of its own accord."

Ned tapped on the wall beside the door, so Grace could hear the hollow resonance.

"The seals," Grace said, aware of her voice trembling. "The magic's been disturbed – the sealing, against the river—"

Whitworth touched the bare earth beyond the door, then pulled back. His hand was wet.

"Oh, God," Grace said, and spun around on the spot. In her mind she was somewhere else – somewhere else dark, perhaps the Salt Guildhall on the day the first bomb fell – but the moment passed and she was here again. Terror fizzed through her veins and a determination she did not feel rose into her voice. "All right, Mr Whitworth, I think it's time we acknowledge the truth. The tunnels will need to be evacuated. Can you and your signal operators start dealing with that? And switch off the power?"

"Yes," Whitworth said, "but there are two trains, stopped just outside the platforms."

"I know," Grace said. "Thanet will do any magic you need to help you get the passengers out and through the tunnels. We can't predict what will happen now," she added, glancing at Ned, who nodded. "There are iron rings in every tunnel, isn't that right? We don't know who might do magic without realising it, or what they might do. Ned, I need you to get Kira out of here, it's not safe. Go as quickly as you can."

"What?" Ned looked up, his eyes very bright in the darkness. "Don't be ridiculous. I should stay. I can help."

"Ned," Grace said, breathing in, hating herself. "You're a liability."

Ned flinched. "Grace…"

"If you stay, you'll be one more thing for me to worry about." And then, softer, "You've done your bit. Let me do mine."

Ned held her gaze for a minute, then dropped his head. "Understood."

Grace reached out and entwined their fingers, not caring about Whitworth's presence. Then she stuffed both her hands in her pockets and took a deep breath.

"Good luck," Ned said, and went back down the passageway along to the steps.

"Miss May?" That was Whitworth, looking at her with confusion, and worry. "What will you do?"

Grace took another breath, and reached for whatever was left in her that wasn't fear. She waited another moment as the great rumbling started up again.

This time it had a sinister punctuation: the rush and movement of water. As they stood, a first gush emerged from behind the door, filtering through cracks in the packed earth and pouring onto Grace's boots.

She thought again of the darkness beneath the bombs, took another breath, and she was ready. "I'm going to seal this off."

※

"Come on, little one," Ned said, his coat sweeping the floor as he turned. "Quickly! Thanet – good luck."

Thanet saluted him ironically. Ned smiled and held out a hand to Kira, who scurried after him with alacrity.

"We're going back up to Temple," Ned said, in answer to Kira's unspoken question, just as the lift doors screeched shut. With a jerk, they began to move upwards. "I think that our next step is to see if we can find the address for the man Grace met at the docks. I wonder if anyone at Temple speaks any Indian languages? Though I suppose there are quite a few – oh, my goodness."

The lift had jerked to an ungainly stop, causing Ned to reach out with his cane for balance. Kira grabbed uselessly against the walls. They both teetered, balanced, and hung motionless for a moment, waiting for the lift to start moving again, but it did not.

"Mr Devlin," Kira said, with a distinct quaver in her voice. "Do you think—"

The lights went out.

Ned swore, listening to the rapid pitch of Kira's breathing in the darkness. He took a step forwards, thinking to reach for her hand – but the lift jerked again at his movement, and this time downwards.

"Oh, that's torn it," Ned said, and his voice was lost in another great screeching as metal grated on metal, and they dropped further.

It triggered something: some back-up mechanism powered by Salt, so the base of the lift was lit up in long threads of strange light. It cast a greenish tint on Kira's face and made the advertisements on the walls, for patent medicines and magically-propelled invalid chairs, into horrible grotesques. Kira whimpered again.

In the end, Ned thought, it was inevitable that it must come to this.

"Little one," he said. "We have about five minutes before the lift falls to the bottom of the shaft. If what I suspect is true, it's the lift shaft itself, deforming around us. So I need you to stay very calm, do you understand? Stay calm, and do exactly as I tell you. What I'm about to explain to you is the sort of thing you wouldn't do for quite a few years yet, in your apprenticeship, and I don't think I'll have time to repeat myself, so listen very carefully. Are you with me so far?"

Kira nodded, her little eyes wide.

"First, you need to raise a light, in the way Miss May has taught you. Name, calling, asking. Use some of your own energy as the gift. That's right."

The light flared into life, a little ragged about the edges, but a comforting yellow.

Ned said, "Now hold it with only one of your hands, and with only one part of your mind. Don't think about it too much. Just let it burn, that's right. Now close your eyes. Think about Salt, what it feels like when you use the power you have, what it's like when you can sense it in the world around you. There's some in the light, it's a Salt light. Ignore that. There's some in the air, we're below the river estuary here. Ignore that, too. What's left should be very bright and intense, but dimmed in the centre. Can you see that? Eyes shut!"

Slowly, Kira nodded, and from somewhere beneath them they heard the great rumbling sound again, the roar taking on the crackle of metal buckling as well as the slosh of water.

"Right. That is my magic – or, what's left of it, that I can't use for myself. Now I need you to reach in and take it. It's magic in itself, the taking, so you need a gift. Use some of the light. I'm going to sit down so you don't knock me over."

It was Ned's habit these days to get from sitting to standing and vice versa with some lack of grace, but he made it a gentle movement, ignoring the pain; his cane would be dangerously percussive on the base of the lift. The green light flickered, and vibration built in the metal beneath their feet, but Kira hadn't moved, eyes squeezed shut.

"Take it, Kira!" Ned said, desperately. "You don't need my permission. Take it."

Kira didn't move. Ned closed his own eyes, listening to the rumbling grow louder, than softer. He fancied he felt movement, although it could be a fevered imagination. "Kira," he said, quietly, "*now.*"

The light in Kira's left hand dimmed. Ned dropped his head onto his knees. He thought, vaguely, that he should have retained some of his own heart, to guide her: so she wouldn't have to guess what to do next with her arms laden with flame and the lift filling with a smokeless inferno. At last there was movement, a great tearing noise and the cracking open of an internal sky, and everything grew dark and strange, and not a little violent, and it went on for a long, long time.

And then: it was still dark. But a long way off a child was crying, and there was something wet on Ned's face and hands. He sat up, his head cracking against the wall, and said, wonderingly, "Rain."

He was in the station, at the surface, and water was curling along the wrought iron awning. "Kira?" Ned called, and then jerked back as she bolted across the deserted space of the ticket hall and landed next to him. "I thought I'd killed you!" she wailed, and Ned leaned back against the wall and breathed.

"It's all right, little one," he said, very softly, "I'm very difficult to kill."

As she cried, he put an arm around her and made wordless, soothing noises, for himself as well as her; there was a great deal of pain, somewhere, that he was ignoring in favour of concentrating on Kira's bright presence, and the rain falling into his eyes.

"Help me up," he said, reaching out for a cane that wasn't there. He leaned on her shoulder to cross the space of the station floor, and came to rest in front of what had been, earlier that day, a London Underground lift. "Oh, my."

"First we knew of it," said a voice from behind him; Ned turned to meet Whitworth's eyes, "the lift hit the top of the shaft like the coming of the end times.

Then the doors opened, and your girl –" Whitworth shook his head. "Well, perhaps she'd better tell you herself."

"I got us out," Kira said, almost apologetically. There was a strange mixture of emotions on her little face, something between defiance, pride, and misery. "I did... do it right, didn't I?"

Ned limped up to the lift shaft. The outer doors had been pushed back with enormous force and bore signs of having witnessed a very rapid exit. Beyond them was only a great writhing blackness, suggestive of further movement far below. Of the lift cab itself, there was no sign. Ned pictured a mangled mass far beneath the earth, and said, sincerely, "Kira, I think you may have saved both of our lives. Thank you."

"Oh," Kira said, more shocked than pleased.

"Mr Whitworth," Ned said. "Grace, and Thanet—"

"Mr Thanet is helping with the evacuation," Whitworth said, with sympathy and concern, "but Miss May hasn't – not yet."

Ned nodded and sat down on the floor. Kira came to perch on her haunches beside him, still with that uncertainty in her face.

"Mr Devlin," she said. "Back when you could still do magic, were you very good?"

Ned leaned back on his elbows and considered.

"I was about the best of my generation," he said, after a minute. "But I think you'll be better than I was."

"Oh," Kira said, again more shocked than pleased, and Ned sat back again and breathed.

Presently, they heard footsteps rising from the stairwell. Whitworth looked hopeful, stepping forwards, and then the first of the people emerged from the Underground. They were the usual mixture of travellers, dignified old ladies and paint-spattered workers, some holding their tickets and some not, but all with the same open-eyed, uplifted expressions. Above them, birds were fluttering, their feathers translucent and crystalline, hovering to guide the way. Ned smiled at them and said, to Kira, "Thanet."

"They brought us out of there," said a woman in a green coat, to no one in particular.

A boy with a splint on his leg was being helped by two other passengers up the stairs. A man in a pork pie hat held up his hands with reverence to the rain. Ned thought he and Kira must present an odd picture, huddled in the corner of the ticket hall on the floor, but no one gave them a second look, and then he was thinking about the signalbox in Boulogne, waking with his mouth full of saltwater, and no thought of being alive.

"What now?" Kira asked, finally, when the great flood of people petered into nothingness, as both trains below emptied out.

"Now, we wait," Ned said. Kira nodded and settled in beside him.

※

"That's the last of them," Thanet called, sending off another handful of guide birds into the stairwell, and began his descent back into the station. "They should make it out in time – oh." His feet had hit water. "Grace! Where are you?"

"Here," Grace said, gasping for breath, appearing at the end of the upper passageway that led to the control room. "It's not –" she coughed and spluttered "—deep enough to cover."

"Yet," Thanet said, and took another risky step downwards. Grace looked up. A light appeared above her head, illuminating the black water, sloshing ominously from side to side. The electricity in the tunnels had been switched off, leaving only magical light.

"It's not too late, Thanet," Grace said. "Mr Whitworth and his signal operators have already gone up. You can—"

"Shut up," Thanet snapped. "Until you go, I stay."

He shivered and took another step, so water began to creep over the tops of his boots.

"No one here but us chickens," he said, hoping it would not carry, but whispering made the echoes more sinister than ever. "Lead the way."

"I think it's just the floodgate seals that have failed," Grace said, stepping out along the passage, raising small waves. "Nothing else. If I can just stop it responding to any more magic, I can fix it. By Salt, or otherwise."

Thanet nodded before realising Grace couldn't see him. "Wait," he said, and caught up, so they were walking side by side. "It's better this way," he said; Grace looked sidelong at him and gave him a wan smile.

At the platform level, the water was now hip-deep, and the shock of the cold held them both in place for a moment.

"Do you think," Grace said, through her chattering teeth, "it's getting harder to breathe?"

It was, the air now foetid and thick around them, but Thanet only nodded. He reached out to grab Grace's hand before they kept on going, steadying her on the steps beneath the weight of water. Another light hung over the water in front of them, against a background of green and cream tiles running off into blackness.

"Careful of the platform edge," Grace said, just before Thanet went over it.

For a second, he was only falling. The track rails came up to meet his feet, sending a bone-deep jolt of horror through him despite what his rational mind was trying to tell him about the power being switched off, and then the water closed over his mouth and nose. His limbs were going slack when a pair of strong arms grabbed him and hauled mercilessly.

"Breathe, damn you!" Grace yelled, her voice shattering into echoes, and then Thanet was on his knees on the platform, the water up to his waist, coughing and coughing while Grace clapped him on the back.

"It's getting deeper," he said, and jumped when Grace shrieked.

"Sorry," she said, spitting water and pushing her braids away from her eyes. "Sorry, that was either algae going past my leg, or an *eel*" – and Thanet began to laugh.

"Sorry," he said, breathlessly. "And thank you, thank you."

"You're welcome," Grace said, smiling at him, and they set off again. "Thanet," she said, after a while. "We'll reach the floodgates soon. If Ned's right, this isn't even our sort of magic. What if I can't fix it?"

Thanet shrugged. "We'll have to improvise. Perhaps –" he mimed a fingernail across a palm "—it's really not superstitious nonsense, after all."

"Urgh," said Grace, feelingly, and kept on. "Although," she said, shivering in earnest now, "given the rate the water is rising, and how long we took to get down here – well. If, we don't seal it—"

"I know," Thanet said, without surprise. "Well, well. Ned will write us a beautiful eulogy, I'm sure."

Grace chuckled. "In beautiful Latin."

Thanet nodded. "Oh, yes. Elegant rhyming couplets."

"I'd have done that for him," Grace said, still grinning, but sounding quite sincere. "Even if I had to learn my Latin to do it. I'm glad I didn't have to."

"Me too," Thanet said, splashing forwards. "But we would have survived it, you know. Oh, dear."

Grace looked up. "Oh, goodness."

They had reached the floodgates. On one side, the water rushed merrily into the dark through the new tunnel. On the other, water was coming through the rusting gaps in the metal. The flow was moderate, but Thanet could see how the force of it would break through all at once, as with a dam in a river.

"Well," he said uselessly. "Here goes."

Grace was quite still, somehow no longer shivering, an expression of utmost concentration visible on her face even in the dimness and the murk. "Got your penknife?" she asked.

Thanet understood the need for desperate measures. He passed the knife to Grace with a shudder, trying not to think about the filth in the water, and Grace closed her eyes and drew the blade across her palm.

"All right," she said, a little shakily, and then lifted her hands. "Thanet, ask me who I am."

Thanet caught on instantly. "Who are you?"

"My name is Grace."

"What calls you?"

"Salt. Although," Grace hesitated. "Perhaps, more than Salt. Perhaps whatever will be the end of this transformation."

"What do you give?"

Thanet followed Grace's gaze down to the black, rank water, then up to the tunnel above, thinking about London, the city that had survived so much: Zeppelins and bombs, strikes and fire.

Grace said, "Everything I have."

"That's what – you know." Thanet said, understanding this for the first time. "That's what Ned gave away."

Grace nodded. "Yes. And even so."

Thanet shivered. "And what do you ask?"

"Safety. And time." Grace inhaled, audibly, above the rush of water. "I ask that the floodgates be closed, that the city be allowed the time for transformation, that those who do magic are only those who know what they do."

Thanet reached out for her then pulled away, aware that this might be the last magic Grace ever raised; or the last thing she ever did. He watched as she placed her bloodied hands on the floodgates.

"Oh," Thanet said, and then all he knew was the screech of metal and the rise of water, and then rankness and darkness and fear, and then, nothing at all.

※

*(v) Remembrance*

At eleven o'clock in the morning on the eleventh of November, 1919, the government's Birds-in-Flight practitioners raised an elegant and beautiful piece of magic, casting great spectral ravens about the city and the City, not as coercion, but as reminder: when silence fell, it was not frightening but expected, even welcome. In the streets the motorbuses rattled to a halt and the street traders stopped hawking their wares; on the river the boats drifted; and in the courts all dockets were suspended, waiting. In the chambers and inside the Temple gardens, even the clocks were stilled. For two minutes they counted out their silence: two minutes for everything that had been lost.

Then Grace breathed out, settled back into her armchair, and said to Ned: "Well. We survived it."

"It and everything after," Ned said. He was sitting on the floor in front of her, hands raised. "Do you want to try it now?"

Grace considered. "All right."

She closed her eyes and concentrated. When she opened them again, there was light where there hadn't been light. As she and Ned watched, it spluttered and failed, sending them back into darkness. But Ned reached over and pulled the curtains, letting in the wintry sunlight, and settled back on the floor. "Well done," he said, and they returned to silence for a while after that.

"A light," Grace said finally, sneezed, and then let out a breath. "I thought – I thought I wouldn't be able to do magic again. Tell me if I'm being horrible and tactless," she added.

Ned shook his head. "It was quite a working you did, Grace. Thanet carried you up all those stairs and by the time she got up to ground level she was dry as a bone."

"So was everything else," said Thanet, from the doorway. "They're talking about reopening the station in the new year."

"I might walk down to the next one along, even if they do," Grace said, a little embarrassed. "Where are you off to, anyway?"

"Back on my rounds." Thanet grinned and rubbed her hands together. "And Kira wants to visit her mum, I said I'd take her. We'll be back this afternoon."

She bowed, grabbed her hat and went out. A kind of fresh determination had come into her movements, Grace thought, since her registration had been restored: a refusal to compromise in the work that she did.

"Grace," said Ned, getting to his feet and colonising another armchair. "Are you quite sure you're all right?"

"I'm – not all right," Grace said, flexing her hands and considering. The cuts she had made, done with an unwashed penknife and then bathed with dirty river water, had become infected with a vengeance, but they were healing better now, with some sanitising magic and patience. "But I will be, I hope."

"You will be," Ned said, certain. "Perhaps we all will. Even Mistress Ferguson – she's drawing her widow's pension, I'm told. Her husband has been entirely exonerated of any voluntary role in the accident."

"How did it go with the railway company?" Grace asked, anxiously.

Ned groaned, and put a hand to his head. "Let us say that I may not be the most welcome passenger on the Southwestern Railway for the next few – ah, decades. But suffice it to say, I am not being brought up on professional malpractice, and Thanet's name has been restored to the roll. They did accept that the accident wasn't our fault, in the end, though that might be something to do with Thanet talking at great length about our *dear* Miss May risking her *life* for the good of the *railway…*"

"Good." Grace smiled and put a hand on his shoulder. "Ned, I want to ask you something."

Ned inclined his head. "Mmm?"

Grace hesitated. "I don't know if you want to tell me, or if you can. But if you can – what did they do to you, in the war?"

"Ah," Ned said, and didn't speak for a minute, rummaging in pockets, and then lit a cigarette. Mrs Throckley didn't like it when they smoked inside, but Grace didn't bring up the point.

"Dear Grace," Ned said, with almost a laugh. "You've been so terribly kind. You've never asked me that."

"I'm asking now."

Ned nodded, and took a drag of the cigarette. "I think the last time I saw you before the Armistice was when the Germans bombed the Guildhall."

"Yes," Grace said. "I thought you might return to practice then. Be invalided out, or however they put it. You were quite beaten up by the whole affair."

Ned smiled at her. "I thought so too. When they asked me to come up to the Horseguards I thought it was something in the way of light duty they had in mind. The Minister for War had dabbled in transport before 1914. He was greatly taken with the silver-bell Salt signalling and recommended me to the War Office. That's how I got sent to France."

"To the front lines?"

"Not all the time," Ned said, still blowing smoke. "It was quite a simple system. Each battalion had its men, its commanding officer, and its practitioner. Salt and Birds alike, though the men liked it to be Salt, Birds could give them courage but Salt could fix the holes in their boots. But every so often the brass behind the lines pulled me out and asked me to think about long-term magical strategies. To devise ways in which we could fight a better war."

"A better war?"

Ned shrugged and overturned his palms. "You shouldn't be able to regret the magic you've done, not really," he said. "You've given a gift of something of yourself: you've done a true thing, no matter what. But there's magic you can do without the full recitation, you know. You don't give a gift. You can drain the salt from a man's bones – Salt and salt both – and force him to sacrifice himself."

"And that..." Grace paused. "That changes people – into what you are now?"

Ned shook his head. "No. It kills them where they stand. The Birds did it humanely, if there is such a thing. Put up great fields of magic and if the soldiers wandered in, they just... well, they lost interest in fighting. I heard German soldiers telling their pals all about how they wanted to take up birdwatching, somewhere far away. But I... well." He shook his head. "The men used to come to me, ask for magic. They knew I was turning men just like them into ash and dust, a half-mile away in no-man's land, and they saw the bar in my ear and they still came to me.

"Then in the autumn of 1918 they started saying it would be over soon. I didn't believe it. That war couldn't end. I was at Boulogne, at any rate. It was a terrible place." Ned dipped his head for a moment, then lifted it. "German soldiers died in the Salt fields without a mark on them. Men were buried three-deep in the frozen ground. It was a better war."

It was said with a faint irony. Grace didn't interrupt.

"Then the message came. The armistice was to be at eleven in the morning: hostilities would cease, and it would be passed down the lines on silver bells. And I –I couldn't sleep." Ned looked up. "The guns would stop. But all that magic – all that Salt in the earth along with the barbed wire. Nothing would grow. Children would have their mothers' fields explode beneath their feet. That war couldn't end, not like that."

"Ned?" Grace said, when he didn't say anything for a minute. "What did you do?"

Ned sighed. "I went to the signalbox, the morning of the armistice. The girl there was from Liverpool, like you. She called me a witch. And then I—I made it safe, I suppose." He looked up and met her eyes. "I raised all the magic on every battlefield. I pulled it into my hands, into my mouth. I put it in a bowl of water. I'd seen some terrible things by then, I thought drowning would be an easy way to die."

"And then?" Grace asked.

"I didn't," Ned said, bleakly. "When I woke up I didn't believe it. But the girl from Liverpool rang the bells, and the war ended, and I poured the water into the harbour."

"It took your own magic with it," Grace said. "That's right, isn't it?"

He nodded, almost imperceptibly.

"But don't misunderstand me," he said. "What I gave, I gave willingly, without regrets. I would have given my life, and yet –" He gestured to take in the room around them. "Here we are." He shrugged again, and lit another cigarette from the first. "That's all. Would you like some tea?"

"Yes, please," Grace said, and as Ned went across to the little gas ring to make it, she raised a light, high above them both, which shone brighter and longer than the first.

⁂

Grace had two visitors that afternoon. The first knock on the door of chambers was tentative, and Mrs Throckley's voice uncertain when she came through to inform them of their guest. "A coloured gentleman here to see you, miss," she said. "Says he knows you."

"Send him in," Grace said. When the man came in, looking around himself nervously, she grinned. "Amir! I'd been meaning to come and see you. Mr Ramanujan over in Pump Court speaks Hindi, we were waiting for him to have a free day – sit down, do. Ned, this is Amir. Amir, this is Ned Devlin, he's my friend and colleague."

She wasn't sure how much of this spiel Amir had understood, but he sat down in an armchair and accepted a mug of tea, and when Ned tapped the sugar pot, offered a small nod in response. After taking a sip, Amir set down the cup and unfolded a newspaper from the inside of his jacket, smoothing out one of the inner pages and pointing at one headline in particular; Grace skimmed the story of the floodgates at Blackfriars and nodded when she got to the picture of herself and Thanet, taken as they left the station with the tunnels sealed beneath. "So that's how you found me?"

Amir nodded. He lifted the cup again, then set it down. It took him a minute to speak. "Well done," he said, finally, with clear enunciation. "And thank you. For – before."

"I'm glad you got away," Grace said soberly. "I was so worried. I'm so sorry that that awful thing happened. I think you're very brave."

Amir nodded, and smiled at her, then set the cup down once more and stood up.

"Surely you're not going already," Grace protested, and he must have understood her tone if not her words, because he smiled again and shook his head.

"Please wait," Grace said. "Oh, I do wish Mr Ramanujan were here. You know about magic from iron. You could – stay." She gestured around the room, at the books on the shelves, at her own and Ned's practitioners' bars. "Ned and some others are trying to recruit people, like the signal operator in the station, and you – people who can do your sort of magic. You could help them. You could help us, too, we could learn so much from you."

Amir held her gaze for a moment, then shook his head.

"No," he said, again with clear, determined enunciation. "Not yet."

He bowed on the last word, took up his newspaper, and was gone, breezing past a surprised Mrs Throckley.

"Not yet," Grace said, thinking of the riots, and the stones thrown, and all that abject fear. "If he doesn't want to help – then we'll leave him be. But I hope he does."

"What an odd bloke," Mrs Throckley complained from the doorway. "Wasn't here five minutes and didn't finish his tea. Grace, dear, do you know if Kira likes pound cake? I've a hankering myself, and all the eggs we'd need."

"I've no idea," Grace said. "But Ned and I would be in favour."

The cake was just coming out of the oven when there came another, much more stentorian knock.

Grace started towards the door, but was prevented from getting any further by the arrival of a stately galleon carrying a horsehair wig. "Ned, my darling, make yourself scarce, this is ladies only. That's right, off with you."

"Good afternoon, my lady," Grace said, amused, as Justice Devlin took Ned's vacated chair and settled herself into it with a deep sigh. "Will you have anything to drink?"

"No, dear, this is a flying visit." Justice Devlin reached into her handbag and began polishing her spectacles with a handkerchief. "I know you've been through the wars. I'm going to ask Ned to surrender the lease on this house, that's all."

"That's *all*?" Grace repeated, horrified. "My lady, if it's a matter of the rent, I know we've been behind – but if you'll allow us just a little more time, I'm sure –"

"Hush, dear." Justice Devlin put her spectacles back on her nose. "Nothing like that. I want Ned to surrender the lease and I want you to sign another, on new terms. Call it a new business proposition."

Grace blinked. "I don't understand."

Justice Devlin leaned back in her chair. "Did you know," she said, after a moment, "that Ned was born in the Temple gardens?"

"Yes," Grace said, surprised. "I was the same – I was brought up around the High Court in Liverpool, my father practises there."

"Grace, my dear, you misunderstand me," Justice Devlin said. "I meant it quite literally. Ned was born *in* the gardens." Off Grace's look, she smiled, spreading her hands. "I had a nasty prosecution I didn't like to leave, and it seems a fourth child may arrive more quickly than the others."

"My goodness," Grace said, faintly, finding her imagination not up to the task of envisaging it.

"Things are different, here in the Temple gardens," Justice Devlin said. "But women must work for what they want: that's the same everywhere. Last Candlemas, did you light Ned's lamps for him?"

That was one of her judicial trademarks, the lightning-fast change in subject. "Yes, my lady."

"Don't do that again," Justice Devlin said, sharply. "I propose a simple arrangement: rent as a percentage of your receipts. Thanet's back on the roll and you'll be sending the little one out to earn pin money soon enough. I trust I'll get perfectly reasonable returns, and handsome ones, in time."

"What about Ned?" Grace asked, gently.

"Ned was the baby," Justice Devlin said, matching her gentleness. "The beloved youngest. Hard to remember sometimes that he's thirty years old and the bravest person I have ever known, save one or two." Her eyes twinkled. "Oh, my boy hasn't outlived his usefulness. Quite the reverse, in fact; I fear there will be others like him, in time, and they'll have need of him then. But that's not for you to worry about, Grace. I'll bring the new lease along in time for the quarter day. Look after yourself, darling girl."

She kissed Grace's forehead and swept out in a flurry of perfume and skirts.

"Is she gone?" Ned peered around the door, and came in when he saw the coast was clear. "Grace, what is it?"

"Your mother thinks I should take over this practice from you," Grace said, spreading her hands.

Ned took a moment to react, but when he did it was only to take some of the pound cake, sitting out on the table, and reach for the teapot.

"You don't need my permission," he said, and poured out.

☙

## (vi) Christmas Day

"The quarter days," Grace explained to Kira, while decorating the tree, "are the days on which people enter into contracts, raise auspicious magic, that sort of thing.

"Begin apprenticeships, even," she added. "It's been six months and change, little one. Shall you be keeping on with us?"

"Yes," Kira said, determined, and Grace grinned.

The new lease had been signed that morning, sealed in Salt, and taken away merrily by her ladyship, whose real errand, she said, had been to deliver a goose. Mrs Throckley was roasting it in the kitchen, filling the house with delicious smells, and Thanet was halfway up a stepladder with two armfuls of holly.

"Why do we always leave our decorating until the last possible moment?" she asked, irritated. "Kira, will you be having your Christmas dinner with us or at your mother's?"

Kira looked disappointed, and Thanet giggled. "Two Christmas dinners is one of the perquisites of apprenticeship, Kira, don't worry."

Kira brightened up. Thanet clambered down from the stepladder, and surveyed her handiwork.

"Now," she said, "come with me for the last touch."

On the windowsill, she carefully sprinkled a layer of table salt, and put down a handful of feathers. "For good luck in the year to come," she explained, to a doubtful Kira. "It's just a tradition, no magic in it."

"Then shouldn't we have iron?" Kira asked, and Thanet nodded.

"Quite right, I should have thought. Ned's got a horseshoe above his desk – run and ask him for it, would you?"

Kira did, and brought it out to hang off the corner of the ledge.

"Very nice," Thanet said, and when they went back inside Grace had almost finished with the tree, raising Salt lights on the end of each fringed branch.

"It's very pretty," Kira said, sounding a little shy, and Grace grinned.

"Glad you approve, little one. Ned, are you quite sure?"

"Quite sure," Ned said, looking up from the journal he was reading. "It shan't be called after iron, after all. Ferrous or Ferric magic, so say the great and the good. There'll be a Ferrous Worshipful Company before too long."

"Ferrous magic," Thanet said, trying it out for size. "I think I'll stick with Birds-in-Flight, myself."

"About that," Grace said, now fetching Kira a footstool, so she could place the star on the top of the tree. "Are you glad to be registered again, Thanet?"

Thanet tossed her hair impatiently over her shoulders.

"Yes, and no," she said. "They hadn't any right to take it from me to start with, of course. And the next time I help a girl with loose morals or some such ridiculous thing, they'll be after me again. But I'll fight the fight when it comes to me. Kamala is doing well, by the way," she added.

Grace smiled at her and helped Kira get back down.

"Right, all. Dinner time for witches," she said, grinning, "and Ned."

Ned threw a popcorn string at her, following which the party arose and descended to the kitchen, where more Salt lights gleamed on every surface in honour of the occasion, and Mrs Throckley beamed beside a plump and crisply gleaming goose.

Everything was delicious, of course. Kira and Ned pulled the wishbone, and Kira got the wish. When the Christmas pudding emerged from the pot, Kira set it alight.

"Name, calling, gift, asking," Grace coached, and the flames rose a lovely blue.

"When I was in the lift," Kira said, a little hesitantly, as they ate it with brandy cream. "With Mr Devlin, and I took the heart out of him – could I, sometime, try again?"

"*No*," said Thanet and Grace together, and Ned only laughed.

"You will again, little one," he promised. "But you've so much to learn, yet" – and opened his palm to reveal the silver sixpence.

They sent her home with it, in the end, alongside with gifts of books and sweets from all three of them, and a Christmas cake in a tin for her mother. Thanet offered to take the walk down the Embankment with Kira to her mother's house, and after they'd gone, Ned and Grace helped Mrs Throckley clean up, presented her with a wrapped gift and a handsome bottle from the Temple cellars, donned their hats and went out.

"It's good brandy, that," Ned commented, in the crisp and frosty air. "There's another one on the side for us, we should crack it open when Thanet gets back."

"That's a plan," Grace said, putting her hands on the railing, looking out across the river. "Speaking of plans, Ned – what are you going to do with yourself, now?"

Ned considered. "I've been asked to help with the new Worshipful Company. After that – well. My mother thinks I could be called to the bar, if you can imagine that."

Grace chuckled. "I think I can."

Ned shook his head, disbelieving. "I almost forgot," he said. "Christmas Day, the last quarter day."

He reached up to the piercing in the top of his ear and pushed, hissing with pain. The metal bar landed neatly in his hand.

"That's that, then," he said.

Grace nodded. "Thanet will be able to clean that up for you," she said, motioning at the old wound. "Though it'll leave a scar."

Ned smiled. "Thank goodness for that. Twenty years of my life ought to."

"Whatever you do next, you should come home often," Grace said, earnestly. "Quite apart from anything else, you'll have to take care of Kira's Latin. I can read it,

I can't teach it. *Forsan et haec meminisse,* quite beyond me, et cetera."

"Grace…"

"The world is changing," Grace said, cutting him off. "All around us the world is changing. It may be that a young practitioner trained for modern times doesn't *need—*"

"All right!" Ned held up his hands. "I will teach Kira her Latin." He overturned his palms in supplication. "There is only so much I can bear. Latin will be taught. Greek also. If she has a yen to learn Sanskrit or hieroglyphs I will arrange for a tutor. Après moi, there will be no deluge."

Grace laughed at his outrage, and settled alongside him on the bench by the water. "I missed you a great deal, when you were gone," she said, presently. "Which surprised me, as you were quite unbearable when you were here."

"Slander. I am a respectable Salt practitioner and an officer and a gentleman."

"One out of three isn't bad," Grace said, wickedly, and wondered for a second if she'd misjudged it: but Ned laughed easily enough, and was still smiling a few moments later, as they watched the boats go past on the river.

"I missed you too," he said, breaking the silence. "And this." He motioned to the water, to the garden steps behind them, to London in general. "What have you decided to do about the lamp-lighting, in the new year?"

"I thought it would be nice if Kira lit your lamps," Grace said..

"They're not mine any more," Ned said, "at least, they won't be. That's as well, though. She can start young."

Whosoever they belonged to, and at whose hands they were raised, Grace was thinking, there would nevertheless come the seven hundred and thirty-second Candlemas of the City of London, that neither war nor peace could dismay: and they would all, as they had always done, raise and make light.

"It's getting cold," she said, rubbing her hands together. "Do you want to go in?"

"Let's stay out a little longer," Ned said, gesturing along the Embankment towpath, and they kept on through the frosty evening, under a clear sky full of stars.

# REFUGEE; OR, A NINE-ITEM REPRESENTATIVE INVENTORY OF A BETTER WORLD

*1. The boy at the window*

The bell, the lantern, the witching hour. (Though this happened to me one time in line at Starbucks – two of us helped the stranger up and the barista got her a chair.) Undone shirt cuffs, unkempt hair. A refugee from the republic of conscience.

❦

*2. Me*

An old woman, now. Lonely, when the kettle whistles and there's no one in the house to wake. Kiran would have helped me get the boy off the floor, and stayed with him while I got something to clean up the blood.

❦

### 3. What we are

Once upon a time, they say in these parts. (Not everywhere, I guess. Where Kiran came from, they don't say anything special at the start of the story, but they always finish with, *and I saw the handsome prince the other day in the market, but he wouldn't talk to me.*)

So, however they say it where you're from. A long time ago, my people came to terms with themselves, and each other. Some people say it was a deal with a higher power, that we signed a piece of parchment (or shook on it, or clicked "Proceed with transaction", or whatever). But I don't think so. I think the time had come and we had come to it. A thousand years of peace and prosperity. Universal basic income; healthcare free at the point of use; happily ever after.

However they say it where you're from.

❦

### 4. Corbie

The boy's name was pretty, like a bird's. You'd know it if I said it. But for now – before he became what he became – let him be Raven the Trickster, or the clever mynah in the folk tales, or ane o' the twa corbies in the poem, who ate the knight's corpse in the wood.

(It wasn't me who loved poetry—that was Kiran. At the water's edge, at the scattering, I read from one of her favourites: of grief that no longer rings within the bones of a people, systematic, symphonic, but chimes in each of us alone.)

❧

## 5. You

You know how this goes. You, who are reading this a long way from here, my kitchen with the high beams and white tiles, the spice jars, the warmth. You, who have stood on the parapet, leaned over the barricades; who have spoken truth to power; who have been torn between what is right and what is easy; you who always took orders, until you said: *no*.

We don't know why or how it happens, that you come to us without crossing the years in between. Only that when it does, it's in pain, in fear, in- all the lightless places of a bloody history; and that it's not to stay. A night, a day, an hour: a respite. Ring the bell as you come in.

(And don't think we're a fantasy. We have alchemists and armourers but also accountants. Kiran could do a corporate tax return at twenty paces. You are the myth.)

❧

## 6. History

"It's because," the boy said to me, urgent, though he didn't have to explain. "It's because I'm a poet. I try—and raise them up, you know? Give them something to sing about. And people used to say that to listen to me, to hear me—was to be run through by a knife so sharp you didn't know you'd been cut. So when they came to take me away…"

Underneath the soaked cloth of his shirtsleeves, hand-carved text whirled and snaked along his forearms. I hissed and swore and put water on to boil. "What does it say?" he asked, while we were waiting.

"You can't read it?"

"No." He looked at me. "I can only—they don't let us learn…"

I thought about lying to him and didn't. There was dirt in the cuts, grit, infection. I cleaned it up and read it out, filth in filth. After a while he started to cry, quietly, and I let him be, making masala chai on the stove so the kitchen filled with the scent of cardamom, and snow gathered in the dark on the panes.

※

## 7. The others

The first time I can remember, I was eight. Parents teach their children about this, to prepare them for what they'll have to do all their lives. So I sat up all night, with my mum and our visiting stranger, a woman who breathed through the pain of delivery and took away two packets of sanitary pads. Later, there was someone we made up a bed for, who wore clothes I'd seen in history books, and a lost child who liked the aloo paratha my father cooked.

Much later, there was the first time with Kiran. We were twenty and twenty-one, just back from our second date, and the stranger was even younger. Her coat slipped to the floor, the pocket spilling blueprints of a public building, and something that gleamed in a vial, with a syringe. "She's on her way somewhere," Kiran said.

Somewhere in our recent history, I thought. Kiran put the vial back so it wouldn't get lost, and made tea for the three of us.

I know what you're thinking. But we feed and water our assassins in this country. Assassins, terrorists, freedom fighters. They are who we are; there is no other.

❦

*8. Kiran*

I put the mug of masala chai in front of him and said, "This was my wife's recipe."

And then cried. Because scent is a trigger for memory, because he had cried, too, and because it was that sort of night. The waves shattered on the shoreline and the wind howled a ghastly sympathy.

"Was," he said, perceptive despite everything, and I wondered if he would think it nothing worth crying about. Not a recent loss, not a whole lifetime's loss. One death, one widow, laid before someone who had received mercy, but not justice; whose loss was human dignity.

But he got up, went across to the window and rang the bell. As they do at funerals, sometimes. "A chime struck for you alone," he said, thoughtful, "though you don't have the whole symphony."

Like the poet said, the one Kiran loved. Written after he landed on my kitchen floor, after running all night from his torturers; before he went back to the battle he was fighting for his people, his language, his occupation of space; and before they fucking killed him.

∾

## 9. Ashes

In the morning, I went down to the gate with him. Kiran used to sit on the bars with her feet swinging, even in the bitter cold, when the snow came down to the low-tide mark.

To her poet, I did not say: this is the way to the gallows; nor, perhaps it was worth it in the end; or even: when the ashes were scattered, when I read, no one cried: it was so new, so sharp, that we didn't know we'd been cut.

(Let no inventory of our better world obscure this: who they were, and how they died, so we could lose our knowledge of grief.)

I said, "Be safe."

"Thank you," he said, picking up a plastic bag of painkillers, medical alcohol, and trail mix, and started off down the path. I watched him grow more distant, along the slough of land into water, until I was distracted by a bird rising from the fog. When I turned back he was gone. No footprints, and no sound but the crack of ice, and the gathering of crows.

# A NOTE ON AKBAR AND BIRBAL

Akbar the Great was the third Mughal Emperor of India, and Raja Birbal was one of his "navaratnas", the nine principal advisers of his court. They are real historical figures (and hardly ancient history at all in Indian terms; Akbar died in 1605) but nevertheless, they're best known for the large body of folklore about them. They're funny, sweet stories, in which trouble may arise but Birbal always comes up with a clever scheme to save the day, and even if he and Akbar quarrel for a time, they're always best of friends again by the end. What I love most about the stories is how relevant they continue to be: Akbar was a social and religious pluralist, a Muslim emperor who trusted his Hindu advisers implicitly. In their bickering, you can catch a glimpse of the modern Indian state, and much else besides. My friend Sumana Harihareswara writes: *"May we all have mythical Birbal's incisive wit and courage, and mythical Akbar's ability to listen to critics about how we use our power, reflect, and change."*

May we have just those.

# ACKNOWLEDGEMENTS

Most of these stories were originally acquired and published by various SFF magazines and anthologies, and I'm very grateful to the editors at *Anathema: Spec From The Margins*, *Goldfish Grimm's*, *Betwixt*, *Middle Planet*, *Expanded Horizons* and *GigaNotoSaurus*. For "Eight Cities", which first appeared in *Sunvault: Stories of Solarpunk and Eco-Speculation* (Upper Rubber Boot Books, 2017), my thanks to Phoebe Wagner and Brontë Wieland. And a special shoutout to my (former) fellow editors at *Luna Station Quarterly*, for their work on "Flightcraft", and to the fiction editors at *Strange Horizons*, without whom my writing career would look very different.

In putting together this volume, I'm grateful as ever to Cathryn and Cara Wynn-Jones of Lodestar Author Services, and to Katie Rathfelder for her patient editing. The beautiful cover artwork is from "Star-sailing" by Katherine Catchpole, used with permission.

# ABOUT THE AUTHOR

Iona Datt Sharma is a writer, lawyer, unrepentant hipster and the product of more than one country. They're just finishing up their first novel, a historical fantasy about spies. Their other work can be found at www.generalist.org.uk/iona/about, and they're on Twitter as @singlecrow.

Made in the USA
Middletown, DE
01 May 2019